Nine

Birds

Singing

Edythe Anstey Hanen

New Arcadia Publishing

Praise for *Nine Birds Singing*

If, like me, you despair for the collapse of the English language, take comfort. In *Nine Birds Singing* you will discover a veritable Aladdin's Cave of delights. Edythe Anstey Hanen not only uses the basic blocks of language, words, to propel her characters and her story, each word has been selected with meticulous care with attention to its meaning and its ability to resonate. The work is a symphony for the logophile. Don't miss it. Patrick Taylor, *USA Today, New York Times and Globe and Mail* best-selling author of the *Irish Country Doctor* series.

Nine Birds Singing is a finely written book, lovingly crafted, poignant and perceptive. A tale of gradual self-understanding, awakening and ultimate release. Nick Bantock, author of *The Griffin and Sabine Trilogy*

In *Nine Birds Singing*, Edythe Anstey Hanen's appealing narrator, Maddie, recalls and examines her own search for independence from her parents' restrictive values. The writer and Maddie, together, gather the reader in to share an intimate, wise, and moving tale. Jack Hodgins, author of *Spit Delaney's Island*

Readers will enjoy the unique views and poetic pacing of *Nine Birds Singing* by Edythe Anstey Hanen. She savors and survives landscapes and relationships in teasing but tasty quick episodes. Her novel takes readers via circular time traveling through decades of Maddie's life in Canada and Mexico. Enjoy this new voice! Bernice Lever, author of *Small Acts*, Black Moss Press, 2016

www.newarcadiapublishing.com

ISBN-13: 978-0-9810241-5-8
ISBN-10: 0-9810241-5-7

Printed and bound in the United States of America

For my children, Aaron and Leah, who will always be my guiding lights.

And to David for believing in me.

Answer, if you hear the words under the words –
otherwise it is just a world with a lot of rough
edges, difficult to get through, and our pockets full
of stones.

Naomi Shihab Nye
From WORDS UNDER THE WORDS (Far Corner Books, 1995)

Prologue

here will you spend eternity? For Maddie, those words have never lost their power to terrify. Sunday night sermons. Stories of the lost ones, the ones who will not ascend to heaven in the Rapture. Two farmers tilling their fields under a noonday sun; one taken, the other left behind. Believers all over the world will vanish, be swallowed up into the universe, inexplicably gone in that final moment of truth. And Maddie's parents will be with them.

The preacher begins his sermon with subdued entreaties for the lost sheep to return to the fold. *There is still time,* he tells them. But it's his table-pounding diatribes on hell's fury that send rivers of fear coursing through Maddie's veins. *There will be weeping and wailing and gnashing of teeth.* Even the water trembles in the glass when he slams his fist against the dais. *Are you right with God?*

Maddie sits in heart-stopping silence, her cheeks aflame with guilt. She is more afraid of the preacher than she is of God. His gray, pin-striped suit, the gold chain attached to a pocket watch that he consults every few minutes. Lavender-tasting Sen-Sens secreted away in his waistcoat pocket. His eyes, bright marbles behind round eyeglasses. The heat in the room like the fevered dreams of childhood.

A framed Bible verse hangs on the wall, demanding: THOU SHALT BE SAVED. The clock in its tall oak case ticks away the minutes, ticks away their lives. The hands circle, move toward the inevitability of those end days. The restless shuffling of feet and the crackling of unraveling bamboo fans during those blazing Sunday evenings in the full heat of a Winnipeg summer.

Maddie remembers her child self creeping down the hallway late at night to listen at her parents' bedroom door. Has she been left like the improvident farmer? Is this the night that everyone has been gathered up in the Rapture? Everyone but her? He will come, her father has told her, reading from the soft vellum pages of his dog-eared Bible, *like a thief in the night.*

The prayers, the incantations: *Please, God, make it be all right and I'll do anything you want. This time I really will. Just make them still be here.*

From the half open doorway of her parents' bedroom, the faint outline of her mother in the dim light, her hair a dark splash against the pillow, one arm flung across her father's back.

Still here. *Thank you.*

But no matter how many times Maddie negotiates with God, there is no end to the fear, to the shame of her unwashed heart. She's like the little boy with his finger in the dike. Helpless against the flood.

The wages of sin.

One

The Island

$\mathcal{M}$addie tips the empty burn barrel on its edge and rolls it out into the middle of the yard. Her anger is restless and mean-spirited, a coiled snake ready to attack. She kicks the rusty old oil drum as though it alone has done her some injustice.

Maddie hasn't used the burn barrel in years, but no better time than now, while the pain of the truth still smolders. Those words. *Something somewhere is calling my name. But it's not your voice. It's life. There's someone else, Maddie, and it's time for me to move on.*

Words of betrayal that she stumbled upon only today. Words hidden in a place where she would find them after he disappeared. Why hidden? *Did he have second thoughts?* Maddie doesn't care. She's tried too long to tear a life out of a thing that has become ingrown and twisted.

She tosses a bundle of newspapers into the barrel and a few cedar strips for kindling. Kerosene from her oil lamps stirs the fire into life. Flames leap out against the night.

What will go first into this baptism of fire?

Maps. Dozens of them. He was a collector of maps, but his journeys have all been odysseys of escape. She drops the maps in, one by one, and watches the long blue highways, the cities and the rivers curl into ash. Next go all his National Geographics, then his copy of *War and Peace* that he never read and an article on a place called Lost Creek Canyon. *Was he ever there?* She feels as though she's burning his dreams.

Maddie gazes out over the water to the North Shore. Fresh snow covers the mountains and the sky is blue black now with the approaching night. She hears the crunch of her neighbor Frenchy's boots in the potholes as he walks toward her.

"You got a permit for that fire?" he asks. A Canada goose straggles up from the beach below and pecks at his trouser cuff. The ducks and geese are all starving at this time of year, scrounging for food. Frenchy nudges it away with the toe of his boot.

"Yeah, of course, Frenchy. You know me. I'm a rule-follower."

It's a lie. Maddie hasn't contacted the fire department for a permit, but there's no wind now and the sky is threatening rain or an early snow.

She stands back from the heat of the fire and the circle of light. The leaping flames of the burn barrel remind her of the grizzled homeless men she's seen leaning over blazing metal drums in the twilit city streets, huddling in the snowlight. Or displaced men like her grandfather eighty years ago during the depression, huddled together in the hobo camps along the railway line, trading stories and dreams. Doing all they could to keep body and soul together.

The ball cap goes next. It was Joey's favorite, a blue Cubs hat. She flings it and it lands on the rim of the barrel, perching on the edge of possibility. *Maybe I shouldn't.* She picks up a stick and pushes the hat into the barrel.

Then the T-shirts. He liked the Led Zeppelin 1977 one best. A faded green, too small for him now. She throws it in, heaps the rest of the T-shirts on top and adds another splash of kerosene. Flames explode from the barrel. She tosses in a few pieces of damp green alder to slow the burn and then waits, listening to the evening sounds, leaning away from the flame and into the dark. The beating of bat wings. The ferry whistle out in the Sound. From far away, she hears the scream of steel on steel as the train hurtles through West Vancouver from the north. Sometimes, when the wind is just right, she can hear the train's call as it drifts across the water and into her dreams.

She'll let the fire die down now. All she can do is let everything that's left of his past twist and writhe until it finds its resting place in the ashes until, piece by piece, it burns out, leaving nothing.

ဆဝလ

Have dreams. Must travel. Maddie stands in front of the fridge and reads the words again. An arrangement that turns shape into meaning. Words that are not hers and meanings that she cannot change.

She's not sure when the messages started. Or when the poems and whimsical juxtaposition of words became symbols for something else. She's had them scattered across the fridge for years. Sometimes, when passing through the kitchen, she moves the words around and puts them together into simple phrases: *kiss the blue morning; linger in beauty; dance me a river.* When Maddie first met Joey, they were reminders to go slow: *Know yesterday. Remember winter heart. Love softly.*

But now Joey's absences have become a measurable thing. His eyes have begun to reflect more distant horizons. The words she assembles on the fridge – *whisper secret moon; open sad smile* – carry different messages now.

Maddie had challenged Joey, looking for answers in his unexplained absences, searching for some improbable secret map that would take her to the truth of the new, cool distance in his eyes. Joey gave nothing away. That day he leaned against the wall, rangy, dismissive, hiding behind that years-old smokescreen – the one she knows is taking him away from her. He scraped a wooden match along the side of the wood stove. It flared into light. The drift of sulfur burned Maddie's throat. He lifted the match to his mouth, slowly, then blew it out. She saw the anger in his fingers as they arced around the wooden matchstick, flicked it to the floor. Maddie moved away, as though there was a possibility of putting distance between them in that small room. She wondered if she had actually said the words out loud or if they were still trapped inside her throat: *Staying stoned all day is for losers, Joey.* What right does she have to demand this of him, anyway? Getting high had been a way of life for her too. But that was years ago.

The razor-edged words of their argument sliced the air between them. They both knew the territory they were traveling now. Rage like bright explosions of glass falling in splintered prisms of light. Wooden doors smashed and split like forked lightning in a summer sky.

Anything was possible.

Maddie felt for the solid safety of the stone wall of the fireplace behind her. The curtain fluttered at the open window, carrying the scent of the winter roses she'd picked by the river that morning. From far away, a dog barked. She turned and slowly walked into the bedroom. He followed.

"You're crazy," he said. "You know that."

He chose that line, Maddie knew, because it carried the most power to hurt. But she had given him that power. She'd told him once how she could imagine such a thing happening: the creeping sense of isolation, the terror of being cut off from the very heart of herself, like Sylvia Plath watching the slow descent of the bell jar.

Joey knew her doubts and fears and where they were hidden, better even than he knew his own. And he chose to hurt her in those soft places, the places that were already bruised. He stood by the window, one hand against the door, his body hard and unforgiving. Maddie smelled engine oil on his shirt, saw the dark hairs on the back of his hand. His anger trembled in the silence of the room like the stirring of leaves outside the window.

Then the reprieve. In one swift movement, he turned from her and strode through the house and out the back door. She heard him wrench the van door open, then slam it shut. His tires spit up stones and dust as he roared down the lane. She wondered when he'd be back. Or if he'd be back.

He did come back. And soon after that she saw those renegade words on the refrigerator door, words that were not hers. Words that hadn't been there the day before: *Have dreams. Must travel.* Before she went to bed, she shifted a few of them around and formed a new phrase: *pick peace perhaps,* and waited to see what would happen.

For days, nothing happened. And then one day, he was gone. He left a note: *I'm going back home.* By *home*, he meant Mexico, the place where he was born, the place that would always be his real home. *I need to think*, he said, *to reassess my world.*

No *Love, Joey.* No *Adios.*

After he'd gone, Maddie discovered a new message tucked near the corner of the fridge door under a glass heart magnet: *wake cowboy prisoner.* It felt faintly scolding. As though she'd lassoed his heart and held him captive all these years.

∞C∞

Winters were hardest before Joey, but Maddie had felt her own strength and power then. There were days that threatened to undo them all in Gully's Grove, a small enclave of abandoned summer cottages that George Gully had bought years ago and made livable. One winter, an unstoppable wind tore Maddie's roof off. Cold rain splashed into pots, jars, cans, anything she could find. By seven in the morning and still dark, everyone in the Grove was up on her roof, tarring, patching, hammering. By nightfall, she had a roof again.

The cold weather always brought frozen pipes and leaking roofs, prophecies of winter etched in frost on windowpanes. Days were spent hauling wood inside from under the tarp, chopping kindling, setting the clock to wake her every two or three hours through the night to feed the fire.

When Maddie first moved to the island and to Gully's Grove, her next-door neighbor, Frenchy, taught her how to split wood one cold afternoon threatening snow. The

8

keening of foghorns, the screaming gulls, the hollow sound of splitting wood in the frozen afternoon hung like warm breath in the air. It was impossible at first. The axe threw her off balance when she swung it over her head; the wood was unyielding. She was enraged by what needed to be done and by her inability to do it. Then the moment of triumph, when the first pieces flew apart with a clean, cold crack.

In those early days of winter, an unforgiving loneliness mocked the smallness of their lives in Gully's Grove. They became strangers for a time, locked into their own shape of solitude, bent figures hurrying through the rain to the lighted windows that called them home. Tending the fire, feeding the cats, reading Ibsen by the wood stove. That was Maddie's life then. A world circumscribed by dailiness. Bone-thin days. A life reduced to almost nothing.

Life before Joey.

⁗⁗⁗

Maddie walks away from the fridge and its mysterious messages left like breadcrumbs on a trail. She forages through her closets and drawers and finds all her candles, then places them around the house and lights them. In Mexico, today is *Dia de los Muertos*, Day of the Dead. For years, she's honored this day by lighting candles and setting photographs on her altar beside her Virgin of Guadalupe. Until now, she's only brought out pictures of her father and Thea, but this time she's added one of her mother who died just this past year.

The picture she's chosen of Thea is one that she always thinks of as a trick done with mirrors and light because Thea looks so happy. She's standing on the wooden deck of their Eighth Avenue suite in Vancouver, dark mountains in the background. She's wearing a dress of Maddie's, a short blue and white polka-dot sundress. She holds the skirt out on either side like a child showing off her party dress. Her shoulder-length auburn hair is in a flip and her smile is open and ingenuous, so unlike who Thea really was.

The photo of Maddie's father has been propped on her desk for years, a close-up of him grinning from under his summer straw hat. He would be disappointed, in his sad Christian way, if he knew that Maddie celebrated Day of the Dead. Depending on how aggrieved he felt, the word *sacrilege* might creep in. *Sinful* would probably make its appearance and *worshipping false idols* would most certainly find its way into the conversation. Maddie's father believed he was the only one who could, with the help of God, hold back the storms of life.

Your dad runs a tight ship, Thea told her once.

Yes.

He was the spiritual captain of the family ship, and with his Bible and his unshakable beliefs, he steered them through the perilous and ungodly shores that might encroach on their life and bring them shame. Maddie had often wondered: to what avail, this dedication to delivering them from evil? Still the rains threatened, the floods came. The boat sank.

Maddie has chosen a photograph of her mother alone. She's young in the picture. It was taken long before Maddie was born. She's sitting on the wooden stoop of the house where she grew up in Winnipeg, her elbows perched on bony knees, head resting on both fists. It must have been summer; she's wearing what appears to be a light cotton dress and tall hollyhocks are growing in the garden next to the steps. Maddie wonders how old she is in this picture. Eighteen? Twenty-one? Had she met Maddie's father yet? Had she even begun to wonder where her life would take her?

Maddie gathers kindling and paper to get a fire going in the wood stove. She searches through her CDs to find music that will honor the day and chooses Henryk Górecki, *Symphony of Sorrowful Songs*. The music lifts and falls; its dark beauty fills the house. She puts the kettle on the propane stove to boil water for tea. On the fridge, she's taped a quote of Virginia Woolf's that she recently found: *Arrange whatever pieces come your way.*

Her therapist convinced her to tape another banner to the fridge during the years she was alone, before Joey came, when all her dreams were about being rescued. The banner said: *Help is not on the way* and it was three years before Maddie understood and accepted its truth. She finally stopped waiting for rescue and took it down. She gave up the therapist that day too.

The kindling finally catches and crackles, sending a cloud of gray smoke out of the chimney, past the window and across her line of vision, obliterating the silhouette of a half-built wharf out beyond the spillway and the rocky shoreline of an empty, low-tide beach. She puts on her work gloves to open the stove and feed it more wood. She finally got gloves that fit after the finger of one of her too-big ones caught fire while she was filling the stove. Her arms are lined with pale half-moon scars from years of burns. She keeps an aloe vera plant in the kitchen window, its sharp spines bursting with the healing gel.

Maddie piles on a few pieces of dry cedar. The wood sputters and leaps into new flame. There is a wind blowing in from the sea in hollow gusts, slamming against the windows, rampaging through the tall cedars and Douglas firs that surround the cabin.

She looks across the road to Claudine's cabin and sees the light in her bathroom, shining like a beacon. Claudine is her closest neighbor, a fiber artist in her mid-sixties who displays and sells her work at an artists' co-op in the city. Their lives have touched over occasional glasses of wine or pots of tea. Claudine is reclusive but always available if anyone in the Grove needs help. She can build and repair things, mend fences, nail down loose shingles or buck up firewood with her chainsaw. They've often looked after each other's cabins when one of them is away, kept fires burning during trips to the city so pipes and plants don't freeze when they're deep in the heart of winter.

Maddie's work is in historical research, most of which she does at home, although she plans a trip to the city at least once a week, usually to the archives or the downtown library. Occasionally, when she had a few days' work in the provincial archives, she and Joey took the ferry over to Victoria. They had a favorite bed and breakfast above an East Indian restaurant where the room was always dense with the odors of korma curry and sweet incense. They hadn't done that in a long time.

Maddie gathers kerosene lamps, fills them and washes the chimneys, in case the power goes out. Her father sometimes told her stories of his childhood on the farm, how he loved watching his mother clean the kerosene lamps' chimneys, her wedding band tapping against the glass. Her father was a man who took deep pleasure in old remembrances, loved to unearth fragments of stories from a lost past. And Maddie was a willing listener, always hoping for unexpected revelations, or some unintended but revealing chink in the family armor.

She drags the rocking chair from its place by the window and sets it in front of the wood stove, gets her wool socks and red plaid jacket that's hanging behind the stove and pulls the thick socks all the way up to her knees. She turns the radio dial to her favorite jazz station. They're playing some scratchy old bebop recording from a long time ago. *Charlie Parker Live at Birdland.* Maddie picks up her journal from the table and looks back at yesterday's entry: *After so many years, island living becomes not just a way of life but a state of mind.* During these long winter nights, it has felt that way sometimes – as though she is marooned, becalmed on a wide empty sea.

In Mexico, Carmelita will be setting up her altar for her mother and for Angela. It is the *angelitos*, the children's spirits that are said to come back first on *Dia de los Muertos*. Lita will place candles around the photographs, set out a bowl of fruit, and grace it with marigolds and sugar skulls. She will not go to the cemetery and sit through the night singing and dancing, and sharing food with other families because that is not where either Angela or her mother is buried. Maddie wishes she could be there with her, especially now, when Lita will be so full of thoughts of Angie, her heart aching with memories of her lost child.

Mexico was the place where Maddie's heart had opened up years ago. The country had grabbed her long before she ever met Joey or Lita. Maddie was in her twenties when she first discovered what she thought of as the *real* Mexico – a land savage and still, a landscape of haunting beauty. She and her boyfriend had hitchhiked all the way from Vancouver, lay in their tent in the Salinas Valley, listening to the wild shriek of night insects. They camped in the cool valleys of California, and slept through the mad crash of Big Sur. Carmel, Monterey, farther down the coast as they moved closer to the border. From the back of a dusty third-class bus that they boarded just over the Arizona border at Nogales, along with scrabbling chickens and hungover mariachis, Maddie's first view of Mexico was of the scrubby flatlands of Sonora.

They'd ridden for days through those dusty mesas, through that land with its ancient history. Maddie came to love its wildness, its unpredictability — tolling church bells, sandstone spires, rough wooden crosses. Even the burros tethered to the *mesquite* trees and standing on the burned earth appeared to be bound there as much by history as anything physical. It was a land where, to Maddie, all things seemed possible. The beaches and the long starry nights below the Tropic of Cancer captivated her, but it was the desert that reined her in and never let her go. She's never been sure what the allure of that barren landscape was, but dusty arroyos and sun-bleached cactus against dry ocher hills can still make her heart sing.

On the wall beside Maddie is a photograph of Joey, an early one. He's leaning over an old guitar that he rarely plays anymore and is looking up at her, questioning. He still has his rangy cowboy look, like a character in an old duster movie. *Joey looks more uncertain these days. The demons are catching up.*

There was a distance in his eyes even back then, when he first came to live with her in the Grove. He has always refused to own any vehicle other than a van. Like a sea creature trapped in its shell, he carries his home on his back, inviolable, safe. But one restless foot is always partway out the door. Primed for flight.

Maddie looks out into the chilly early morning light. She imagines what it would be like to be in Mexico again. Salmon pink and scarlet bougainvillea blossoms, purple jacaranda blooms that drift from the trees like confetti in the time of the winds, the white-faced ibis arcing across the sky at sunset, winging its way toward the lake.

She'd love to see Lita; it's been a while since they've visited. *I could leave right after Christmas.* Most of the research for the project she's working on is done and can easily be finished during the next few weeks. The writing can be done while she's in Mexico. If Joey isn't back by the time she leaves, Claudine will look after the house.

There's no use pretending this isn't about Joey too. The leaky boat that's kept their life together afloat has been sinking for a long time and Maddie sees now that she's been the only one rowing anyway. She can't stay here and wait for the other oar to drop but she doesn't want to chase Joey down like prey either.

She paces the house, waiting for answers to come, some revelation that will tell her what to do. She gets her angel cards and slides one from the purple box. This has become her daily ritual. *Discernment.* That's not much help. Or maybe it is. She puts the kettle on the stove again to make more tea. The fire crackles and snaps. The only other sound is the slap of the wind hurling raindrops against the windowpane.

All her inner compasses are pointing south. If she sees Joey, she sees him, and if she doesn't, she doesn't. It's time to set her body free, to let her feet wander again over the cactus hills and into the sunlight.

She'll book her flight tomorrow and be in Mexico for Epiphany.

Two

Mexico

Maddie has never in her life arrived anywhere unannounced. Yet here she is, streaking through the mountains of Mexico, breaking two of her own prime rules: Never drop in on anyone, no matter how well you know them, and never follow a man anywhere, for any reason. Ever.

Carmelita won't mind. She'll be surprised, but she won't mind. Maddie can't begin to guess what Joey will say. She thinks of this journey as blazing a trail to the source of her fear. Learning how to be free again and once and for all settling the score.

Maddie leans against the bus window and watches the fleeting landscape as though in this very movement, her body will be absorbed by the burnt sienna hills of this high country. It is a terrain that is both alien and familiar. Deep in the hills is a flash of movement of a *vaquero* on his horse, here, then gone, reclaimed by the bleached beauty of the countryside.

How Maddie loves this land. Rolling hills of cactus; *saguaros, agaves, nopales.* The soft sweep of *mesquite,* stone walls that appear out of nowhere and trail off into nothing. Steep olive and ocher valleys, the soft purple blush of *jacarandas* against the green mountains.

She leans back against the high, comfortable seat and unwraps the ham sandwich on brown Bimbo Bread with the packet of *jalapeño* relish that is provided on these deluxe first-class buses. These days, she no longer rides with chickens, hungover mariachis, and fretful, sleepy babies tucked into their mothers' *rebozos,* the way she did when she rode buses through Mexico all those years ago.

Maddie loves flying into Mexico City. She always arrives late at night and each time the journey thrills her. That last hour of flight over the Sierra Madres, peering down into the immense cavern of darkness, broken only by the scattered lights of *pueblos.* Tiny settlements clustered like diamonds in the dark. They soar above the sea of lights, below them one of the biggest cities in the world, carved deep into the *Valle de México* and guarded by the fierce presence of high, cold mountains and steaming volcanoes. Popocatépetl, Iztaccihuatl.

Descending. The world below takes shape in the darkness like a photograph pulled from its watery bath. An emerging familiar. Pyramids to the Sun and the Moon at Teotihuacán huddle somewhere in the darkness. The Avenue of the Dead. Farther away in the heart of the city, the dark forests of Chapultépec. The castle ramparts where during the 1847 Mexican-American war, cadets – some as young as thirteen – wrapped themselves in the Mexican flag and leapt to their deaths rather than be taken by the enemy.

The plane banks, the glittering landscape fans out on either side of the plane windows as far as the eye can see. *Avenida Insurgentes*, a long river of lights like a bright pulsing vein that snakes through the city for twenty-eight kilometers. Finally, the long glide along the tarmac, past the terminal *Aeropuerto Internacional Benito Juárez.*

Home. That's what she feels with every landing.

Maddie arrives at the bus station early the next morning. Each time she makes this familiar journey north from Mexico City, the time goes by more quickly. Small settlements on the city's outskirts peopled with stray dogs, shanties sprouting rebar. Laundry flutters in the hot, dry wind. The bus hurtles past roadside *tiendas* and *restaurantes*, their tables covered in greasy flowered oilcloth. The road becomes gravel and dust as the bus approaches the highway that curves down into the town, pink, orange, and blue adobe houses dotting the hills above the city. Even from here, Maddie can see the Gothic spires of the parish church, the *parroquia*. The evening sky is a misty blue, the horizon smudged from the smoke of brick factories.

The station is cool, cooler even than the air-conditioned bus. Maddie is glad she's wearing her jean jacket. She heads across the wide expanse of gray and white marble floor to the telephone, finds the phone card that she kept from her last visit to Mexico, and dials the number she knows by heart. Lita answers on the first ring.

"*Bueno.*"

"Lita? It's me."

"Maddie. Hey."

"I'm here."

18

"Here? You mean *here* here?"

"Yeah. I'm here. I'm at the bus station."

"Wow," she says, and there's a beat of silence. "You're really here?" Her voice is quiet. "He's not around, Maddie. I mean, he's in Mexico, but he's not staying with me. At least not right now."

"It's okay, Lita," Maddie says quickly. "It doesn't matter. I didn't expect him to be here." She sighs. "It's a long story. As usual."

Carmelita laughs. "Well, you'll get to tell me all about it in five minutes. I'm coming to get you."

Maddie sits down on one of the hard, blue bus station chairs and waits. Carmelita is her oldest friend. They've known one another for almost forty years. No one knows Maddie better, has seen more deeply into her secret hidden places, and is familiar with her frailties and her moments of grace. That's why Maddie knows it's okay to be here now.

Both the front doors and the doors to the loading bay are open and the cold, high mountain air drifts through the building. The grating call of crickets resonates from outside. Even here in this small, beautiful town, Maddie can smell the familiar miasma that is Mexico, and the odor of the garbage-strewn *arroyo*, now just a dried-up waterway. Lita calls it Stinky Canal.

Maddie picks up her backpack and drags her wheeled tote bag over to the door to watch for Carmelita. Lita pulls up to the curb and parks across from the taxi pickup area, then leans out the window with a big grin and waves. She gets out of the car and Maddie picks up her backpack and runs to her. They hug and Maddie breathes in the warm, spicy vanilla scent that is Lita, smells it in her long dark braid, in the silver and turquoise braceleted arm that encircles Maddie's shoulders, in the wool of her soft green sweater.

"I can't believe this," Lita says as she slings Maddie's bag into the back seat. "You look great, by the way." She hesitates. "Are you okay?" She puts Maddie's tote bag into the trunk, slams it shut and climbs into the car.

"I am," Maddie says. She surprises herself because she knows it's true.

They're curving down around *Avenida de La Guadalupe*, heading into the *colonia* where Carmelita lives.

"I know it's weird, me showing up like this," Maddie says. "Especially with Joey here in Mexico too. I guess something perverse in me didn't want to let you know I was coming." She rolls down the window and breathes in the cool night air. The fragrance of frying tortillas. Tamales, spicy gorditas. "He doesn't know I'm here either."

Lita waves to an old woman crossing the street. She is small as a gnome in her blue-checked apron and carries a basket of dried flowers on her head. "Okay," says Lita, "I'm listening."

"Tomorrow," Maddie says.

Lita looks at her and nods. "Sure," she says. "However it is, is okay with me. You know that."

They turn down one of the narrow, cobbled streets, power lines slung low, still hung with remnants of Christmas. It's January 4, two days before Epiphany – Three Kings' Day – the most exciting day of the holidays for Mexican children. Yellow lamplight falls along the narrow stone sidewalk and pools from under the heavy closed doors. Maddie is suddenly filled with the happiness of *right now*. This very moment in time fills her to the brim and is sheer perfection. *I'm glad I'm here. It's the right place to be. I'm home.*

Lita parks on the street in front of her *casita*. She unlocks the heavy, carved wooden doors and Maddie remembers all at once how much she loves the familiarity of Lita's flower-strewn courtyard, the now-silent green-tiled fountain, gardens filled with red and pink hibiscus, mounds of bougainvillea climbing old stone walls, tall cactus in round clay pots or jammed into rusted red and gold Carbonell olive oil tins.

They bring in Maddie's things and then sit at the kitchen table drinking apricot tea sweetened with agave syrup. A gas heater illuminates the room and casts a soft, shadowy glow on a small white statue of *Santisima Virgen de Juquila* that stands next to a pot of geraniums in Lita's grotto altar. Books and pottery fill wooden shelves. A bright Oaxacan carpet covers part of the tiled floor. A thick Mexican blanket is flung across the couch beside an open book and Lita's reading glasses. The *mesquite* tree outside the window throws long, lacy shadows against the wall.

"Were you reading when I called?"

"Yeah. Doing some prep work for a class."

Carmelita teaches writing workshops during the winter, and throughout the summer she travels, mostly on buying trips to Oaxaca for her shop in town near the *zocalo*.

"And being alone is still good for you?"

Lita is silent for a moment. She takes their empty cups to the sink, rinses them and turns them upside down on a brightly embroidered red cloth carefully folded on the tiled counter. "For me right now, life is perfect."

"I'm glad," Maddie says, not knowing what else to say, feeling so acutely the imperfection of her own life. But it's true - if Lita's content, then Maddie's glad.

She collects her things and finds her way to the room that is always hers when she's visiting Lita. She pauses at the door, looks back.

"Where is he, do you think?" The absence of Joey in their conversation leaves a space between them, too awkward to sleep on.

"He talked about going on the *cabalgata* to Cristo Rey," says Carmelita. "He's always wanted to go." She begins unbraiding her hair. It shimmers blue-black in the light from the stove. "He has a friend in Guanajuato who has horses. They'll ride together."

The *cabalgata* is a cowboy pilgrimage to the site just a couple of hours away, the home of a sixty-five-foot statue of Christ that resides in what is thought to be the geographical center of Mexico. Christ at its very heart. On the day before Epiphany, thousands of cowboys from all over Mexico and the U.S. snake their way on horseback through cactus-covered meadows, high, green cornfields, across mountain switchbacks like a long river of the faithful, until they reach the feet of *el Niño Dios* at the top of Cubilate Mountain, his outstretched arms waiting to encompass and to bless.

"He's never said that he wanted to do that," Maddie says. "I'm surprised he never told me."

"You know my brother. I don't think he knew himself until he actually left." Lita slides a white cotton nightgown over her head and shakes her hair free. "He said he might spend some time in D.F. afterwards. See a friend in the city. So he may not be back for a while, Maddie. A few days, anyway."

"That's okay." Maddie has no idea what it is she'd want to say, even if she does see him.

"Sleep well then, Mad. We'll talk tomorrow."

Maddie lies in the bed, wondering if she'll be able to sleep. An iron cross hangs on the wall above the carved headboard, a sturdy presence and symbol of faith that always pleases her. She listens to the familiar sounds of barking roof dogs and the rasping song of crickets outside. The soft slap of Lita's bare feet as they move across the floor.

Maddie studies the framed photograph of Angela on the wall. She has Carmelita's eyes and her long dark hair. Richard's grin. She looks about six. The picture must have been taken not long before the accident. They were living in Vancouver then, and it was before she and Carmelita met. Maddie remembers Lita telling her about going to the Buddhist Centre after she put the twisted remains of the bike into the garage and closed the door on it forever. Lita wasn't a Buddhist but she didn't know where else to turn.

"What do I do now?" she asked the Lama. "What do you do when you've lost your only child?"

"You never stop being grateful," he said, "that you had her for six years."

She and Richard were so solid in the beginning. They were strong, held one another up. But Maddie knows that it takes more than strength to survive the death of a child. She doesn't know what it takes and since she has no children, she never will. In the end, the sorrow tore at their marriage, tugged at its weave, until in its unraveling it became unmendable. The hollow place of their sadness, the torn places, became valleys too deep to traverse. The silence grew tighter, frozen into a cold war until the final door slammed shut. What was a scream of sorrow became a deep, painful silence. Carmelita moved back to Mexico and for eight years she has lived alone, just a few miles from where she grew up.

Maddie feels angry, knowing that Joey is going on the *cabalgata,* though she doesn't know why. Is it a pilgrimage of atonement? The anger she's kept so long at bay threatens her now. It has been nipping at her heels like an unbridled pup. The betrayal. Whose? His betrayal of her or hers of herself?

When Maddie thinks of their life together now, it's not Joey she thinks of but the place he came from, a town not far from where she was visiting Carmelita now. A village set in the bleached, burnt hills of the Mexican highlands with escarpments that push out into mesas and benchland where the sun burns white and hot all year round. A pueblo so otherworldly and different from her island on Canada's West Coast, with its foggy bays and inlets like long, cool arms waiting in a perpetual welcoming embrace.

Something about that place in Mexico where Maddie and Joey first met fills her with a strange hollow sadness. Maybe it has to do with the indifference of those dusty streets, the emptiness of those dry, inhospitable hills, sere, brown and yellow. Uninhabitable. That desolate, empty place turned out to be the person he has become, as though what they had has collapsed in on itself, lost its heart. But the difference between him and that dusty little pueblo is that the town promised Maddie nothing. He had offered her his soul.

A weight settles in Maddie's chest like a cold stone, and a rush of adrenalin reminds her of where she is. What will she say if she sees him? Their life together circled back on itself, ending up here, where it all began.

The wind gusts and branches of bougainvillea brush against the *casita* walls, a restless scrabbling at the door. Scattered raindrops fling themselves against the window. Wind chimes sing in the tangled trees and leaves skitter like tumbleweed across the bricks of the courtyard. Maddie pulls up the quilt and waits for the slide down into the long deep canyons of sleep.

୫୦୯୫

Maddie wakes to the familiar scrabbling of cactus wrens on the adobe roof tiles and remembers hearing rumbles of thunder sometime in the night. She's amazed that it's already light. She lies in bed for a while, eyes closed, listening to birds, their scrappy morning conversations, the calling of doves. Footsteps run down the street, then fade into the distance. From far away a train whistle; two long, one short, one long, and she remembers how train whistles everywhere sound just the same.

She gets up and rakes the filmy white curtains across the window. A wren swoops down from the white bougainvillea and lights on a branch of the *mesquite* tree. The tangerine sun washes the yellow plaster buildings across the street in morning light. The sky is blue and white clouds hang suspended outside the window. Cool air drifts in and Maddie smells the earth and damp streets from last night's rain – the clean scent of a new day. There are no sounds from inside, nothing to indicate that Lita is up or even at home. Church bells clang, calling the faithful to mass, or chiming out the hour perhaps. She counts the gongs. Nine.

Morning light falls on the photograph of Angela. She has the smooth skin of her mother, the untroubled smile. Even after Angela's death, about the time Maddie met her, Carmelita's face reflected a unique serenity. As time went on, Lita became even more tranquil, but in a strange, unreachable way. Looking at her, you could almost imagine that her body had absorbed the terrible sadness, turned it into an inner light so pure and bright that it was as though she had swallowed the moon.

She would not be defeated by life, Lita said in the days after, or be done in by despair. She bore no grudge. Maddie remembers how many of Lita's friends thought she was crazy to even think of forgiving the person who had taken away her child, the man who had hit her, then dragged her and her mangled bike for a block, half underneath his car. They thought she should have raged against the terrible truth of what happened, that she should have kept her anger honed, clean and sharp like the steel edge of a knife.

"They don't understand forgiveness," Lita told Maddie then. "Forgiveness isn't about somebody else, it's about yourself." Other people's anger only made her sad. "Anger is like a fire inside you, tearing at your guts," she said. "An unfixable pain. I'll never find peace in anger." She told Maddie again and again, "What I can't forgive, I'll have to live with every day of my life. I won't do that."

When Lita moved back to her home town, she set up a shop selling Mexican folk art. She traveled through the villages of Oaxaca buying hand-dyed carpets woven on backstrap looms from Teotitlán de Valle, black pottery from San Bartolo Coyotépec, ceramics from the Aguilar sisters in Ocotlán, baskets woven with smoked palm fronds, and hand-pounded tinware from villages farther north.

Maddie pulls on her jeans and a T-shirt and opens the door to the living room. Lita has left the gas fireplace on. Maddie's glad. She'd forgotten how cool mornings can be in the highlands.

She hears the scratch of a straw broom on the cobblestones outside the *casita* door — probably one of the *senoras* or a maid from a *casa* nearby. A key turns in the lock and Lita comes in, breathless from climbing up the hill from the market.

"*Hola.* Good morning. How did you sleep?" She is carrying a bunch of freshly cut red roses. "The flower lady was on her corner today," she says. "I haven't seen her in a while. I'm glad she's back." She takes vegetables and fruit from her red and yellow plaid *bolsa* – guavas, avocados, tomatoes, fresh tortillas, yogurt, a couple of limes, and a bag of dark coffee.

"I slept like a baby," says Maddie. She reaches for a clear blue glass vase to put the roses in. Lita makes coffee and pours it into bright Mexican mugs and they sit out in the courtyard under a canopy of jacaranda blossoms to catch up on each other's lives. Maddie tells her about Joey's leaving with only the frailest of explanations.

"Just words on the fridge," Maddie told her.

"What words?"

"Have dreams. Must travel. Open sad smile."

"And what are those words supposed to mean?"

"I don't know, Lita." Maddie pours herself another cup of coffee. "They're just words."

"There's only one problem with that, Mad." Lita pushes the agave jar across the table to Maddie. "He doesn't live his words. He never has."

"Well, I guess I know that now, don't I?"

Words were the wall that Joey hid behind. The place where he lives. He can build a country out of words. He just doesn't always choose to live there.

"Well, you asked him, didn't you? What he meant by *open sad smile*?"

"No."

"Really, Maddie?"

"I didn't want to know. Not then, anyway."

But Maddie did know. She's known for a long time. Lying beside him these last few months, tracing the ridges and hollows of his body in her mind, feeling the sea drift widening between them. All those sleepless nights. She'd get out of bed, make tea in the dark, having long ago memorized the morphing night shapes of the kitchen. Then she'd pull the rocking chair in front of the fire and sit alone with her tea until dawn crept through the blinds and fell across the floor.

She knew.

৪০৩

That first warm summer night they met in Mexico, Joey and Maddie sat outside in the rain, lost in a storm of words against the backdrop of solitary hills and a black, empty sky. They stayed there long after Lita had gone to bed. Joey showed Maddie the treasures he'd collected when he first came up from Texas through an underground movement, and was living on a ranch in the Kootenays.

He told her about the place where he had first settled, where the Columbia River runs cold and fast, cutting a swath through the valley floor. "The river," he told her, "once carried pioneers and adventurers north to the gold fields." It was by that river that Joey, an explorer of sorts himself, staked out his claim on a piece of the past, camped out with his gold pan near its quiet bends and dark, still depths.

He had not always lived in that place or even in this country. He had left Texas and escaped to Canada when his draft number came up. After their mother died a couple of years later, Carmelita followed him west and emigrated from Texas to Vancouver. Maddie had met Carmelita in Vancouver then but she didn't meet Joey until years later when they were both visiting Lita in Mexico at the same time.

Lita and Joey had lived a hardscrabble existence. Their mother, who raised two children on her own after their father left, had been beaten down by the struggle and had taken them to live in Texas in search of a better life.

"We moved so much," Joey said. "Even when we were in Texas. I needed some kind of connection to the places we'd been. I needed a polestar." He leaned across the table toward Maddie, his intensity an almost tactile thing. "So I started collecting things."

"What kinds of things?"

"Just things from the streets at first," he said. "Shards of colored glass, old bottles I'd find in empty lots. Then when I got to the Kootenays, I started finding really old relics. Chinese stuff. Bottles, purple from the manganese in the soil they'd been buried in, jars and rusted cans, old coins, shards of blue and white pottery, tarnished silver buttons. Sometimes tiny nuggets of gold."

"Chinese? In the Kootenays?"

"For sure," he said. "A lot of people don't know that history. The Chinese came for the gold rush, settled in mining camps in the Columbia Valley sometime in the mid-1860s. Later they headed farther north into the Cariboo where the bigger fields were. But there are lots of ghost towns in the Selkirks and the Monashees, even now. I've found beautiful artifacts there – blue pottery like the kind you see in Chinatown, glass medicine bottles, Chinese coins. Moving around got to be part of me. Part of who I am. I had no attachments except for this stuff." He waved his hand in the direction of his treasures. "No roots. So the collecting got into my blood. I didn't feel like I belonged any place, so I took parts of places with me."

He had carried all of this – his whole universe – with him like a talisman. A lifetime of collecting, pulling from the earth its secrets. It was the only currency he knew. He'd spread that life out in front of Maddie that night as they sat in the soft summer rain. A gesture that promised everything. And Maddie, with her whole body leaning toward his every word, the grazing of her hand against his arm, soft murmurings of affirmation, in her wordless way, had made promises too.

The most powerful offering Joey gave Maddie the night they met was his confession. He'd been in jail. For kidnapping. And she was underage. Fifteen. "A trumped-up charge brought about by the girl's parents," he said. There was never a kidnapping. She was his girlfriend and they were in love.

"But she was younger than I thought," he told her. "Fifteen. Too young obviously, since I was thirty. The thing is, I didn't know that then. She told me she was twenty. And she looked twenty."

Maddie didn't know what to say. He was Lita's brother and Lita had never said much about it. Or had Maddie just refused to listen?

"Everyone deserves a second chance," she said. "You've paid the price, haven't you?"

He'd told her that he had. But was that true? As soon as the words were out of Maddie's mouth, she realized that she didn't really know. Had he paid the price? And was he remorseful? He looked at her and smiled but didn't answer.

He had to wear one of those neon orange jumpsuits, he told her. Because of the age of the girl, he was kept with the other sex offenders.

"You have no idea," he said. "The humiliation. Making us wear those monkey suits."

Up until then, Maddie had always assumed that the men who ended up in those neon orange jumpsuits, housed with other sex offenders, were there because that's where they belonged. She felt confused. Compromised in some way.

"I'm not like them," he said. His voice was edged with anger.

But don't they all say that? Maddie had pushed that thought from her mind. He told her that when the girl's parents found them traveling in his van through Alberta, they'd confronted him and turned him in. He'd lost the heart for running, anyway, he said. He'd run from Texas all the way to the Kootenays. And by then, there was no place left to hide.

When Joey came to her that first night with his story, his head bowed low in humble apology, Maddie was overwhelmed. Drawn by his sadness, his shame. *He's so honest, telling me his darkest secrets.*

Later, after he'd gone, Maddie couldn't sleep so she went outside and sat alone in the courtyard. An almost imperceptible breeze rustled the lacy fronds of the pepper tree. Other than the soft glow of the gas lamplight against the earth and the diamond piercings of the stars against the blanket of black night, there was only darkness. Just that pool of ghostly light like an oasis in the middle of the desert landscape. The heat was almost palpable. She could smell smoke from the brick factories in the hills. Somewhere in a nearby compound the twang of a guitar.

31

Laughter. The spicy scent of carnitas, onions, tortillas. Maddie sat for a long time thinking about Joey that night, of something he'd said: "Maddie, you're a gift to me."

"What makes you think that?"

"Your openness. Your acceptance. I've told you things. Things I haven't told anyone else."

Maddie remembered the way he'd walked toward her that morning when Lita first introduced them. Stooped, his head lowered, as if bent with an incalculable weight. Little did she know then, the weight he carried.

He had given her his life, his story, all his sorrow and pain, lifted up the burden of his sadness and handed it to her like precious cargo. So she took it. Grateful, humbled at such openness. He was offering his soul.

On Maddie's last day in Mexico all those years ago, before she flew home, Joey arrived at Lita's to retile her adobe roof. Maddie sat in the sun and read *Love in the Time of Cholera*. Every hour or so, he climbed down from the roof, carefully unstrapped his leather knee pads, and sat and talked to her.

"So," he said. "What're you reading?"

She held up the book so he could read the cover.

"Good?"

"I love it. I've read it once already."

"Read me something."

"Here's the first line," she said. "It's one of the greatest opening lines ever." And she read: "*It was inevitable. The scent of bitter almonds always reminded him of the fate of unrequited love.*"

He smiled and said nothing. But while Maddie read, he pulled his chair closer, watched her with such intensity and purpose. If such a thing were possible, she may have even thought she could feel the hand of Fate touch her shoulder. She sometimes amused herself with thoughts like that. It might have been a warning too, but she never thought of that then.

On the bus back to Mexico City, Maddie leaned against the window and thought of this man who had hijacked her thoughts. The next day on the plane as she neared home, she looked down at the rugged coastline that hugged the granite slopes, plummeting waterfalls, narrow railway bridges that spanned swift, sullen rivers hundreds of feet below. By the time she reached the ferry to the island, the soft curves of the coast and the blue familiar of Howe Sound, a yearning had already begun and Maddie knew then that her life had changed forever.

Three

Vancouver: mid-Sixties

s for me and my house, we will serve the Lord. Those lofty words proclaimed themselves from picture frames that hung slightly askew on their living room walls. The embroidered scriptures were scalding reminders to Maddie of her family's rigid life. The preacher's pronouncements of hell doomed them if they didn't repent. The hymn singing, ragged and thin without the accompaniment of worldly trappings like an organ. Prayers at night, kneeling on the cold floor, alone with God.

Maddie's parents' beliefs were unshakable. They were not to be questioned or denied. Their home was a fortress for their faith and Maddie's prison just as surely as if it had been built of bricks and mortar. A place to contain their lives, to keep them safe from the minefield that was the world outside their door. The rules were unforgiving, impossibly stringent: no movies or dances. Maddie could not date or listen to music. She was not allowed to wear pants, earrings or makeup of any kind. She kept those things hidden at the houses of her friends, or tucked away under a beam in the garage. They didn't own a radio or a TV.

Maddie had no faith at all. Fear was her guiding light. The disappearance of her parents in the Rapture was a terror she could never get beyond. No matter how many times she pleaded with God to not leave her behind, she feared always that her prayers would never be enough to save her. She saved herself in the end. But it wasn't the kind of saving her parents had in mind.

Maddie's family had been lured west from Winnipeg by an opportunity to buy a nursery business where they could work together and be self-employed. A splinter group from the Winnipeg Brethren Church had settled in Vancouver years before and enthusiastically welcomed Maddie's family into their midst, pleased that they would be adding four more bodies to the meager numbers of those who clung to their truth. For Maddie and her brother, the move brought some relief. The Vancouver preacher was mild-mannered and friendlier, although still rabidly devout. Not above cornering Maddie and questioning her as to the state of her soul.

In the end, nothing changed much in their day-to-day lives in Vancouver except that Maddie and her brother were allowed to forgo Thursday night prayer meetings. They still had to go to church three times on Sunday: the morning breaking of bread, Sunday school in the afternoon, and the Gospel Meeting at night. The hungry flames of hell still tore at Maddie's dreams.

When Maddie was sixteen, Thea moved into the neighborhood. She and Maddie fell into a rhythm of hanging together in Maddie's basement room, listening to music, and sneaking out at night to folk clubs and the after-hours jazz club that was just a few blocks away. Their world was exploding with the beginnings of a new era – the 1960s. It was in those secret places they found a home, a world on the fringe, a place where the limitations and boundaries Maddie had grown up with were beginning to crumble and fade.

As Maddie got older, she learned to navigate the traps and undertow of her parents' faith. That meant treading water to keep her head above the stifled world she had grown up in. Thea was fearless. She hadn't grown up in Maddie's world and could navigate life's edges without a moment's hesitation. She was always the first one to peer over the rim of the precipice to assess its possibilities and decide whether to jump. Thea lived by her own rules, lawless as a stray cat.

It was a cold fall afternoon, one of those fretful gray days that left Maddie moody and anxious, when Thea's presence first crossed her line of vision. Thea and her mother had moved into the house across the street a few days before. Maddie was standing at the upstairs window, watching the shadows of distant trees and wondering how it would have been if they had stayed on the Prairies. She had come to feel the unique rhythm of the city deep in her bones, that restless movement of the coast, its shifting tides, the comings and goings of ships. She had never before had that ability to watch her world from a distance. It was not only the empty Prairies that had held her. Her family had lived their whole lives on a flat plane, unable to see anything move or change.

Maddie leaned out of the window into the early evening light. Is this what *gloaming* was? Dusk with a lonesome feel to it? She'd have to look it up. A stillness enveloped her, as though the clamor and hum of the day had finally settled into evening, a time of quiet contemplation before darkness fell.

Then Thea pirouetted past the window of the house across the street. Maddie couldn't tell what she looked like. The dark silhouette vanished as abruptly as it had appeared. She thought then that there was something magical in that vision, something that was perhaps even auspicious. Later, she realized that Thea had done it with great calculation for the benefit of Maddie's brother, Tom, whose room faced Thea's.

From the beginning, Maddie was both shocked and delighted by Thea's boldness, her extravagance, her brash, sure presence. When Thea's mother was away, Thea would stay with Maddie on weekends. Sometimes, she would creep downstairs and slip perfume-scented notes under Tom's door. She never told Maddie what they said, but Maddie once found a folded-up piece of paper that Thea had left in the drawer of the bedside table. It was a Walt Whitman quote from *Song of Myself*. Maddie recognized it from her high school English class. *I believe in those wing'd purposes*. That was all. The note was as enigmatic as Thea herself.

On the nights Thea stayed over, Thea would lie in the dark and tell Maddie stories with strange, nightmare endings. Innocent objects – sinks, tables, and chairs – became threatening and untrustworthy in her stories. Nothing was safe. Her voice was drowsy and unfamiliar in the dark and she often drifted off mid-story. She ground her teeth in her sleep.

Maddie was startled one day during their graduation year when Thea told her she had been accepted into the same nursing program that Maddie was enrolled in. For months, Thea had been vacillating about whether to find a job or apply to a college.

"When did you apply to get into the program?" Maddie asked. She had applied the year before and had been accepted months earlier.

"A few weeks ago. When you told me about it."

"And you got in?"

"Somebody had dropped out so they had a space," Thea said. "Just for me." She laughed. "I'm glad you came up with the idea."

It hadn't been Maddie's idea for Thea at all. She had been mulling over her own future and had simply told Thea what it was that had lured her into nursing. Being an LPN – a Licensed Practical Nurse – involved only a year's training with a guaranteed job at any hospital in the city. For Maddie, that meant independence. Freedom. A life that would be her own.

Thea had already claimed her life. Her father had left them years before and her mother worked long hours and was rarely home. It was Thea who made the rules in her house. She strode through each day as though life owed her something – a promise perhaps, of some serendipitous occurrence that waited around the next corner, or at the very least, a small but recognizable nod from the Universe for simply being who she was.

Thea collected words. Like a scavenger unearthing lost treasure, she found them, wove them into phrases, polished and refined them, so that by the time they leapt from her mouth, they had been shaped into objects of utter perfection.

Thea had been staring out the window of her living room one day and said, apropos of nothing, "Dilettante. I suspect I am one. A very shallow person." She turned to Maddie. "Dilettante. My word for today."

"You have a word for each day?"

"Well, not every day. Just when I think of it. I collect words."

"Why?" asked Maddie.

"To use. That's what words are for," she said, as though Maddie was too stupid to have figured that out on her own. "But I use them well. I choose carefully."

"But why?" Maddie asked again.

"Because it pleases me." Thea walked into the bedroom. For her, the conversation was over. Thea didn't ever want to be caught without words, and she rarely was. She wanted her armor intact, her weapons at the ready. And her weapon of choice was always words.

ᏸᏆᏸ

Maddie is looking at a photograph taken in 1965 on the day she and Thea graduated from nursing school. Forty-nine of them are standing in the bright fall sunshine, uniformed and smiling, forming a green Z on the college steps. A girl in the bottom row is holding a sign that says *Vancouver's Fifty-Second Class of Practical Nurses.*

They are all smiling eyes and practiced innocence. Bouffants and beehives are piled high; auburn, black, bleached blonde. Maddie's own face, perplexed and serious, reflects a clear-eyed youthfulness. Her hair, shorter then, frames her face in a pale golden storm, rebellion hidden in the beaded bracelet and the patchouli oil on her wrist. But the real rebellion – in a world that was sliding into the chaos of war and protest – was the one that was rumbling inside Maddie's heart.

Maddie remembers the photo and the day. Can see it now. Thea leaning against the wrought iron railing, insolent, fingers playing idly with a pack of Player's Filter, which she has hidden in her uniform pocket. Her long dark hair is tied back from her face with a narrow, green velvet ribbon chosen specially to mock the drab green cotton uniforms.

The picture makes Maddie laugh. Thea was never innocent.

Bitch, Thea would say if she could. *What do you mean by that? I was your best friend, Maddie. I loved you. I gave you poetry, silver, and moonlight. I gave you words. I gave you a voice to speak.*

And yes, she had given her all those things. In their conversations long into the night, Maddie often heard what she hadn't wanted to hear. Thea opened doors to her past and lingered there. Her evaluations were brutal, her criticisms cut to the bone. She scorned Maddie's father with his religious tracts and his out-of-the-blue sermons. *He's a bully*, she'd say, *with all his God talk.* And though Maddie knew Thea was right, it made her unaccountably angry. *I'm just trying to be honest*, Thea would insist. *You'll thank me one day.*

Soon after they graduated from nursing school and found jobs, Thea and Maddie moved into an apartment on the middle floor of a rambling old house near the hospital. The house was one of a group of three-story turreted mansions that were eventually torn down to make way for the pastel, look-alike Mediterranean-style condominiums overlooking False Creek, a neighborhood that became all the rage in the eighties. A stone walkway climbed from the street to an overgrown yard, continued past a weeping willow tree, and then joined another path bordered with heather and wild poppies. A long flight of creaky wooden stairs led to the second floor and their suite. They took turns sleeping in the bedroom and on the pullout Murphy bed in the living room, depending on who was working the night shift. They were rarely on the same shift together.

In the bedroom, the lumpy double bed was covered with an old patchwork quilt that Thea had inherited from her grandmother. A window ledge ran along one side and the end of the room. The ledge was cluttered with early-morning coffee cups, a bedraggled spider plant, a lopsided fern, copies of F. Scott Fitzgerald's *Tender Is the Night*, Steinbeck's *Cannery Row,* and a thin and battered copy of the *Baghavad Gita*. A door led to a small wooden balcony. The view of False Creek was industrial then – a wasteland of grit and smoke, dilapidated factories, and mills linked by rutted dirt roads. Maddie would stand on the balcony at night after the factory noise had ground to a halt and the dust and smoke had settled, and wait for the wind. The wind always carried the sharp, salty scent of the sea, even where they lived in the heart of the city.

On the wall, they'd hung a poster advertising a mantra rock dance, with proceeds going to the opening of the San Francisco Krishna Temple. Featured were the Grateful Dead, Allen Ginsberg, and Big Brother and the Holding Company. *Krishna Consciousness Comes West* the headline proclaimed. A faded imitation Chinese carpet graced the living room floor. Mice skittered across the countertops at night. Their furniture was simple. Bookcases made of bricks and boards, an old horsehair sofa, lamps and cushions from the Sally Ann.

Maddie's brother Tom came over sometimes and played his sax in the bathroom because it was a small room with no windows and the notes leapt off the walls and ceilings, clear, bright bubbles of sound: *Stardust, Begin the Beguine, Take the 'A' Train.* He would bring his jazz records: Dizzy Gillespie, Billie Holiday at the Cotton Club, and Louis Armstrong playing *West End Blues,* tender, edgy, heartbreaking.

The kitchen was even smaller than the bedroom, equipped with only an icebox and a gas stove.

"Great," Thea had said when she first saw the stove. "Gas. That'll come in handy if I ever decide to kill myself."

"Jeez, Thea."

"I'm giving it until I'm twenty-two," she said. "If I haven't pulled it together by then, I'm outta here. Let's face it, Mad, it's my inexorable fate."

"Meaning?"

"My destiny."

"Uh huh," was all Maddie said. She pushed open the wooden door to the balcony and looked out over the city. Let Thea's words fall away across the ocean, over the mountains, and into forever.

Maddie had heard it all before.

耂C&#x8

Charlie and Dogface were friends of Thea. Maddie didn't really know them but she'd met them a few times when they'd picked Thea up for one of their weekend hikes. Charlie lived in the neighborhood where Thea had grown up and they'd been good friends for years. It was only in the past few months that Charlie had begun bringing Dogface around, the tag-along misfit, so named, Charlie said, because of an accident that had left his face profoundly disfigured. Thea told Maddie that she was pretty sure Charlie's explanation of Dogface was the sanitized version and that the real story probably came from deeper and more dangerous waters. Although Dogface was kind and gentle, always – the quintessential Quasimodo with a heart of gold – Thea suspected that there were things she didn't and shouldn't know, things that existed far beyond the riptide of her imaginings.

Charlie loved guns and worked in a gun shop downtown. He'd given Thea a pearl-handled derringer for Christmas. She carried it around in her handbag sometimes. There was something about its secret presence, she said, the sweet heft of a thing so forbidden, that made her walk taller and check out her own image as she strode past glass windows on downtown streets. The gun had no bullets in it, but Thea didn't care. It was the aura of danger, the beauty and mystique of that hidden secret that intrigued her.

Charlie used to take Thea and Dogface into the forested backcountry north of Squamish or high up in the mountains above West Vancouver. They'd line up cans on a log and shoot them off with rifles. Charlie taught Thea to shoot, bought her a rifle that rested perfectly in the hollow of her shoulder. Once she got the feel of it, she loved everything about shooting. The kick, her sure, clear-eyed aim, the *blam* as the cans sailed off the log. She was a good shot.

Those days with Charlie, Thea said once, were among the happiest moments in her life. She stood tall and sure in the cold sunshine and bright fall leaves, the rifle on her shoulder. The clear, sharp crack of the explosion echoed through the frozen air.

One day Charlie just stopped coming by. When Maddie asked Thea about it, Thea shrugged and told her she wasn't seeing him anymore. "He was a friend," she said, "nothing more." As if that explained anything.

Maddie knew that Thea missed those forays into the hills, and Maddie missed Thea's stories of the rugged wilderness, the untamed land. It was a place where, in Thea's stories, life felt bigger than anything Maddie could imagine.

"So where is he?"

"That, Maddie, is an imperspicuity."

"Thea . . ."

"It means it cannot be explained."

No matter how many times Maddie asked Thea about Charlie's disappearance, Thea would never say more than, "He's gone, Maddie. Just leave it at that."

So Maddie finally stopped asking.

৪০৫৪

Coming face to face with death was something Maddie hadn't counted on, although she must have known it was inevitable in a down-at-the-heels geriatric ward like B6, a boneyard stalked by death. It was a prison of sorts where nurses became custodians, reluctant witnesses to the daily humiliations and the savage betrayal of flesh and bones.

Thea and Maddie worked on a medical-surgical ward with a few orthopedic patients thrown in. In truth, the ward was just a home for the outcasts, the last bastion of care when beds couldn't be found anywhere else in the hospital.

Maddie was on the morning shift, responsible for opening the ward and getting everyone up, or at least getting those up who were capable of getting up – not many – and just waking the others, shoving thermometers into sticky morning mouths, handing out mouthwash, basins of tepid water, towels.

Maddie surveyed the ward – twenty beds on each side divided by a long corridor. Dim morning light seeped through cracks in the closed curtains. It was not yet seven. An early riser fumbled through the drawers of her bedside table. Someone woke and rolled over with a groan.

She had half an hour to prepare the ward for breakfast, opening curtains, giving bedpans and wash water to those who couldn't get up, assisting those who could. She wound up beds to a sitting position and slid bedside tables over, ready for trays of food. Tin pots of brackish tea, gluey porridge, wobbly eggs and cold, unbuttered toast. It should have been simple enough and would have been, if it weren't for the additional requests. Someone who wanted their dentures cleaned or another bottle of mouthwash. Fresh towels or a pill for pain. There were smells, unpleasant and sometimes unidentifiable, of sickness and decay. Maddie couldn't have known then that she would dream of those rooms and those smells years later, bewildered, her dream self adrift, lost somewhere in the maze of the hospital.

After the breakfast trays had been collected, Maddie began her morning's work with the seven patients who would be her responsibility for the day. Only Mrs. Eldridge required a bed bath. She had Parkinson's disease and sat propped like a china doll against the white pillows. Her face typified the disease, a vacant mask that gave no clue as to what delight or terror hid behind the silence. Only her eyes moved, darted like small, trapped birds. Her body trembled.

"Are you cold, Mrs. Eldridge?" Maddie asked.

Mrs. Eldridge nodded and wrapped thin arms around her body.

"I'll hurry then."

Maddie filled the metal basin with hot water and removed all her blankets, then covered her with a flannelette bath blanket. Flesh, almost transparent and thin as paper, stretched over bones, her breasts withered to almost nothing. Nipples like two hard raisins. Maddie could hear the residents and interns making their morning rounds, coming nearer. Suddenly, one of the residents was behind her, poking his head through the yellow curtain.

"May I come in?"

"Of course." Maddie covered Mrs. Eldridge with another blanket, then stepped back and knocked her elbow against the wash basin, spilling some water over the bedside table. It ran in rivulets down the side of the table and onto the floor.

Shit.

Maddie gathered the dirty laundry and tried to wipe up the spill. The resident bent over Mrs. Eldridge and took her hand in his.

"Hello, Sweetheart," he said. "And how's my favorite patient this morning?"

Mrs. Eldridge didn't answer. Her thin, blue-veined hand tightened around the resident's. His white coat brushed against Maddie's face as she leaned over to pull up the rest of the covers. He smelled of laundry starch and disinfectant soap. He straightened up and grinned at Maddie.

"You look a little flustered, nurse," he said. He laughed. "I don't bite." He raked open the curtains and moved off to the other end of the ward.

Maddie was uncertain and anxious around men and boys. She was nineteen then but hadn't ever had a real boyfriend. From the time she'd been old enough to understand that her family was different, she'd struggled to keep the world inside her home separate from the world outside, ever vigilant to ensure the two would never collide. The world she lived in with her parents was a minefield of embarrassing possibilities. Her father would shove Sunday school papers and Bible tracts into the hands of her unsuspecting friends. *Messages of Love*, the paper was called, but the stories had titles like *How Will You Spend Eternity?* Or *Will You Be the One Who is Left Behind?* All the titles threatened doom and destruction. There were no messages of love.

As dating was out of the question, Maddie wasn't allowed to go to movies or dances or parties, so she made a point of never putting herself in a position where she might be asked. She learned early to distance herself, to keep intimacy at arm's length, to never need or want what she couldn't have.

Thea and Maddie sometimes met boys on the street or at the hamburger drive-in, older boys who were dark and slightly wild, who might not expect traditional dates that involved meeting the parents. There was the occasional grappling in the back seat of an old Chevy with boys they met on their Saturday night prowls down Broadway. It was their territory, the place to strut their brash but naïve youth. The whistles, *Hey, Sweetie, you've sure got a nice pair* and the catcalls as they strolled past Lions Drive-In and Dairy Queen. Maddie loved it. And she hated it too.

After Mrs. Eldridge's bath, another nurse helped Maddie put her into one of the faded green plush armchairs in the alcove where she would sit while they made her bed, tied in with a stained white cotton restraint jacket. There were other chairs there, empty now, and a table strewn with magazines: *Cosmopolitan, Redbook, True Confessions* and several out-of-date newspapers.

"She sings, you know," said Diana, the other nurse. She spoke into Mrs. Eldridge's ear in a voice that was too loud. "You sing, don't you, Dear?"

Mrs. Eldridge looked down at her pale blue-slippered feet.

"Why don't you sing for the girl?" she asked. "Maddie, you'd like that, wouldn't you?"

"Sure," Maddie said. "But only if she wants to."

I hope nobody calls me 'Dear' when I get old.

"Sure she does. Go on, Dear, sing."

Mrs. Eldridge looked up at Maddie, then folded her hands carefully in her lap, one over the other, and began. Her voice was high and sweet, frail, like a child's: *My love, I am lonely, life is so long, I want you only, and you want my song.*

She stopped as abruptly as she had begun and closed her eyes. She had gone as far as she would go. Her thin white hair had been wet-combed back. There was barely enough to cover her head. She looked sad and vulnerable, naked as a newborn chick.

"Do you think she knows what she's singing?" Maddie asked. "I think she just made that up."

Diana shrugged. "Doesn't matter. She likes to sing."

After the lunch trays were gathered, Maddie and two other nurses wheeled a few patients outside, the mobile ones, the ones least likely to make any trouble. It was a relief to get away from the stink of the ward. No matter how much they cleaned and changed, the smells always came back, permanent, indelible. The smell of dying.

Later, the ward was darkened and the curtains drawn for the afternoon rest period before visiting hours began. Thea and Maddie's names were down on the roster to clean the utility rooms and service rooms, shake down thermometers, sterilize equipment in the autoclave, and scrub bedpans. They hadn't seen each other all morning because Thea had been working on the men's side. It was one of the few times they were on the same shift.

"How was your morning?" Thea asked when they met in the utility room.

"Awful. A little old lady sang for me. It was so sad."

"It's disgusting over there." Thea nodded toward the open service room door. "Spittoons and urinals. Men are pigs." She slammed an empty enema can down on the countertop and began washing bowls and instruments that were to be put into the autoclave. "Sometimes, I really wonder what I'm doing here."

Maddie laughed. She knew why she was there. Girlhood dreams. The angel in white, hovering over a deathbed, cool fingers pressed against a quickly fading pulse. Heroic rescues attempted at great risk to her own life. But it was not those dreams that had taken her there. It was the promise of a way out. Escape from prayers and Bible verses, commands that hung on the walls of her parents' house. It was the belief that she'd be leaving fear behind. She hadn't yet learned that fear cannot be put out and forgotten for a while like a household pet.

"I only went into training because of you," said Thea, accusingly. "And because I had nothing else to do."

A lie. Maddie had never had that kind of power over Thea. No one did.

Thea spoke with a trace of a Swedish accent. It wasn't the accent that made her speech unusual, but a manner of speech that was precise and literal. Maddie never got used to the fact that what came out of Thea's mouth could so often be malevolent. Words flung out in anger or pride, heedless of their mark or their impact. Yet she had moments as soft as any Maddie had known. Thea was not afraid of loving, of hugs, or of throwing her arm around Maddie's shoulders while she read to her from *Vanity Fair* or *Jane Eyre*. But just as suddenly, she could strip the unexpected gentleness from her tone as if to deny that part of her had ever existed. It was as though she had caught sight of herself in some invisible mirror, hated what she saw, then turned in anger, trapped in the new light. Betrayed.

Maddie's mother had once said that Thea was like a queen without a court, but Maddie knew that was not true. Thea had her court and her courtiers. Anyone she'd ever known would testify to that.

Maddie continued to wash and shake down thermometers, then place them in clean, soapy water. Thea silently filled the autoclave with urinals and enema cans. The day was nearly over when the charge nurse came into the service room, appearing without a sound in her rubber-soled shoes.

"Have either of you had a death yet?"

They shook their heads.

"I thought not," she said. "We've had a death. Perhaps the two of you could prepare Mrs. Eldridge for the morgue. She's just been pronounced."

Maddie gasped. "What happened?"

The charge nurse looked at her. Raised an eyebrow. "Nothing happened, Miss Kaslo. She just died."

"But she was sitting up only a couple of hours ago. I was—"

"She was old, Miss Kaslo. Her kidneys had stopped functioning properly. These things happen." She took a bundle of linens down from one of the shelves. "This is a mortuary pack," she said, placing it on the counter in front of them. "Bring it and come with me."

Maddie and Thea followed her through the ward, past Mrs. Eldridge's stripped and empty bed. The charge nurse stopped outside the storage closet at the far end of the ward.

"She's here in the closet," she said in a lowered voice. "We can't have you preparing a body in the middle of the ward during visiting hours. She'll be out of the way here and we can wheel her to the morgue later. Her family hasn't come for weeks and I've not been able to contact them. I don't think any of them are likely to show up now."

She opened the door of the closet and yanked on an overhead light. The body was lying on a stretcher that had been shoved to the back of the closet among the mops and wheelchairs and extra equipment. "The instructions are on the mortuary pack. Let me know when you're done." She left, closing the door quietly behind her.

Thea leaned against the door as though she wanted to get as far away as possible from the body under the sheet. "This is too macabre for me," she said. "*Macabre* as in *ghastly*. As in *ghoulish*."

They stood there for a minute, not speaking, not looking at each other. Maddie unfolded the mortuary pack and removed the itemized list. *Instructions for the Preparation of a Body for the Morgue*. They closed her eyes gently, fingers pressed lightly against cool flesh. A chin strap to keep her mouth closed. Name tags, one around her neck and one attached to the big toe of her left foot.

Eldridge, Mrs. Kathleen. Time of death 1:25 p.m. January 9, 1967.

They washed the body all over with cool water. The temperature didn't matter anymore. Washing the body again seemed pointless to Maddie, but she knew they had to. It was on the list. She thought of Mrs. Eldridge's small body shivering under the thin covering only a few hours earlier. Dying even then. They wrapped her mummy-fashion, in cloths so white they reminded Maddie of the stories of Jesus in the sepulcher. The flesh offered no resistance now.

"Did you hear about that woman over in Neuro?" Thea asked.

"No. What woman?"

"Violet. Poor dumb Violet," said Thea. "She tried to kill herself by jumping off the Lions Gate Bridge. Certain death, you'd think, right? But not for Violet. She didn't see the tug coming out from underneath the bridge. She landed on the deck on a pile of ropes and pulleys." Thea moved away from the stretcher and leaned against the wall. "You'd think she'd smash like a pumpkin, wouldn't you?"

"What happened?" Maddie asked. She saw in her mind's eye the kind of pumpkin you carve on Halloween, splattered against the oily boards of the deck, its leering grin still intact.

"Poor Violet," Thea said. "Couldn't even kill herself properly." She paced to the end of the narrow closet and back. "She's in a wheelchair. For the rest of her stupid life. All she has is that wheelchair to forever remind her what a fool she was. She'll never be able to end it now, will she? She took pills before. I guess that time they found her too soon."

"You mean they found her in time."

"No," said Thea. She shoved the gurney against the wall. "They found her too soon. No one has the right," she pronounced slowly, as if explaining a difficult concept to a child, "to stop *me* from dying, if dying is what I want to do. Violet is a prisoner in that body now. Can't you see that? Can't you see how wrong it is that she has to live, when all she wanted was to be left alone to die?"

"I can't imagine wanting to die at all."

"No," Thea said. "You wouldn't, Maddie." Her voice was hard-edged, brittle. "But I can. I'm not a survivor. I'm not like you."

This old argument like a foreign language between them. Maddie's fear of death, Thea's pull toward it. *This business of living*, Thea always said, *is highly overrated*.

"We have our whole lives ahead of us, Thea," Maddie said. "It's our world now. It's *our* turn. You can't not *want* to live." The intensity in her own voice surprised Maddie, as though she hadn't said the same thing to Thea many times before. "I read somewhere," she continued, "that you have to be able to imagine yourself in the place you want to be. It's like Olympic high jumpers. They imagine themselves vaulting over the bar, flying through the sky, before their feet ever leave the ground. If you can't believe it and see it, it can't happen."

"How can that mean anything to me, Maddie, when I don't have a plan, when I don't even have a place where I *want* to be?" Thea stalked over to the sink and rinsed the basin. "How is it being *our turn* supposed to mean anything to me?"

"I know, Thea, I know. But we've argued this one to death, don't you think?"

"Yes, *to death*. Ha ha."

Thea carried her sadness and rage with her, a burden, barely visible, like an old scar. But its edges were hard, unpredictably sharp. Maddie would see her sometimes, trapped in her own lost place, staring out a window or lingering in the pages of a book, her eyes not moving over the words. Or sitting on the edge of the sofa, braiding her hair, adrift in one of her daydreams.

Just the day before, she had watched Thea as she sat staring into nothing, a hair barrette in her mouth and one hand clutching the long braid, trapped mid-movement between her thoughts and the hair she was about to pin to her head. A Carl Sandburg poem had tumbled through Maddie's mind like a soundtrack to that moment: *The woman named Tomorrow sits with a hairpin in her teeth and takes her time.* Thea in that empty room, perplexed, trapped in a place from which there was no escape.

When they were finished, Maddie went into the washroom and locked the door. Why was she so afraid of dying and of death? Childhood nightmares. Mr. Cooper, their Winnipeg preacher, had trapped her once by the rear exit of the church hall and reminded her that if she was to die, filthy in sin and unsaved, she would never see her parents again. *If you should die tonight,* he said, *where will you spend eternity?* The place of forever and ever. In the dark pit of hell. Alone. Maddie thought of Mrs. Eldridge, alone, just a body now, lying in a storage closet waiting to be wheeled to the morgue at a more convenient time.

Her song. *My love, I am lonely.*

Death should never be like this, Maddie thought. But when is it really ever any different?

After all the hymns and fine speeches and the weeping, it still comes to only this. A bundle of bones and flesh to be given back to the earth. A life over, gone, forgotten.

In the end, we cry only for ourselves.

Four

Mexico

The morning sky is streaked with high cirrus clouds and the air is still cool. Maddie's legs feel strong, striding through the morning. At home in Canada it's been cold and the damp winter has already insinuated itself into her bones like a mold. The familiar ache in her joints and in the muscles in her legs loosens here in the dry mountain air. Maddie has promised herself a massage. She walks alone along the narrow, cobbled sidewalk on her way to the spa. Carmelita is heading to the *biblioteca* to do some research.

"Go, go," Lita said. "The spa is a good way to spend a day. Think of it as a kind of cleansing."

A cleansing. A stripping off of the armor that Maddie's clung to for so long, long after the war has ended. Old history is what the doctor tells her is the cause of her pain. Ancient cargo from her past. Muscles that rage against old invasions, a body that has not forgotten, that's still desperate to escape.

It's time to take all those old walls down. Maddie wants stillness now. Finding that still place, she knows, will expand her writing into the places she's wanted to go for a long time. She's loved writing history but she wants more. She wants to tell her own stories, the ones locked inside her body, stories dreaming of their own release.

It's early and shopkeepers are sweeping outside their storefronts. The scratching of straw brooms against cobblestones and the raw smell of soap and bleach is such a part of morning life here. In the distance, Maddie hears garbage collectors making their way down the streets, banging their metal rods against iron triangles – the familiar song of garbage collectors all over Mexico. Doors are thrown open and trash containers are hoisted into the street and carried in the direction of the clanging sound. The sidewalks are so narrow that every few minutes Maddie has to flatten herself against a stone wall or a wrought iron grate, or step down from the sidewalk into the roadway to let someone pass.

"Perdón." A soft murmur, heads bent as one of them yields. There is a hierarchy of sorts. Women walk pressed against the walls. Men move to the street side to let the women pass. But everyone – men and women – steps into the street to let the old ones by. Beyond the steep and narrow street, the city drowses, pink and blue and orange adobe against the distant green hills. Maddie dodges the drips from rooftop spouts where plants are being watered, terraces swabbed down above her. Propane tanks with their cupolas like spires of little churches squat on rooftops. Women fling buckets of water against the cobblestones and sweep away the grime of yesterday's dust and traffic.

Maddie pushes open the wrought iron gate into the courtyard of the spa, now a jungle of flowering poinsettias, tall palms, and potted ferns. The manager says she can fit her in, introduces her to one of the young women who stands waiting with a shy smile.

"Lupe," she says quietly, and motions for Maddie to follow her into a room lit only by candles. Vivaldi's *The Four Seasons* plays quietly. Draped walls are hung with altars to the *Virgen de Guadalupe*, flaming hearts of hammered tin, whimsical *retablos,* niched statues of the *Virgen de la Soledad,* The Virgin of Sorrows.

Maddie takes off her clothes and stretches out on the narrow massage table, then covers herself with the thick blue towel. Lupe enters the room without a sound. She is wearing a loose white top and white trousers, like a nurse. Long black hair hangs to her waist and is tied back with a blue satin ribbon. As far as Maddie has been able to make out, Lupe speaks no English and conversation is not initiated or expected. She's grateful for that, and sinks into the soft, fluid quiet of the room, filled only with strains of Vivaldi and the scent of crushed strawberries.

Lupe's hands move gently, expertly over Maddie's back, seeking out the taut muscles, the hollows, the mysterious kinks and knots. Her hands are tender, accommodating. Maddie allows that, keeps the fear at bay, reins in the apprehension that a foreign touch can bring. Memories surface. Shades of other hands, rougher hands. Her father's and her grandfather's. The preacher's hands as he pulls her out of the river . . .

In a narrow forest along the banks of the Assiniboine River, they traipsed down a long trail, through stands of birch and cottonwood, to a place where the river pooled into a still lagoon edged with slough grass and Virginia creeper. Maddie was about to be baptized in the river along with a few recent converts to their church and a couple of children her age, twelve, approaching thirteen – which, according to the Bible, she's been told, is the age of responsibility. In the ritual of baptism, they were about to atone for their shameful state of sinfulness. The church's meager band of worshippers sat on the riverbank, the women's heads covered with scarves or black lace mantillas, the men wearing fedoras and carrying gold-embossed leather Bibles under their arms.

Every once in a while, there was a burst of singing, ragged as an old coat, and Maddie's mother's voice, as always, rose high above the others. *Yes, we'll gather at the river, the beautiful, the beautiful river; gather with the saints at the river that flows by the throne of God.* Maddie's mother was proud of her voice, although without a piano or an organ – deemed worldly and therefore sinful – that skill had never been of any practical use.

When it was Maddie's turn, she scrambled down the riverbank. The hand of Mr. Cooper, the preacher, reached out and clasped hers to lead her into the cold, unwelcoming water. His grip was rough, proprietary. As she reached to take his hand, she saw a thin thread of blood trickle down her arm where she had caught it on the broken-off branch of an oak tree. She threw a handful of water on it and watched it dissolve into a pink puddle and roll off her arm.

Mr. Cooper was wearing regular clothes, not his Sunday go-to-meeting clothes. When he preached his sermons, she knew he was speaking to her. Her sin clung like a dirty shirt. All the adults in the room were saved, so she knew he had to be preaching to the older children. Her, her brother Tom, and their cousins. She hadn't yet put herself forward to be saved and her parents' expectation and disappointment were palpable.

Maddie stood in front of Mr. Cooper in the river and waited. He placed one hand at her neck and another at her waist. *Repent and be baptized in the name of Jesus Christ for the remission of sins,* he intoned in his flat, cold, baptismal voice, so different from his Sunday night accusing voice, *and ye shall receive the gift of the Holy Ghost.* He pushed her backwards into the water. Maddie smelled the rich, resinous scent of sweet gale on the riverbank. A meadowlark sang on a branch above her. Then her nostrils filled with the brackish smell of stones and mud as cold river water closed over her head.

When the preacher pulled her back to the surface she was already shouting. *No! No! No!* Maddie leapt away from his grasp and ploughed through the water, back to the shore. She sat on a log on a strip of muddy shoreline and tried to still the panic that had overtaken her. She was flooded with images, images of her grandfather pushing her down on the bed – his bed – his hot breath, his arms taut as baling wire holding her down. The smothering heat of that summer afternoon. Her grandmother playing hymns on the piano upstairs, who wouldn't hear her even if she screamed.

The final explosion of panic as she tore herself away from him, running, running, running, the screen door banging behind her. She scrambled through a ragged hole in the fence, tearing the hem of her dress when it caught on a nail. Tall hollyhocks grew like guardians at the gate. A steely blue hatred gleamed in her grandfather's eyes from that day on.

Memories too of her father with his nightly Bible stories of punishment and loss that drove terror into her dreams. He pinned her to her bed with blankets tucked tightly from head to toe. His stifling love. Those were the walls within which her life was contained.

"What's the matter?" Maddie's mother called down from her perch on the bank.

"It's not deep," Mr. Cooper called back. "She was only under a second or two."

"Oh, she's okay," said her mother. She threw a towel down to Maddie. "Come up and get dressed. You can change in the car."

Maddie wrapped the towel around her and climbed back up the riverbank.

"What was all that about, for Pete's sake?"

"Nothing." Maddie ignored her and everyone else on the bank and ran back to the car to change. She didn't feel any different. Maybe she hadn't given the baptism enough time to take, running off like that. What had she done, anyway, that she needed to 'die to her old life,' as her father had explained it to her? She barely had a life.

We must strive for holiness, her father had told her, *honor the life of the spirit over the flesh.* But Maddie saw no evidence in their lives of this purity of spirit. There was nothing that felt like holiness in their home beyond the ritual prayers at every meal, the long treks to church twice a week and three times on Sunday.

Maddie only felt how their lives were permeated by a rigid devotion to an angry and punishing God. She thought of that flock of believers sitting on the riverbank, praying for atonement, praying for the promise of a key to the magical Kingdom of Heaven, as though the waters had become rivers of forgetting. But where were their sins while hers were being washed away? Was the gift of the Holy Spirit still alive and well in their hearts?

Maddie didn't think so.

 howl

The first time Joey visited Maddie's island was just two weeks after they met. He arrived without any warning and knocked on her door. He wore a blue Cubs cap and a red T-shirt. Maddie was pleased, surprised, and completely unprepared for the reality of his presence. What would they do with the rest of that long sun-drenched day? What would she feed him? How long would he stay?

So they walked through the shadowed trails to the lake, across the meadow, a cloud of purple with the Canada thistle in full, sweet bloom. Along the pathway to the fish hatchery, across rickety wooden bridges over dried-up creeks, then back through the trails, the lagoon and home again. It was somewhere on the trails on the way home that Joey took Maddie's fingers in his and held tightly. He was careful not to claim any more than just fingers. Not yet.

Maddie cooked curried chicken and jasmine-scented rice. They drank a cold beer, sitting on the front porch watching the ferry pull out of the cove, past the lighthouse and into the Sound. He still hadn't said when he was leaving. It wasn't until the shadows lengthened and a cool evening breeze swept through the cabin, rustling the wind chimes, when the last ferry pulled around the lighthouse and into the Cove that he asked if he could stay.

"Do you think . . .?" he said. He paused.

"That you can stay?"

He grinned. "Is it too soon to ask?"

"No, but . . ."

"But?"

"I'm not sure how to do this. I've been on my own for a long time." Maddie hesitated. "There hasn't been a man for a long time."

"I know," he said.

"You know?"

"Well, I do know a little bit about you," he said, "and I surmised that. Lita is my sister and your best friend, after all."

"It's just . . . I need to go slow. I'm not sure how ready I am for this."

"Maddie." He brushed her hair off her face. "I just want to be with you. I'm not asking you for anything you're not ready to give." He smiled. "Go. I'll be in to find you in a while."

Maddie washed her face and brushed her teeth and put on her white cotton April Cornell nightgown with the pale blue embroidery. Joey didn't come to her bedroom for a long time. She heard the scrape of a match as he lit a cigarette out on the porch, smelled the smoke as it drifted in on the evening breeze. When he finally came in, he lay beside her and folded her into his arms. Easy as that. She imagined she was breathing in those dusty, dry hills of the place he had come from and the clean smell of his sweat.

He was just a cowboy lover with a lonely soul. She fell asleep in his arms, dreamed the sweet scent of his sadness and his aloneness. Maddie was lost in a world of possibilities.

ഇൗരു

After the spa, Maddie spends the rest of the day exploring the familiar cobblestone streets, standing for a long time at the gates of the children's graveyard, where the *angelitas* are buried. The gate is locked and chained. The graves and stones and whitewashed tombs are so small.

She wonders if Lita wishes Angela were buried here instead of so far away in Vancouver. Maddie sits for a while in the *zocalo* and watches the life of the street. A woman sits under her green and red-striped umbrella, mangos and papayas piled high, tortillas stacked on an earthenware plate on the blue and white oilcloth-covered table. She smiles at Maddie as she scrapes the spiny thorns of the cactus pads into a yellow plastic bucket.

"*Hola,*" she calls out to her. "You eat." She waves Maddie over. Her two children scurry behind her skirts at the approach of a stranger.

Maddie can see that she's proud of her English so she speaks to her in English.

"No," Maddie says, "I'm not hungry. Maybe *mañana.*"

The woman laughs. She doesn't believe her. "Mangos very good today."

"Mangos are good every day," Maddie says. "I'll come back tomorrow."

A dusty cowboy who looks as if he has just ridden in from the hills on his horse leans against a lamppost and sings a *ranchera* song, *Cielito Lindo,* eyes closed, arms raised to heaven, his voice catching in his throat. His heart seems to break with the depth of rising sorrow. *Ay, ay, ay, ay Canta, y no llores Porque cantando, se alegran Los corazones.* Ay, ay, ay, ay, sing, don't cry because singing, pretty little sky makes hearts grow happy. He is awash in his suffering, but cherishes it too. Either drunk or hungover, he holds out his palm for pesos. Maddie gives him a few.

"*Gracias,*" he says, and grabs her hand to kiss it, bending deeply at the waist in a mock bow.

It's a hot day, unusual for January in this mountain town. Maddie's scalp prickles with the heat, rivulets of sweat run between her breasts. On the way home, she stops in the cool shadows of the doorway to the coffin shop. It's always a jolt, seeing this place right in the middle of a street full of tortilla makers, a rug store, a butcher shop, and next door to the market where Lita buys bags of rice and *guanábana* yogurt that tastes like flowers. On a ledge outside the coffin display window, an array of thick honey-colored candles has been arranged. Babies' and children's coffins are stacked in the window, tiniest ones on top, lids open to display the white silk brocade, the tiny satin pillows edged in lace.

When Maddie gets back to the house she is greeted with the fragrance of chorizo bubbling in garlic and cumin. Carmelita is in the kitchen making dinner – rice and beans, and a salad. She is slicing vegetables on the wooden cutting board and listening to the Dixie Chicks. Lita has the longest fingers Maddie has ever seen. The flash of the knife against the plump, ripe tomatoes, the slivering of spring onions, the slide of oil on romaine and the glint of her silver and turquoise rings and bracelets create a symphony of movement that Maddie has always loved to watch.

"Hey Mad, pour us a glass of wine," Lita says. "I'm just getting rolling here. How was your day?"

"It was quite a day." Maddie opens the glass-fronted kitchen cabinet and takes out two blue-edged wine glasses. She opens the bottle that Lita has set on the edge of the tile counter and pours them each a glass.

Lita turns down the music. "Tell me."

Maddie tells her about the massage and the memories that surfaced. The baptism at the river. Memories of her father's hands. Her grandfather's. The preacher pushing her under water, his grip on her wrists angry, as though he wanted to drown her. Joey.

"Maddie, it was abusive. All of it. You know that, don't you?"

"God, Lita, that sounds so . . . definitive." Maddie sits down on the sofa and pulls her knees up to her chin, wraps her arms around her legs.

"Well, wasn't it? And your grandfather. Abusing you was his *intention,* wasn't it? He knew it was wrong. And your father? All those stories he terrified you with night after night. What is different about those memories now?"

"The details, I guess." Maddie pulls her legs in closer. "I remembered the cold water covering my head as I sank, the preacher's rough hands pushing me down. It all felt so hateful. And I remembered too, how frightened I felt when my father tucked me in like that, so tight that I couldn't move. And I could never tell him how much I hated it. How afraid I was. I felt helpless. It was remembering those details that made today different."

"Somebody said the devil is in the details."

"I thought that was God."

"Yeah, well, him too. But those images," says Lita. "They came to you with such intensity. Don't you think that means something?"

"Yeah. I guess."

"You've always protected them, Maddie. Your dad and your grandfather. Why?"

"They were so cruel to my grandfather," Maddie says. "My mom, my grandmother. They hated him. All of them hated him. I guess I always hoped that one day some kind of good would surface. I wanted to believe that he was a good man. And he wasn't."

"No," says Lita, "he wasn't."

"But you forgave the man who killed Angela."

"Yes."

"Why?"

"Because it was not his intention to hurt or kill. He wasn't drunk or careless. It was a terrible accident," she says. "A terrible burden that he will live with all his life."

"And Joey?"

She paused. "I think he set out to deceive. He knew how wrong it was with that girl. I love Joey; he's my brother. And he's damaged too. I forgive him because he's my brother but I hate what he did. But I can't forgive your grandfather. Not for that."

Maddie nods.

"And what about your father? Why have you said nothing about that for all these years? What he did was abusive too. You know that. All that Bible-pounding. Scaring the hell out of you. You were just a child."

Maddie shrugs. "I guess because he's my father. He thought what he was doing was right."

Lita stirs the chorizo, holds her wine glass up to the light as though she has only just discovered its rich beauty. She tips the wine into her mouth. "God and the devil are both in the details, Maddie."

Maddie lies in bed that night and thinks about Lita's words and her own fear of venturing very far into her past. She tries to picture her grandfather, what he looked like when she was a child. An image forms, a scene from Maddie's life back in the time when her grandparents lived next door to them in Winnipeg.

The chalky basement smell of her childhood: cement and dust, the sharp tang of paint, cleaning fluids, turpentine. And another smell crowding out the others.

What is it? Is it real, or is it just here, skulking about in her imagination, pushing her to a place she doesn't want to go?

The sharp metal smell of roller skates and rusty keys. She used to roller skate in her grandparents' basement, glide past the furnace on the gray painted floor. Around the workbench where her grandfather had his tools hanging against the back wall, tin cans of nails, screws, washers, mysterious odds and ends. A vice painted red and attached to the bench end. And the door beyond that led to his room. *His* room. Not her grandmother's and his, but his room in that house in Winnipeg, right next door to where Maddie lived as a child.

She sees it now. Her grandfather's room in the basement, distanced from the family, darkened, blinds pulled against the smothering heat of a summer afternoon. The sun is invasive, barbaric, relentless. A knitted brown and rust quilt made by Maddie's grandmother is folded carefully across the end of his single cot. A cross-stitched scripture framed on the wall proclaims GOD IS LOVE.

He pushes her to the bed. She is ten years old and not nearly strong enough. He is a small man, but wiry. Gray hair falls over his face like a curtain. Sweat glistens above his upper lip from the heat and exertion of holding her down. His arms are taut, veins standing out like a thin blue highway. His Bible lies open on the wooden table beside the bed, next to his hymn book and reading glasses. In her head, Maddie can hear his raggedy voice as he sings hymns in the emptiness of his room. She can sometimes hear him from upstairs in her grandmother's flower-scented living room.

She pushes against him with all her strength. The air is dense with the heat, her grandfather's indomitable will, her unvoiced screams. She's never going to get away.

But she does. Something reaches up from deep inside, reaches out into the room, into the choked space between them. She pulls herself away from his grasp, pushes off the bed and runs across the room, then across the cool, painted cement floor of the basement and out the door where a huge bluebottle fly drones against the screen. In the dazzling afternoon, the hollyhocks have grown as tall as the fence that separates her grandparents' yard from hers. She climbs into her yard through a gap in the boards, hears him following close behind. He shouts one word: *Bitch!* He hated her then for getting away. And he has hated her ever since.

Why does his hatred of her still hurt?

There are stories of Maddie's grandfather that her mother and grandmother retell as often as they can, keeping their loathing honed, weapons at the ready. Maddie can see the scene unfolding, her grandfather standing in the garden, leaning heavily against his bent wooden rake. He's wearing a starched white shirt like the ones he wears to church on Sundays, but with the sleeves rolled up above his elbows and secured with an elasticized arm band. Sweat beads across his forehead. He brushes a damp strand of limp, gray hair from his eyes.

Maddie's mother is standing at the kitchen sink with her hands in soapy dishwater, watching him from the window. "He's at it again," she calls to Maddie's grandmother who sits knitting in the living room. "He still can't tell a weed from a delphinium."

Maddie's grandmother says nothing. The angry click of her knitting needles is the only sound in the room. This is how they see him, have always seen him. A foolish old man, barely worth the cost of his feed and the roof over his head. They hated him in ways Maddie couldn't begin to understand then.

They knew his stories by heart. How he'd grown up in an orphanage in Quebec and was taken away to a farm by a stranger when he was just a child. The man tore apart his childhood, beat him, abused him in every possible way.

"Worked me like a beast," he'd told them. "Spared me nothing."

His voice was soft, almost a whisper, but it didn't belie the rage that hovered so close to the surface of his wry smile. "He was pretty familiar with the whip too."

And later, the escape. The farm banked down to the river where one day he discovered a small wooden boat in the reeds by the water's edge and made his escape by moonlight. Young and green, but tough, he made his way south and signed on as one of the Gatineau loggers driving the booms down the Ottawa River.

Maddie imagined him: ill-fitting boots clamped to the wet, rolling log, his arched body young and strong as he fought to outwit the temperamental river. Perhaps it was the only time he had power over his life, power he has long since surrendered – or had torn away.

Neither Maddie's parents nor her grandmother believed his stories, but Maddie did. She had not forgotten his touching, his angry need pushing against her body. She hated him for doing what he did, but she stubbornly refused to align herself with them against him.

From her earliest beginnings, she had known that he was a broken man, a man who had been robbed of his soul. As a child, Maddie thought they were the ones who had done that to him, her parents and her grandmother.

But as she grew older, she understood that his soul had been killed long before he hoboed his way across the country, rode the rails, knelt by night fires in vagabond camps along the tracks of the railway lines, long before he found Gran and her God. He played the role, read his Bible alone in his room at night, sang hymns in his rusty old voice. But Maddie didn't ever think he'd found God. He was too broken in too many places to even claim or believe he held God in his heart. Surely, he must have thought that of all the betrayals in his life, the greatest was God's.

Maddie knew, long before she ever had the words to name things, that in her home he was a man dispossessed. As she grew older, she knew he had become – like her – a stranger in his own life. She had no way to unravel the secrets that surrounded him and so she let him go until he became just a tiny figure in a distant landscape, a small shadow on her heart. Faded, and except for the occasional stabbing pain of memory over the years, all but forgotten.

ଚ୬ୠ

Joey came to the coast often. He stacked Maddie's wood and chopped her kindling, had plans to paint, do repairs, clean up the yard. He was there to anticipate her every need. A man of a thousand promises. He wove his dreams into hers so expertly that she lost track of where her dreams ended and his began.

Joey was tall and rangy, more lean than thin. Fair hair was lightened from years of being outdoors. His skin was the color of chestnuts, smooth as burnished leather, from a life spent under the sun, riding the Kootenay hills. When Maddie first met Joey, there was a permanent ridge in his hair from wearing a cowboy hat all the time. He worked on a ranch in the mountain country of southern B.C. near the U.S. border, and on weekends played drums in local taverns, roadhouses, and hotel bars along highways of the old gold rush trail.

Sometimes he'd call her late at night from one of the taverns or a hotel lobby in some town: Kaslo, Smithers, Grand Forks. They were all just names on a map to Maddie. He'd have to shout to her over the laughter and music and it was at these times she would feel a different Joey emerge. She often sensed he wasn't really saying what he intended, as though the real meaning was being hijacked by the tide of energy in the room. Or by another person. But it was much later when she thought of that.

In the beginning, she'd shown him how to email from the computer in the local library near where he lived: *Lady Moon to Paladin – are you out there somewhere, riding the range?*

Have drum, will travel, he wrote back. Shades of what was to come. But he hated the technology, hated having to hunt down Internet cafés and trying to figure out different computers. He'd never typed in his life. They soon went back to phone calls.

"You're all I can think of," he said. "I think you, I dream you, I breathe you."

"Joey, that's a pretty big piece of cake you're offering me."

"Too much?"

"Yeah, a little."

"I don't mean to scare you."

"No."

"And I don't want to lose you."

"I'm not going anywhere."

The third time he phoned, he told her he loved her. No one had ever said that to her before. She couldn't say it back because she had no idea what love was. She had no clear sense of what love looked like, or felt like, but she longed for what she imagined to be its cloak of tenderness, its mantle of safety. She could only be grateful for his declaration. Stunned into silence.

He visited on weekends and Maddie ached for him when he was gone. Every time he left the island to go back to his town and his work, she would sit on the front porch with a glass of Grand Marnier over ice, smoke cigarettes, and watch the ferry pull out of the Cove, past the lighthouse, carrying him out of her life again and again.

They laughed together between arguments. He bought her things. Silk scarves, turquoise and silver bracelets, glazed bowls from a local potter. He taught her how to make tortillas the way his mother did. And every day he told her he loved her.

The day he moved to the coast and into Maddie's life permanently, she wrote a goodbye letter to herself in her journal. A farewell to the life she'd been living and that she knew she'd never have again. She'd been anxious for days, wary about this move, not quite ready, although she denied that back then. He arrived with only an armful of belongings along with a boxful of his treasures, as though he were bringing nothing but himself into this life they would share. Her world was to become his. Her home, her friends, her family. Gradually, he wove together the pieces of her life and claimed them for his own.

Lita had warned Maddie. She had been purposeful in everything she told her. She reminds Maddie of that the next morning. They're up on her roof and Lita is pruning her bougainvillea bushes. "I know it must have been hard to live with Joey, knowing what you knew," she says. "But Maddie, you *knew*."

Although Lita had chosen to stay connected with her brother, she could never come to terms with his past. What he had done, she believed, he'd done with intention. He'd known.

Lita told Maddie a story about something that happened to Joey when they were children. "But no one," she said, "ever found out what actually occurred."

"My mother found out. It involved one of our neighbors. One day she made it clear to both of us that we weren't to go anywhere near that neighbor's house ever again. When we walked by, my mother would look across the street or off into the distance. She made her feelings clear without saying a word."

"Did you know the guy?" Maddie asked. "The guy who supposedly did whatever he did?"

"That's the weird part," Lita said. "It wasn't a guy. It was a woman. She and my mom had been pretty friendly before that. They had coffee at each other's houses. They watched *telenovelas* together. She even looked after us a couple of times when my mom had to go out."

"A woman. That's a twist."

"I always thought it was strange that she'd call for him all the time. To help with little things. She'd call and say: *Can I get Joey over here for a minute?* But never me. I always wanted to go, but Joey said I couldn't. He wouldn't say why.

"Then Joey started acting strange. Angry all the time. Shut himself in his room and wouldn't talk to us."

"How old was he?"

"About ten by then, I guess. Ten or eleven."

"How did it stop?"

"One day he just refused to go. He wouldn't answer the phone when she called. It was around then my mom cottoned on to the fact that something was wrong. She went into Joey's room and closed the door. She was in there for a long time. Then she came out and marched right over to this woman's house, enraged. She was spitting mad."

"Then?"

"Then nothing. Nothing was said. It was all hush-hush. The woman – Lucille was her name – just disappeared from our lives. She moved away soon after that. Joey got quieter. I tried to talk to him about it but nothing I ever said or did could drag it out of him."

Lita made no excuses for Joey, nor did she ever try to talk Maddie out of being with him. Only once was Maddie stunned by what Lita said when Maddie told her how honest a man she thought Joey was. He had opened his life to her. "No, he's not honest," Lita said, so quietly that Maddie almost thought she hadn't heard her.

But she had.

"And that's the thing," Maddie says now. "I knew what he was and what he'd done. He'd become abusive. Cursing at me. Smashing things. I hated him for that, but I stayed. That's the thing I can't forgive myself for. I'd lost all respect for him. I didn't even love him anymore. And still I stayed."

"What are you going to do now?" Lita leans her face into the morning sun that is streaming over the *casita* wall.

"I'm going to face him," Maddie says. "I'm going to make him tell me to my face what's going on. At the very least I deserve the truth."

He'd been too cowardly to do that at home, Maddie thought, and she'd been too cowardly to push it. Too scared to hear the truth, whatever it might be. All her life, Maddie had lived with other people's silence and because of that, she'd lived all her life in fear – of the unknown, the dark corners, the hidden truths. "But I know . . ."

"What do you know?"

"I know this is it. I'm done."

Lita nods. "I've been wanting to ask . . .," she begins, then stops. Maddie waits. "I don't want to be presumptuous," she says, "but I've been wondering if your mother left you anything, anything you can do something with. On your own."

"You mean, like buy my own place?"

"Well, wouldn't that be an amazing thing? For you to own your own place?"

"It's what she wanted for me."

I want you to get out of the Grove, she had said to Maddie in those last weeks. *I know how much you love your cottage, but I want to know you're in your own place. You'll be able to have that now.*

Maddie hadn't wanted to think about it then because she didn't want to think about her mother being gone. But now it's something she can do. The lawyer told her that by the time she got back from Mexico, the estate should be settled. And she knows it's time for Joey to go – past time. Much has been dark and furtive with him. She's hidden who he is from so many people for so long that she's created a life where she's been able to hide the darkest parts even from herself.

෨෬

"I lied." Lita comes out of the bathroom with a white towel wrapped around her head and slams the door on the cloud of rose-scented steam enveloping her.

Maddie glances up from the book she's reading: Barbara Kingsolver's *High Tide in Tucson*. "About what?"

"About not seeing anyone." Lita pulls the towel off her hair and gives her head a shake like a wet dog. "I am," she says. "I'm seeing someone."

"Why would you lie about a thing like that?" Maddie sets her cup of chamomile tea on the table beside the sofa and folds the bookmark into the page she's been reading.

"Because I'm unsure," Lita says. "It's still so new."

"Unsure of . . .?"

"Unsure about whether I want it."

"Want the relationship? Want the feelings?"

Lita sighs. "All of it. I'm not sure I can believe in it. Love. Relationships."

"Uh huh. Well, I get that."

"But it's more than that." Lita throws the wet towel over the back of a chair and rakes her fingers through her hair. "Remember *Becket?*"

Maddie remembers. She's seen the movie twice, the first time in the neighborhood theater near where she grew up. The Hollywood was old world, beautiful in a weary way, like a rich but slightly tattered dowager draped in furs and pearls. Worn burgundy carpets, seats in faded claret-colored plush. Spangled walls and brass sconces. The vanishing glamor of another era. At nineteen, Maddie hadn't had words for how the movie had stirred up a small quiet thrill in her heart, or understood then that it was a story about the impossibilities of love. She knew nothing of love other than the imposed love of God in their family, a frightening, bullying kind of love that felt as though it were torn from her. *Have you accepted God into your heart?*

"So what about Becket?" Maddie asks.

"He's King Henry's closest friend. His only friend," says Lita. "Henry makes him Archbishop – for his own purposes, of course, so that he can divorce his wife – and Becket betrays him by falling in love with God."

Maddie laughs. "In manner of speaking, yes he does."

"He closes the door on Henry. Abandons him. He loves God now." Lita crosses the room, brushes dust off her niche altar and rearranges the candles, then lights one. She blows out the match and tosses it into the sink. "So much for love."

"He pays the price," says Maddie. "Murder in the cathedral."

"But anyone can love *God*, Maddie. That's not real love."

Maddie smiles at Lita's certainty. "What *is* real love?"

"It's the kind of love that tears your heart apart, grows you wings and convinces you that you can fly."

"A pretty high bar."

"I'm afraid that maybe I'm like Thomas now. Incapable of real love."

"That's crazy, Lita. You know that, don't you?"

"What makes it crazy?"

"Your life, that's what. The one you've lived up till now. Don't tell me that you didn't love Richard. And what about Ange?"

"That's different."

"No, it isn't."

"So why does this relationship feel so impossible?"

"Because you're scared, Lita. And you're really smart. Anybody who's smart would be just as scared as you."

Lita tells Maddie about him. Sebastian owns a bookstore in Mexico City. His family lives in one of the villages near Lake Pátzcuaro and he wants to take her there to meet them. "I've been putting him off with lame excuses."

"Just tell him," Maddie says. "Tell him you're scared. Any man who's worth the trouble is going to understand. It's not like when we were twenty, back when we thought we had to be whatever some guy wanted us to be."

"I know. But."

"You've gotta go with it, Lita. See where it takes you."

"I've been dodging this one for a long time," Lita says. "There've been opportunities. It just never seemed worth the effort. But I do like him."

Maddie wonders why the thought of Lita in a relationship surprises her. Lita's seemed so content being alone, so self-contained. Maddie has always admired that. She can't see Lita in what Lita calls "the mess of love" again.

"And you?" Lita says.

"Me." Maddie laughs. "I seem to get into the wrong kind of love, don't I? I don't trust myself, or love, anymore."

"I'm not sure there is a wrong love or a right love," Lita says. "Love comes in all shapes and sizes. Some love fits. Some doesn't."

"Still. I haven't made good choices."

"Do you think you're going to want to look for love after Joey?"

Maddie stands up and wraps a quilt around herself, gathers her book and reading glasses, and heads for the patio. "I can't even begin to contemplate that now. It's scary territory. Thin ice, Lita. Thin ice."

৪৩৫৪

The first time Joey touched Maddie with anything other than kindness or tenderness was on a summer afternoon about a year and a half after he came to live with her. By then they had bound their fortunes together like partners in a chain gang. Maddie hadn't even considered the possibility of escape. They were arguing and as always, his anger hovered on the cold steel edge of rage. He was acting out what had become his pattern – to leave when Maddie attempted to present her point of view. Joey had devised ingenious ways of leaving, of refusing to let her be heard. He closed his eyes and dismissed her or left the room and sometimes even the house. Often the abuse he hurled at her was so hurtful that she would be the one to leave. That became his chosen weapon of power because the tables were turned. *She* walked out on *him*, he would say.

She put out her arm to stop him as he was about to walk out the back door. In an instant, his hands were around her throat. Squeezing. She felt his body tremble as he fought to come back from that place of deep fury that wanted to keep squeezing until she was silenced forever.

But what if one day he didn't come back? Or couldn't? Was too deep into his rage to find his way back?

It was her questions that he hated the most. For an explorer and a man who loved more than anything else to unearth buried treasure, he displayed an astounding lack of curiosity. He erupted in rage when Maddie asked him something for which he had no answer. Sometimes, instead of attacking her, he would smash things. He smashed his fist through wooden doors, slammed the telephone to the floor, swung his arm against a lamp and sent it reeling to the floor in a chaos of exploding light and broken glass.

What hurt most was the shame. The shame of being so unworthy. She would walk through the Grove with her head down, stained with the knowledge of the things he had said. The humiliation of what she was, there for the world to see.

In the end, she'd become the enemy. Joey had to leave because Maddie knew too much. She was all too familiar with the backcountry of his inner landscape and knew far too well the dark chasms of the places from which he'd traveled. She could never again mirror back to him the proud hero he so much needed her to believe he was.

80C3

Maddie's been in Mexico almost two weeks and there's been no word from Joey. As the days pass, she feels the tension gripping her body. Last night she dreamed that a man with a lariat followed her down a dark, narrow street in some unidentifiable Mexican town.

In the dream, lamplight streams across the cobblestones, casts eerie shadows on rust-colored adobe walls. She escapes into a shadowed doorway. He passes her by, but she knows that one of these nights in one of these dark dreams, she will not be so lucky.

With each new morning, she feels edgier. Frightened sometimes. He's already gone, she knows that, but the *why* of it holds her in its grip. Not just *why did he leave me?* To that she can almost answer *why not?* The biggest *why*, the one that is giving her the most sleepless nights is, *why didn't I leave first?* The shame of it haunts her.

☙⊗☙

There had been men in Maddie's life before Joey, but no one she had ever wanted to settle with. Even as she yearned for a profound and heart-opening connection, the very intimacy that implied frightened her into a speechless isolation, distanced her from any awareness she might have come to – through her father and her grandfather – of how brilliantly she had learned to disappear into the uncharted shallows of her own heart.

During the years when Maddie was still nursing and living in the city, men drifted in and out of her life, good men, but few lasting longer than two or three months. Lanky, blue-eyed Christopher was a sweet California boy a few years younger than she was. She met him in a bar and took him home to her bed. He had been hitchhiking for days and needed a place to stay before heading off to look for more work so he could keep traveling east. Christopher stayed with Maddie for a month until he got a job baling hay on a farm in Alberta.

They laughed a lot together and sometimes stayed in bed all afternoon on her days off, propped up on pillows, sunlight sifting through the bamboo blinds and dancing across the sheets. They drank cold Chablis right out of the bottle, threw the *I Ching* and read their destinies to one another. They were two children playing house, savoring each moment because they knew they only had each other for a while, that with one of the next waves, they'd come crashing down on different shores.

"*Earth over thunder changing to mountain over marsh/mist,*" Maddie read, after she'd thrown the coins and created her hexagram. "*Sacrifice two baskets of grain even if that is all you have.* I wonder what that means."

"It means just what it says," said Christopher. "That's what you've done. You've shared your basket of grain with me. Metaphorically, of course."

Maddie was sad when he left. She gave him the Chinese coins she'd found in an antique store in Chinatown and her copy of Wilhelm's *I Ching*. They wrote each other for a while until he told her he was moving on. *With this baling hay all day*, he wrote, *I'm turning into Superman.*

Like all the men who passed through Maddie's life over the years, Christopher eventually disappeared into the landscape, leaving not so much as a fingerprint, nothing she could hold or touch to remind her that he had ever been there.

David was an orthopedic resident at St. Simeon's. He was married with two young children and she knew that about his life early on. Like most of the men she chose, he came with an escape clause and no promise of a future. Maddie liked it that way, the dance of intimacy loose and uncomplicated.

He took her to his room in the doctors' residence where he stayed while on call. They made love quietly on the narrow cot with the backdrop of a perennially dripping tap, the muttering of traffic on the street below, and wailing ambulances pulling into the emergency bay across the street. Maddie was fond of David, warmed by his soft ways, his gentleness. He was the only one who could make her heart stumble at odd, unexpected moments, make her wonder what it could be like to wake up to a warm pair of arms around her every morning. But she knew love was a lot more than that.

And a lot less too.

Maddie's feelings for David changed after she finagled a date with one of the new interns so she could get invited to the end-of-the-year party on Grouse Mountain. She had hoped David would be there, but hadn't considered that if he was there, in all likelihood his wife would be there too.

His wife was lovely. Long chestnut hair and a green dress that shimmered. Maddie watched them slow dancing to the song *Cherish*. David held her lightly, his hand grazing her back. Her eyes were soft with distance, as though she was tethered by an invisible thread to her other life, the one of children, old dreams, and promises once made. Lightly they danced, together yet strangely apart. They were two people who had memorized one another's stories, who could fill in the empty pages of the other's life when memory faltered.

Before then, Maddie hadn't thought that the fact David was married had a lot of meaning for her. She hadn't thought of his wife as a woman perhaps only a few years older than she was. Certainly more tired. She imagined her bent over a sink full of soapy dishes and tucking a loose strand of hair behind her ear, wiping up children's spills, reading *When We Were Six* to them at bedtime. Folding heaps of fresh, clean laundry late at night when everyone else was asleep and she finally had a few peaceful hours to herself. A woman crying softly at night, alone, even when she was lying beside his long, tense body, knowing that the chasm between them was widening.

After that night at the party, Maddie was often visited by images of his wife's long chestnut hair, her green eyes, her tired smile. She became uneasy with the truth of who this woman was: Mother. Wife. Somebody else's.

Soon after that, Maddie told David she couldn't see him anymore.

"But it's you I want," he said. "You make my life possible." He actually cried. He'd been unhappy for years, he told her, and planned to leave his wife as soon as he got his Fellowship under his belt. But Maddie had no use for the idea of David leaving his family for her.

"You'd better find another way to make your life possible," Maddie had said, "because you can't do it through me. I don't want that burden."

In the end, David stayed with his wife - as Maddie knew he would - and they moved to Vancouver Island, to a coastal town with oyster shell beaches overlooking oily black hulks of fishing boats pulled up onto the shore near an abandoned cannery. He commuted every day to the hospital in Victoria.

Once Maddie moved to her island and Gully's Grove, there was a long stretch of time with no men until she met Lorenzo at a Royal Canadian Legion dance. Lorenzo was a fisherman and they'd arrange to meet on the dock after his day out on the ocean, his long, black, curly hair full of salt and wind, brown arms pulling her against his body, taut and ropy from hauling nets and lobster traps.

Summer days, diving into the sea from the side of his old wooden boat, sliding deep like an arrow shot into the shadowy depths. Gliding deeper and deeper, her breasts free and floating like something separate from her, released from the prison of clothes. That was the best time of all, that beautiful, perfect glide into the sea. Then surfacing, laughing, licking the salt from her sun-browned arms. They made love rocking on the tide, once in a storm that unmoored the boat and set them adrift, slammed them against the government wharf and tore up the boat.

Maddie took that as a sign.

Lorenzo was an alcoholic. He would phone Maddie in the middle of the night and they would have long, circuitous discussions about something he'd read in the latest *Time* magazine. Then he'd fall asleep or pass out mid-sentence, tying up his phone and hers. She'd have to get up, dress, walk over the causeway spanning the lagoon that drowsed on one side of the bridge, where the sea crashed against the stone wall on the other side, hike the trail through the abandoned apple orchard and down the path to his cabin. She'd let herself in, put the phone back in its cradle, cover him with his quilt and leave. Sometimes she'd stop and watch the moon as it rose over the mountains, wait for the geese to scrabble up from the beach looking for handouts, even in the middle of the night.

Maddie was ashamed of Lorenzo and kept their relationship hidden. Her friends, she knew, would hate her for dating a drunk. A small community has eyes everywhere and is not always forgiving. *What is she doing with him?* Maddie imagined their questions and knew she wouldn't have answers. So she sat with her friends on the other side of the bar from where he was and didn't acknowledge him in the General Store or on the ferry. They'd meet late at night at the lagoon, like Shakespearean lovers, blinded by passion and by the uncertainty of the fragile craft they sailed in.

Lorenzo grew tired of the subterfuge. "Either you acknowledge me in public or I'm out of here," he said. "If you don't want anyone to know we're together, then we shouldn't be."

He was right, of course. What Maddie was doing was deceitful and unkind. It was her own shame that made her hide him. And it was that deeper shame of being caught in the storm of her secret yearning for connection that made her decide when she met Joey, that it was time to learn how to truly commit to a relationship.

"You'll thank me for this someday," she told Lorenzo, as perpetrators of breakups always do. "This is about me, not you."

That was true too, of course. But she had no idea she was about to execute a high dive into a very shallow pool.

🙰🙳

Maddie is on the rooftop patio when she hears Lita calling her from the kitchen where she's frying tortillas.

"Maddie, he's here."

Maddie doesn't have to ask who. She glances over the edge of the roof and down to the street. She's not surprised to see a truck parked on the street below. Joey gets out, slams the door hard, looks back once at the truck, then ambles toward the house. He always looks more Mexican in Mexico, wearing a straw cowboy hat that he never wore on her island. His usual bent-over walk makes him look as though he feels he doesn't quite belong in the space he's occupying. Maddie used to think he was carrying the weight of the world on his shoulders but she knows now that it's shame he carries.

"Joey." Maddie calls and he looks up. He doesn't look surprised. "Can you come up here?"

Joey nods, puts his key into the locked door of the *casita* and slams it behind him. He doesn't come up right away. There is the familiar sound of a beer tab popping open. Maddie waits and listens. Then the clang and echo of his cowboy boots on the metal staircase to the roof.

"What are you doing here?" Joey pulls his hat off, tugs a hand through thinning hair and settles into a chair. His hair is fair for a Mexican. Some Spanish blood somewhere down the line. "Dumb question, I guess. It's kind of obvious."

It isn't until he opens his mouth and speaks that Maddie realizes how angry she is. "No, it isn't obvious," she says. Her tone is clipped, defiant. "You would think it's obvious, of course."

He shuffles his feet and looks down, wearing a half-stifled grin. She'd like to smack him.

"I'm here, Joey, because I want answers. Answers you should have given me a long time ago. To questions I should have asked and didn't."

"What answers?" he says without looking up. "I told you I needed to get away."

"I'm here," Maddie says, "because what you gave me was a story, not an answer. Poetic, yes. But still just a story."

He looks up. "What are you talking about? What story?"

"The story, Joey. *Have dreams. Must travel.* How you have to *reassess* your world. *Wake cowboy prisoner?* That story."

As Maddie speaks, she watches his anger rise, like it always does when he feels panicky, unsure where to go in his mind. The more panicky Joey feels, the more he stumbles, grows defensive, then angry. She doesn't want him to get too angry. That could slide into dangerous territory.

"Okay, so it was a mistake," he says.

"No." Maddie will not allow him this escape. "After all these years, Joey, you owe me the truth, no matter how much I don't want to hear it. The truth, not some bullshit story about cowboys and dreams and the sudden need to travel." Her heart is pumping with fury now, but her fear is rising. Fear of the truth she's demanding from him.

He takes a pull on his beer, rubs his thumb along the rim of his hat. "I had an affair. There. Now you know." He walks over to the edge of the patio, looks down to the street as if talking to someone just below. "But like I said, that was wrong. What more can I say?"

"The truth would be enough," she says, although she knows this is not a completely honest answer. "But telling the truth has always been difficult for you, hasn't it?"

Joey wheels around. "Don't you think I know what you think of me? Don't you think I know what you're thinking when you look at me? You hate me for what happened to that girl. And you always will. Do you think I don't know that?"

"It didn't *happen*, Joey." Maddie is shouting now. "That's the problem. Behind your smokescreen, your convenient hiding place from the truth, you still tell yourself it's something that *just happened*. Well, it didn't *just happen*. You did it. You slept with a fifteen-year-old girl and then helped her run away from home."

Maddie's afraid she's gone too far now. Not afraid though for saying what she's said because she knows it's the truth.

"You think you know everything," he says. "Well, you don't. Yeah, she was young. But like I said, I didn't realize she was that young. And I did love her. In the *Latino* culture, we express our love differently." He sounds like a child now. Taunting.

"Your culture? You went to jail, Joey, and you're still telling yourself that it was just about your culture?"

"You know what I mean," he says, and Maddie sees that he's backpedaling, playing for time so he can get back on his feet, pull his thoughts together - something he's not good at, especially when he's stoned. "My culture is different," he finishes lamely. "You should understand that."

Maddie stands up tall and straight. She feels enraged, but strangely calm. "Are you talking about your '*Latino* blood,' Joey? That same '*Latino* blood' that made it okay for you to smash things and threaten me?"

Neither of them speaks. It is as though they are both holding their breath. Joey looks at Maddie with naked scorn. He has nowhere left to go. This is the first time she has ever laid out his crimes for both of them to see. He looks for some escape.

"Well," he says, "that's my point. And now there's someone who doesn't feel the way you do. Someone who doesn't look at me the way you do." His voice is arrogant, self-satisfied. He looks pleased with himself, as though he has won a contest.

"Someone here?"

"She lives in D.F."

"You mean to say your traveling cowboy prisoner dreams are really about going off with another woman who lives in Mexico City?"

"I didn't know how to tell you. And I didn't want to leave you."

"How long have you been seeing her?"

"A few months. I don't know. Six, maybe."

"In Mexico?"

"She came to Canada a few times. To the city, not to the island."

These are words Maddie can't comprehend. She sits down again. Another woman. So many times during the last few months, she'd asked him if there was someone else. Wondered at his coldness in bed. His petty meanness. Again and again, she'd asked – when he started coming home at odd hours or didn't come home at all. He was working in the city and had to sleep in his van, he said, to get an early start on the job. Waiting in ferry lineups was too time-consuming. He was on a deadline. Always he answered with the same words: *Of course, there's no one else. I love you more than I ever did.*

And she had believed him. Why? Maddie knows the answer, although she doesn't want to. She had thought no other woman would want him. In her own arrogance, her hubris, she had believed she had all the power. *I was the one who accepted him and loved him, in spite of his history.* He would never have been able to share with anyone else the secret he had shared with her. That was what had made him hers.

How wrong she was. It was that very history that was the allure, the seduction. He would have gone to his new woman in the same way he came to her. Bent low and humbled with the beauty of his sadness. He would have handed her his love, his shame, his very life. And she would have accepted it as Maddie had, like a gift. The allure of being given someone's deepest, darkest secrets was too seductive to refuse.

"When were you going to tell me?"

"I came here to figure it out. And I did. It's you I want, Maddie."

He hangs his head in that shamefaced victim pose Maddie has come to hate. "I know I've hurt you," he says. "But I can make it right. I know I can."

"No, Joey, you can't."

"But Maddie."

"What can you possibly have left to say?"

"That I still love you."

She is stunned. In some crazy way, she knows he believes this. Maddie says the first thing that comes into her head. Flings the words like cold hard stones in his face. "Then get over it."

She crashes down the metal stairway and leaves the house, slamming the door behind her as hard as she can. Joey doesn't call out to her and he doesn't follow.

ꙮ

Years after they'd met, Maddie finally found the courage to ask about the girl he'd run away with. They were out in the yard, Maddie sitting at the picnic table cutting up plums from their tree to can. Joey was pruning the lilac bushes.

"So, what really did happen, Joey?" she said. "With that girl."

"It wasn't what you think. What you've always thought."

"How do you know what I think?"

"It was really about love."

"About *love*, Joey?" Maddie knew she shouldn't be asking this. It couldn't possibly take them to a place either of them should go.

"Don't mock me." A blast from the ferry horn sounded out in the bay. "I loved her," he said. He spoke so quietly she hardly heard him. "And that's the part you'll never understand."

"How did it happen? How did it start?"

"She hung around the ballfield on weekends. Watched our games with her girlfriends. One thing led to another . . ."

Maddie tried to shut out the image of his hungry eyes tracing the curves of her young body, his hands drifting over her dreaming flesh. Perhaps if she had allowed that image living space inside her skull a long time ago, she would have left him then. But that would have been another story.

"Maddie, she *wanted* to be with me." He was trying to gain his ground back. No humility now. "Strutting around the baseball field, where all the guys were, wearing almost nothing. She wanted *something*. She wanted *me*. What did she think was going to happen, dressed like that?"

"What did she *think*? Thinking has nothing to do with it, Joey. That's what fifteen-year-old girls do. They strut their stuff, show off their womanly bodies. It's what they *do*. They don't think about the repercussions or the ideas they might put into guys' heads. You were the adult. It was up to you to not act on her naïveté and lack of judgment. She was a *child*."

He didn't bother answering. By then he was deep into his own story, his own truth, and had long since decided that in his world of explanations and justifications, he owed her nothing.

Maddie didn't ask him to leave that day, a truth that still lives with her. A shameful secret. He didn't seem to have any remorse for what he'd done, for any hurt he may have caused, or for the fact that he was a man of thirty and the girl was fifteen.

In the end, Maddie let it go. She wanted him and that was the cargo he came with. He was in love with the girl. That gave him certain rights, he believed, a kind of license.

It was done in kindness, he'd said. It wasn't something he understood, but he knew it was all about love. Love needed, love wanted, love offered. It was love that made it okay.

Like so many women who believe they have found their heart's mirror, Maddie closed the door on the pain of this new knowledge. And locked it tightly.

∞⌘∞

Maddie climbs the narrow cobblestone street and watches the city drop away behind her. Green and red Christmas bells and wide, loopy flowers and stars are draped over power lines and slung above the street in a haphazard, gimcrack way. Church spires and domes fade into hilly green spaces and the lake beyond is a storm-colored blue-gray that dissolves into the distant mountains. The winding stone stairway climbs to the top of the city. Its perimeter road reaches even higher into scrubland and cactus-lined pathways through red dirt, then levels out into a rocky bluff and a panorama of the city. *El Mirador.*

Partway up the stairway, a rust-colored dog uncurls from where he is sleeping in a doorway beneath a potted fern and follows Maddie. He trails behind, but ignores her, as though on a journey to a place that has nothing to do with her. When she looks back, he stares at the horizon, disinterested, but twenty minutes later when she reaches the top of the bluff, the dog is still with her, nosing through the prickly pears, sniffing the hot, dry air.

Maddie sits for a long time, looking out over the city, talking to the dog once in a while when he ambles over to see if she's still there. Her rage at Joey tears at her and this perch above the city offers no refuge. She had thought

94

she'd come back down from here with some deep knowledge, clear-eyed insight that has thus far eluded her. Isn't this the metaphorical mission of journeyers – to come down from the mountain and bring home the wisdom? But the knowledge she has is unwelcome. Her shame. It's not the knowledge she wanted.

She thinks again of the day Joey towered over her, his face bent with rage she had never seen before. The day he'd tried to strangle her when she'd put out her arm to stop him from leaving. His hands around her throat, squeezing, then stopping just short of twisting. She'd been stunned, horrified. His face clearly warned that all his boundaries had been crossed, that he was no longer the person he had been just a few minutes before.

He had been splitting wood. Wood chips were caught in his hair. The strong smell of his sweat. In the distance, the innocuous and gentle sound of tinkling glass wind chimes, a sweet bird call, the barking of a dog. Everything in the house had an air of innocence. The soft glow of the lamp in its pink shell shade, the vase of rust-colored chrysanthemums on the table, the view of the bay from the window. Maddie's cat cowered in the corner, as frightened as Maddie. She knew. Innocence overlaid with violence. His body, huge, solid, impenetrable, was pushed against hers.

That first time, he wept, swore he'd never done such a thing to any woman. Promised to never do it again. She believed him. The second time there was no apology, no excuse. No tears.

And still she stayed.

But why? Had living with fear also become her shelter? A place shadowy, but familiar? In choosing Joey, had she locked herself into a prison of her own making? It was her dread of being abandoned and left alone that had troubled her childhood nights. The stories: The farmer left standing alone in his field, the unprepared virgins. It was in the dark silence of those nights where those first primal fears had taken root, invaded her dreams. Was her terror of being left greater than her fear of intimidation and shame?

From her perch on a rock in the rust-colored earth, the city below is a sea of adobe brick. A dusty road circles the outskirts of the city and beyond that rise the blue Bajio Mountains. Tears come, slam her body, tearing up her throat. She wraps her arms around her knees and rocks back and forth, the way she did as a child. What she has come to Mexico to do is done. She feels an ache deep inside. A longing. She lets it all come, feelings she's been holding at bay for so long, afraid of where they'd take her. She is filled with a grief as deep and burning as the blood in her veins. Grief for this place she'll be leaving soon, this place that has for so long connected her so fiercely to who she is and where she's going.

Leaving Mexico means letting go. Not the letting go of Joey but the letting go of the dream, everything Maddie believed in. Her future. Letting go of the dream is a lot harder than letting go of Joey. And that's why she didn't leave after the first time he humiliated her or threatened her. Or the second.

Or any time after that.

The next afternoon, Maddie finds Carmelita on the roof, doing yoga. She sits on the whitewashed wall and watches for a while.

"I think I've been hooked on the idea of love," Maddie says finally. "Not in a good way – as though being hooked on anything can ever be good."

"What do you mean?"

"I've been thinking a lot about this since I've been here."

"Tell me." Carmelita stops what she's doing and sits down on one of the wrought iron chairs facing Maddie. Maddie loves that Lita is someone who always gives you her full attention. It's one of the things that's so special about her. She doesn't ever say, *Go on, I'm listening*, while she keeps doing the thing she's been doing. Lita always looks you right in the eye and waits for you to say what's on your mind.

"Like with Joey," Maddie says. "No one before Joey ever told me they loved me." It was true. Her parents had never said it. No man had ever said it. "So when Joey came along and told me he loved me every day – sometimes three, four, five times a day – it got to be like a drug. I loved it. And I felt secure. That was the biggest trap of all. Feeling secure. *He'll never leave me*." Maddie moves into a shady spot by the purple bougainvillea bush.

"What do you mean by 'secure'?" asks Lita.

"I guess I thought that anyone who told me he loved me that often would never leave me. I'd never be alone – although I'd never minded being alone. In fact, I used to love living alone."

"But it wasn't good with Joey. It hasn't been good for a long time." Lita starts unbraiding her hair. "Why do you think you stayed?"

"It was a fix," Maddie says. "And once I got a taste for it, I didn't want to let it go. It was gas in the tank. It kept me going."

"Did you think you wouldn't ever be loved again, that if you let this one go, you'd never find love?"

"Oh, yeah. That scenario was always in play. Front and center. It was always *what if . . .?* I'm ashamed of that, Lita. Ashamed to admit that."

Maddie knew that what she had always wanted was easy love. Love that asked for nothing, demanded nothing, expected nothing. Love that carried no ability to hurt or be hurt. The only thing she had never contemplated was its loss.

Lita sighs. "The real problem is that we expect way too much of love. We think it's going to save us. And it can't." She combs her fingers through her long hair. "I thought that," she says quietly.

Maddie looks up. The quietness of Lita's voice reveals that she is saying something important, something she's never said before.

"I thought love would save Richard and me. Maybe because we both loved Ange so much and we both lost her. But in the end, love had nothing to do with it at all. We almost came to hate each other for what we'd lost. It still makes me sad," she sighs, "that I could never fix it."

Five

Vancouver: mid-Sixties

After working at the General for a year, Thea and Maddie moved to St. Simeon's, the small Catholic hospital downtown. St. Simeon's offered an intimate atmosphere, a familiarity that was so unlike the bright steel-edged coldness Maddie had become accustomed to while walking the General's long, antiseptic corridors and its white and green glinting underground tunnels.

Maddie worked in Obstetrics and Gynecology. She felt oddly comforted and sheltered, working in the company of women. She even liked the silent authority of the nuns in their long black robes and the pictures and statues of a supplicating Virgin Mary in every room.

The priest gave communion at six o'clock each morning, shuffling along the half-lit corridors, head lowered, hands folded under his white robe, tinkling a brass bell to announce his arrival. Maddie found that display of faith reassuring in a place where the business of life and death was a game often played too close to the surface and without rules, a place of stark vulnerability with little to cling to that was familiar.

This foreign terrain of nuns and priests was a long way from Maddie's parents' truth that shunned the crosses with their bloodied, crucified Christs and their statues of a munificent Mary. *Worshipping false idols,* they called it.

In the world of obstetrics, there was death too, even where life began. Maddie never really got used to it, never came to terms with that world of loss. Death in a place of new beginnings felt like a betrayal in a world where that new, burgeoning life was so precious, a thing to be salvaged at any cost.

It was an hour before midnight, half an hour before Maddie went off shift. The halls were darkened and still. The charge nurse sat at the nurses' station writing the evening report. From the nursery down the hall came the muted sound of babies crying, a chorus that rarely stopped. In the first days after Maddie started to work there, that sound was a clamor inside her head long after she was home, even while she slept. The sound was persistent, never-ending. Diabolical. Months later she discovered that every nurse who worked there had at one time or another dreamed of flinging screaming babies from the nursery window.

Across from the nurses' station, the elevator door whirred open. Thea emerged wearing a purple silk dress and a black lace shawl. Her leather coat was slung over one arm. She came toward Maddie with a wide grin. She was a little drunk.

"Well," she said, "are you coming?"

There was a party in the interns' residence across the road. Maddie had been listening to the music all evening, distant yet slightly raucous, giving an edge to the night.

Thea was in love with one of the new interns from St. Simeon's. He was dark and secretive and seldom spoke unless addressed. The image Thea had pulled from her arsenal of words was *inscrutable. Mysterious. Unfathomable.* She called him Heathcliff. He was from an old moneyed family in Toronto and that added to his appeal for Thea. Maddie thought Thea probably frightened him.

"I'll see how I feel when I get off," Maddie said.

"Don't think about it," Thea said. "You think about everything too much. Just come." She giggled and leaned against the desk, brushing her hair back from her cheek. She looked beautiful, Maddie thought, leaning like that, loose and uncomplicated, hooking a long strand of copper hair behind one ear.

"How do I look? Tell me the truth."

"You look perfect."

"The truth, Maddie." Thea laughed and pulled the shawl off her shoulders. "Do I look slutty in this dress? I don't want my entrance to look like the arrival of the whore of Babylon."

Bitch and *whore* were two of her favorite words.

"You look stunning," Maddie said. "Go. I'll see you in a while."

Thea sighed and tugged her shawl back over her shoulders. "Try and make it, Mad." She got back on the elevator and waved as the doors were closing.

A few minutes later the elevator door opened again and a stretcher was rolled into the corridor, a new admission right at shift change. The charge nurse was in the service room with the door closed, taping her report for the next shift, and Sandra, the other nurse, was busy. Maddie would have to admit the new patient. Who knew when she'd get off now.

A woman lay on the stretcher, a girl really, not much older than Maddie. She was lying perfectly still, eyes closed, one hand underneath her head. Long silky strands of blonde hair had come loose from her soft chignon. She was wearing what appeared to be stage makeup; it was immaculate. She did not open her eyes or say anything. The ambulance attendant slid a sheaf of papers across the desk.

"She spontaneously aborted," he said. "Doesn't speak much English. She was dancing with a troupe from France tonight at the Queen Elizabeth Theatre. She aborted in her hotel room right after the performance."

Maddie headed down the hall and the stretcher followed soundlessly on rubber wheels. She pointed to the empty bed and pulled the curtains closed. The emergency nurse had taped an identification tag to the railing of the gurney: *Arsenault, Miss Francine.* She was twenty, the same age as Maddie. She was shivering. Maddie covered her with an extra blanket. She turned to leave but the girl motioned to her. She folded back the clean white sheets and lying beside her under the edge of her nightgown was a green and white towel. HOTEL VANCOUVER was woven into the border. She lifted up the folded bundle and unwrapped it carefully, ceremoniously. Inside the towel was a fetus about three inches long.

"How many months?" Maddie asked. She must have hidden this from the ambulance attendants and the emergency staff or it would be on her chart. Someone would have said something.

She frowned. Maddie pointed to the girl's stomach and gestured in a measuring motion. "The baby. How big?"

"Ah," she said and held up three fingers. Three months.

Maddie carried the bundle to the utility room and called Sandra. "What should we do with it?"

"It'll have to go to the lab, I guess," Sandra said.

Maddie wondered what they would do with it. Did it just get flushed away? Or get incinerated with the garbage? She placed it in a metal basin and put it on the counter in the utility room. She covered it with a towel. She didn't want to have to look at it.

A few minutes later, Sandra called to Maddie and waved her over. "It *moved*," she whispered. "It actually *moved*, Maddie."

"What moved?"

"The fetus. It moved. It's still alive."

Maddie felt cold. "Jeez," she said. "What should we do?" She said *we*, but she wasn't in charge. It wasn't her call.

"Nothing," said Sandra. "I'll wrap it in a paper towel and Nights will send it to the lab. It's kind of creepy."

"I know. I really don't want to look at it."

"You can go," Sandra said. "I'll deal with it. Anyway, the night shift's here."

So Maddie went. But for a long time afterward, when she thought of that night and saw in her mind's eye that tiny fetus in a basin in the utility room, she could not help thinking of it as anything other than Francine's lost baby.

୫୦୯୫

It was a quarter to one when Maddie finally changed and left the hospital. She heard the faraway murmur of voices, bursts of music, fading sounds of the dying party at the interns' residence. There hadn't been time to think about the party and now it was too late. She left through the

Emergency exit and headed down the street toward the bus stop, thinking about a hot lavender soak in the tub while she played some old Billie Holiday records on the stereo. Maybe she'd even have a glass of wine.

It was a cold evening with a breeze. Maddie smelled the salty sea air. The vapor street lights hummed. She buried her hands in her pockets for the three-block walk to the bus stop, past the shabby apartment buildings, the second-hand bookseller's, the locked and barred antique shop. Shadows, alleyways, crouching possibilities.

A car pulled up alongside the curb. The driver rolled down the window. "Hey Maddie. Hop in." It was Jackson, one of the new orderlies who had recently begun working on her floor. He was still wearing his hospital whites. The Mamas & the Papas were singing *California Dreamin'* on the radio.

"Hey, Jackson." Maddie walked over to the car and got in.

Jackson was one of the American boys who had recently been hired on at the hospital. Maddie thought of them as boys because that's what they were – boys her age. Boys who had fled the draft. Jackson wasn't one of those. He'd been to Vietnam.

Maddie had been hanging out with Jackson for the last few months. She liked him, felt a bond with him through their friendship. She admired his strength, the way he connected with patients. He was someone who stepped up to the plate. She'd watched him wrestle a man with DTs into quietness, and he'd done it not only with physical strength but with kindness and respect. She saw his vulnerabilities too, those times when she caught him unaware, haunted by ghosts, his face a map of sorrow. *War ghosts*, Maddie thought.

Both Maddie and Jackson lived near the hospital. They often met and walked late at night when neither of them could sleep after their four till midnight shift. They sat on the swings in the park, smoked a joint and laughed together. They talked about books – he loved *Moby-Dick* – and he told her stories about his childhood on a farm in Missouri. He pronounced it Missur-uh.

Sometimes they spent Saturday nights at a folk song club downtown, listening to one of the locals singing old Woody Guthrie songs. They lingered in coffee shops and talked long into the night, both of them restless, half-dreaming that they were drifting toward some new life, were on a moving track to a destination that had not yet revealed itself. Neither of them had any idea where that nebulous road might lead.

"How about a drive through the park?" Jackson said, "Is that cool with you?"

"I'd love it," she said. "Love to turn off the noise in my head." She was still thinking about Francine and the baby.

"Hey, I'm hip," he said. "My brain's on overload too."

"Tough night? I didn't see you."

"Yeah, I was filling in on Neuro. It's been one of those nights. Carrying the war around in my head."

He drove for a while without speaking, into the dark labyrinth of the park, curving around the seawall. He turned the radio off and the silence filled the car.

Maddie had asked him very little about the war and he rarely spoke of it. She didn't know how to begin. "Can you tell me something about Vietnam?" she asked.

He shrugged. "I was what they called a band-aid," he said. "A medic. I only saw one tour of duty. That was enough. Too much." He leaned out of his window and adjusted the side-view mirror. "That world of frag wounds and body counts just about did me in."

"That must have been true for a lot of guys."

"Game gets rough pretty quick out there."

"Does it still freak you out? The dreams, the memories?"

He laughed, a short, humorless laugh. "I'm buried in it. Still."

"I guess you saw a lot more than you ever wanted to see."

"I was a medic," he said flatly. "I saw it all."

"It's almost impossible for me to get my head around the idea that it's *boys* who are fighting out there," said Maddie. "Boys like you, boys my age. Dying. Hundreds of them coming home in those flag-draped coffins. I watch it, night after night, their stories, their deaths, all across the evening news."

"Yup," he said. "We're the ones dying. About six thousand of us so far." He rubbed his hand across his eyes as though whatever movie that was projected on that inner screen was too painful to watch. "But it's those old bastards in Washington who're pulling the trigger. Knowing that can sure mess with your head. Gives you some pretty hard edges."

As he spoke, Maddie sensed a part of him was still lost in that green jungle of memory. He'd gotten what he called an "early out" from Vietnam, he told her. And like so many of those boys, he was trying to get landed immigrant status in Canada. All the conversations Maddie had overheard between the American boys in the hospital cafeteria seemed to have been about "getting landed."

"I've watched you," Maddie said. "You're kind. Whatever you saw in Vietnam didn't give you hard edges.

106

But I've seen a lot of it in others. Barely hidden anger, impatience. Never in you. It's sad to watch."

"Yeah, we all think we know how things ought to be in this world. Fair. Just. But they never are." He wheeled into a parking spot at Prospect Point where they sat in the brilliant light of the North Shore shipping yard across the dark water with its containers heaped with dazzling yellow sulfur. Above that, Maddie could see lights on Grouse Mountain and the rainbow arc of the Lions Gate Bridge.

"It sure ain't like that in Nam." He said it quietly, as though speaking only to himself. "No justice there."

"Was there anything good?"

"There's a song. *He ain't heavy, he's my brother*. Know it?"

"I love that song. Not that I claim to understand it. Not really."

"Yeah, well, that's our story. We carry each other. Dead or alive. Nobody's ever too heavy."

He started the car and they continued on through the dark shadows and arbors of the park. He began to sing.

"It's an old Robert Johnson song," he said, "*Sweet Home Chicago*. I used to play blues guitar before . . ." He stopped. "He's the guy," he went on, "who sold his soul to the devil. Met up with him at some crossroads in Mississippi."

"Why'd he do that?"

"He wanted to be the greatest blues singer ever. That was the exchange." He laughed. "I guess he was the musical *Dorian Gray*."

He began singing again.

Maddie wound down the window and a cold breeze blew through the car, carried the melody into the night.

For a few moments, it was as though she wasn't there at all, just part of an audience listening in the dark.

They stopped at Second Beach. It was black there and still. The mountains and outcropping of shoreline were dark, distant shapes now. Maddie could feel him coming back from whatever place he had been in his mind, easing into the cool stillness of the car like a phantom recovering its lost body.

"When I was young, growing up in Missouri," he said, "I thought I'd be a singer. I loved music. Especially the blues."

"And what happened?"

"Nam happened." He touched her arm just then. "Come back to my apartment with me. We can smoke a little weed. Talk."

Maddie said okay. She wouldn't be able to sleep now anyway. She'd never been to his place.

They drove back through the night streets in silence. His apartment was in an old dinosaur of a building a few blocks from the hospital. In the hallway, he pushed the button and the elevator shook and rattled its way down to the main floor. Maddie laughed as he pulled back the cage door. It reminded her of elevators in the Hudson's Bay store when she was a child. Operators in their perfectly white gloves pulling back the cage doors of gleaming, polished brass. *Ladies' dresses, Notions, Linens. Going up.*

They stepped onto the fourth floor and he unlocked the door to his apartment. The elevator disappeared with a clang and a whir. They sat on his bed and smoked a joint together, leaning against the wall amidst the soft orange blur of the Indian scarf he had draped over the lampshade. Candlelight flickered against the black and white poster of Bob Dylan hunched over his guitar in the corner of an empty room, ash from the cigarette stuck to his lip just about to fall. Jackson put Dylan on the turntable. *Highway 61 Revisited.*

"Stay over," Jackson said. He hesitated. "We've never talked about it, but I'm sure you've figured out that sex isn't what I'm looking for. Not now, anyway. I'm not queer or anything. I'm just . . ."

"Jackson, I'm cool with that." It wasn't what Maddie wanted either. She hadn't been attracted to him in that way and their friendship had never come close to moving in that direction.

"Just think of me as a non-practicing heterosexual."

She laughed.

"We can still be close." He pulled up a quilt from the bottom of the bed and covered them both, nestled into the curve of her arm. She wrapped her arms around him and held him. Somehow it didn't feel strange. It felt right.

"Out in the jungle," he said, "there's no soft place to put your head. But I was one of the lucky ones. I had a *mama-san*. For a while anyway. She massaged my feet. It was the best thing I ever had in my life. Her foot rubs."

"What's a *mama-san*?"

"Just that. Love. Warmth. Connection." He laughed. "A great thing if you were lucky enough to find one in the middle of all that craziness. And I was."

"I don't know what to ask you about Vietnam. I can't imagine the things you've seen."

"Well," he said, "I can tell you." He lay there for a long time, silent. Then, "It's pretty simple. There's Nam," he said. "And there's the rest of the world. And there ain't nothin' in between."

They fell asleep listening to *Just like Tom Thumb's Blues*. When Maddie woke, deep into the night, Jackson was shaking her, calling her name.

"What's wrong?" she said. She pulled the quilt around herself, pushed away the hands gripping her wrists. "What's happened?"

"You're alive," he said. "You're okay."

"Of course, I'm okay. What did you think? What happened?" She put her arms around him and rubbed his back as though he was a child waking from a nightmare.

"I couldn't feel you breathing," he said. "I didn't know . . ."

"You thought I was dead?"

He nodded. "I know. It's stupid."

"It's not stupid, Jackson. But you're not there anymore."

But even as she said those words, she knew that for Jackson, it might never be over. Vietnam had permeated every cell of his body.

He lay down again and curled into a fetal position. "If you wake up and I'm gone," he said, "don't worry. Sometimes I just gotta go."

"Where?"

"Anywhere. I just walk."

"So if I wake and you're gone?"

"Go or stay. Either is cool with me." He grinned. "We'll see each other again."

Maddie couldn't go back to sleep so she read his *Time* magazine. Indira Gandhi was on the cover. The headline read: *Troubled India in a Woman's Hands*. She read for a while, then finally drifted off.

It was almost morning when Maddie woke, chilled and disoriented. Jackson was gone. She went into the bathroom and threw water on her face and brushed her hair. Her reflection in the mirror looked veiled and remote, as though something in her had been mysteriously altered. She stepped from the building into the still morning streets and walked six blocks home, thinking of the last thing Jackson had said before he fell asleep: "The word we used in Nam for crazy was *dinky dau*. And I can tell you that by the time most of us come out of there, we're all pretty goddamn *dinky dau*."

᎒ᏅᏨ

As Maddie neared home, the house appeared in the half light, an apparition, tall, gray, turreted. There were no lights in any of the windows and no sounds except for the background rush of the city beyond the Granville Street Bridge, like a long, slow out-breathing. A gust of wind came out of nowhere and picked up a few abandoned leaves, spun them and dropped them. The sky was beginning to lighten, pale blue and pink, and the streets were gleaming and wet from an overnight shower.

She thought of all the mornings like this that she and Thea had shared, elated and powerful after long nights on acid, wandering the neon-washed streets of downtown. Even the rain on the gray pavement glittered and shone. Through the park and over the bridge and back again. They were dazzling then and dazzled. There were miracles. Molten suns lifting out of a bruised morning sky, the first shy blossoms of spring. Miracles performed, they believed, for their eyes only. Their psychedelic drug-taking, they had vowed, would never be recreational or incidental. Journeys into inner space were planned and guided by what they were reading at the time: *Lao Tzu, The*

Tibetan Book of The Dead, Siddhartha. They were amazed at the perfection of the universe. They were not yet cynical.

Maddie paused on the wet pavement outside the house, in the flat gray light of early morning. Something had stopped her. The sky lowered. The air smelled of ozone, rusty nails and rain. She felt a chasm between where she stood and where she was about to go. She recognized the place; she had been there before. A place that harbored a secret knowledge. The sea change that washes in just before the flood.

Words spilled into her head. *After the deluge. Fate.* They rolled over her tongue. But it was too soon to lean that far into the future. Her senses hummed like a high-tension wire. She was standing on the edge of something not yet spoken. Some dark imagining.

This isn't going to end well.

Maddie approached the house from the side, passed a straggly rose bush and climbed the first flight of stairs to their suite. At the landing, she felt an odd sense of fear as she unlocked the front door, and stepped into the living room. It was quiet. Nothing was amiss. Thea had left a note on the table: *Don't wake me in the morning. I've already called in sick. Where were you last night? You promised, you bitch.* The clock on the wall said six twenty.

Maddie tried the knob on the bedroom door, but it was locked. Why would Thea have locked the door? Maybe she had Heathcliff in there, but Maddie didn't think so. There was something wrong. She and Thea had a strong connection, a psychic intertwining that bound them in a way neither of them really understood. Maddie felt that pull now. She banged on the bedroom door and called out to her. No answer.

She lifted a sweater from the hook by the door and ran into the hall, down the stairs, outside and around the house, past the rose garden, and through the back gate to where the fire escape began. Even though Maddie was frightened of heights, she climbed the narrow wooden stairway to their balcony. The bedroom window curtains were open and she peered through the rain-spattered glass. Thea was asleep, still dressed, lying across the bed in a familiar pose. One knee pulled up to her chest, hands folded under one cheek, like a child. She was still wearing her glasses. On a table beside the bed was a Mason jar filled with daffodils she had bought at the Chinese grocer's down the street.

An almost imperceptible movement caught Maddie's eye. From beside Thea, a drifting curl of smoke. The window was locked but she knew that if she opened it, she'd fan the smoke into fire.

"That landlord's a dirty, spying pervert," Thea had said just days before. "He pretends he's washing the windows, as though I don't know what he's really doing. Spying on me." Thea had been on nights and was sleeping during the day.

Maddie climbed down, ran faster now, through the cold, yellow grass, around to the front, back up to the suite, and called the fire department. After she hung up the phone, she banged on Thea's door again, but knew Thea wasn't likely to waken.

She ran back down and out into the street. There wasn't a sound. The streets glistened. The sky behind the mountains was pale violet. There were no sirens, no clamor of trucks. *Where are they?* She wondered if she should be waking the other tenants.

Then they were there, unfurling hoses. *Which door, Miss?* Boots pounding up the stairs. A few sleepy faces peered over the railing on the landing. Maddie followed the firemen and stood back while they pushed their shoulders against the bedroom door, then slammed at the lock with an axe. *Shit. The landlord will kill us.* The door reeled inward and a curtain of smoke drifted into the living room.

Thea was still stretched across her bed. She hadn't moved. Her hair was spread around her on the pillow like a dark fan. One of the firemen picked her up and carried her into the living room. He leaned her back against the pillows on the couch and pressed a green plastic oxygen mask to her nose and mouth. She woke coughing and rubbing her eyes. Swore.

"What the hell are you doing with that thing?" Thea pushed the mask away. She was still drunk. The smell of scotch on her breath – her favorite drink – mingled with the smoke. She punched the fireman. Screamed. "You bastard! Get the hell away from me with that thing." Then she leaned against the pillow and closed her eyes, dismissing all of them. Her glasses had been knocked off by the oxygen mask and were lying beside her on the couch. Maddie picked them up and put them on the bookshelf.

The fireman's face was bloated and red. A grimy line of sweat rolled down the sides of his face, disappearing in his sideburns. "Your friend here just saved your life."

"I do *not*," Thea said, then repeated it, "I do *not* need *anyone* to save my life."

The fireman looked at Maddie and rolled his eyes. Maddie paced across the living room and back. She wanted to scream.

"You burned the bed, Thea," she said. "You could have burned down the whole place."

Another fireman came into the room, rubbing a fist across his damp forehead, leaving a long, dirty streak. "The mattress is a goner. It's in the yard. We got it out just in time."

"What about the room?" Maddie asked.

"Water damage," he said. "And it'll smell of smoke for a long time. You'll want to paint for sure."

After they left, Thea picked up a blanket from where it had fallen on the floor and swept it around her shoulders. "I'm going back to bed," she said.

Maddie looked at her. "There is no bed, Thea." Maddie knew she should comfort her, offer to make tea, create some sort of order out of what was left of the night. But she couldn't.

Thea paused at the bedroom door, glanced back at Maddie. "You stupid bitch," she whispered. "You stupid, stupid bitch." She slammed the door. It reeled back against the broken lock.

Maddie sat on the couch for a long time, staring into the thin morning light. Thea's journal lay open and face down on the end of the table. She hesitated for a moment, then picked it up. The last entry had been dated just the morning before.

I tried to kill myself the other day. It was one of those lonesome days, cold and raining, those damn foghorns crying in the harbor. Wailing, as though they could push through all the goddamn fog and confusion of my life. I lay down on the cement under Heathcliff's car, breathing in the exhaust fumes. Everything turned red as though the whole world was on fire. I got out of there as fast as I could because I knew that if I went any further, I would be going straight to hell. I'm not ready for that. Not yet. I didn't mean for Heathcliff to know, but he came out to the garage for something and caught me choking and gagging. I was out from under the car by then, but he knew what I'd been up to. He said he'd had enough. He doesn't want to see me anymore. I guess that was the last straw. Ha. What a joke. He has no idea what the last straw could really be. There'll be other Heathcliffs. There's always a Heathcliff somewhere. But afterwards, when I was back at home by myself, I felt so lonely. It was as though I could feel the cold cry of foghorns, like bruises on my skin.

A palpable sadness. Palpable: able to be touched or felt; readily perceived.

Maddie closed the journal and sat for a long time looking out the window into nothing. Had Thea left it open and lying there hoping Maddie would read it? There was a terrible sorrow in Thea's words. Even so, Thea was the queen of duplicity and deceit. Cynical, self-mocking, she was capable of anything. Maddie wondered what Thea was thinking as she sat alone on the floor beside the empty bed frame and her jar of yellow daffodils. Regal, even in her defeat. She couldn't guess. But she knew that Thea would probably come up with a word for it before the day was done.

ॐ

Jackson sat on the living room floor and leaned against the couch, his long legs stretched out in front of him. Maddie enjoyed his company but knew he wanted more, not a physical kind of more, but more of her time, more of her insights and understanding. She loved the times when she stayed with him and they would talk half the night. Those times when his past didn't hijack his dreams. He rarely spoke of the war but when he did, it was as though his memories were taking shape slowly, piece by piece, from some long ago dream he had not quite forgotten. The words spilled out like dark poetry. *We came home to an America torn apart. Not the America we knew. No more Norman Rockwell. Streets bleeding. Kids dying.*

It was in the night, though, where his dark secrets mushroomed. Cries torn from his throat. Staccato rhythms. Night flights, border skirmishes. Faces of terror crawling out of his burned-out dreams. His body was taut, always, never still. Poised for escape.

Sometimes he had softer dreams of boys like him, boys who made it home. Or boys who never left. Boys dreaming of Canada. Dreaming of getting landed, like winged things, butterflies, Luna moths looking for a safe place to light.

All this as they slept under the pale blue silk of a parachute he had carried home with him. Still, he lived with a small sliver of hope that he would someday fly free, released at last from the night's dark fist.

Maddie thought that what he wanted was another *mama-san*, a soft place to lay his head, someone to tell his dreams to and spin out his nightmare. She had decided that wasn't going to be her.

The war in Vietnam was exploding across television screens all over the world. The KKK night riders were murdering blacks, protesters were on the march and dying, and all of it was fueled by an uncontained passion and a belief that this generation – her generation – could change the world forever.

This is the world Jackson knew and needed to stay connected to, a world that was gritty and raw and, despite all its growing horror, promising too. It was through her friendship and caring, he had told Maddie, that he could believe anything was possible. That she could be the one to tame his nightmares, to show him the way back to himself.

"When I'm with you," he said, "I don't feel so numb. I'm coming alive."

"It will be okay, Jackson. But you've got to give it time."

"I love Canada. I'm grateful to be here. But it's not my home, Maddie. Sometimes I feel like that. Like a homeless person. It probably sounds crazy, but knowing you're around makes me feel safe somehow."

"Trust me," Maddie said, "I'm not the one who can keep you safe. You have to find that safe place for yourself."

"I know that."

It was late, long past midnight. An evening windstorm had knocked the power out and they sat together and talked by candlelight. Thea was working nights. Maddie was wrapped in a blanket to keep warm. Jackson refused a blanket and kept his jacket on.

"What will you do now? Now that you and Thea have been evicted?"

"I'd like to find my own place," Maddie said. "I've decided to go back to school to study writing. I've got an application in."

"What kind of writing?"

"Maybe historical writing. That interests me."

"What will Thea do?"

Maddie sighed. "I don't know. We have to leave, obviously, but the landlord is letting us stay until spring. I won't stay though. I can't. It's time to go. Time to get away from Thea."

"What is it about Thea?" he said, uncrossing his legs and propping himself higher against the couch. "I don't know her very well, but why is she always so angry, so bitter?"

"She's always been cynical. She's got a lot of rage around her father. Lots of unresolved stuff."

"What's that about?"

"He left them. Years ago. Thea just dances around the periphery of the story when she talks about her life before she knew me. I think it was a bad time for her, his leaving when he did."

"Why?"

"She was a girl on the threshold of womanhood, a daddy's girl, I think, and needed a father to witness that. The metamorphosis. She needed to know she was beautiful in his eyes, needed him to tell her that she was growing into a lovely creature. Chrysalis to butterfly. Instead, he walked out of her life and never came back. So she got stuck somewhere in between, before she could grow her wings and fly. Out of all the things she's said to me over the years, that's what seems to have hurt her the most."

"That's sad."

"Yeah, it's sad," Maddie said. "And she's been acting strange ever since Charlie left. He was an old friend, a kind of boyfriend, although she's always insisted he wasn't. They spent a lot of time together. She really cared about him. Then he vanished. One day he was just gone. And she won't talk about it."

"You have no idea what happened?"

"She refuses to say."

Maddie ran water into a tall, skinny wine bottle and put the yellow rose Jackson had brought her into it, then set it on the table. "Thea's enraged by life. Enraged by what could have been. She sees its beauty too. She sees beauty in poetry and music. But it's as though she can just never get close enough to it, can never hold it long enough to keep it fixed in her mind or remember how it feels. Now it's all about loss."

"Why did her father leave? Did she ever say?"

"Not in so many words. No. But there was some deep, ugly stuff. Her mother's humiliation. Her father's rage. She told me once that her father hung a red light above their front door. Told her again and again that her mother was a whore. And this was after he'd already left.

She said something really strange. It was just after the firemen had left and she was determined to go back to her room even though the mattress was gone and the door was wrecked. She said to me, 'You stupid bitch.' Just in that way, and then said it again. 'You stupid bitch.' It was as if she'd wanted to die. Had planned it even, and hated me for interfering."

"Do you think she really wanted to die?"

"I don't know," Maddie said. "At first I couldn't imagine that scenario. But later . . . it was eerie, the look on her face and the way she spat out the words, as though what I had done was the ultimate betrayal."

"Has she ever talked about suicide?"

"Yeah, sometimes. In that cynical way of hers."

Maddie told him about Thea's journal that she'd found on the table the morning of the fire. "But I'm never really sure how serious she is. Not long ago she said that if she hasn't pulled her life together by the time she's twenty-two, she'll kill herself. But that's Thea. There's always so much drama."

"She actually said that?"

"Yeah, she did. 'I'm outta here,' is what she said. 'Unless a whole lot changes.' But she loves the attention. Loves the reaction she can provoke."

"Have you told her you're leaving?"

"Yeah, I've told her, but she's pretending I'm not really going. She doesn't want me to go. Or to leave her. But, both of us have to go."

The candle sputtered and Maddie got up to find another one before it went out.

"If the power was on I'd play *La Mer* for you," she said. She came back with a thick candle and a saucer to put it on. "Sometimes Thea and I would put a blanket on the floor and lie in the dark to listen to the music. We'd smoke a joint, then pretend the sea was rising and crashing all around us while we were safe on our little square of blanket." Maddie lit the candle and the shadow of the flame leapt against the wall. "I just liked that feeling of knowing I'm safe while the sea rages. Stupid, I guess. I used to write stories when I was a child and they all had the same theme."

"Which was?"

"Survival," Maddie said. "They were all about kids who had been abandoned by their parents. But they survived. On their own, that was the key. They all survived without parents. My favorite book was *The Boxcar Children*, about three children who lived in an abandoned boxcar. I can still see the pictures, of all the rooms they fixed up with odds and ends from scrap heaps and people's leftovers, and a garden outside the door, full of red geraniums. They were safe and they survived in their own little world, a world they made themselves. They weren't dependent on anyone. Their whole life was lived on their own terms. I loved that story. It was always how I wanted my life to be."

"Not dependent on anyone else?"

"Yeah." Maddie sat in the stillness and looked at Jackson's face, his fair skin and blue eyes, profile so thin, features sharp and angular like carved driftwood. She wasn't in love with him and never would be. He wanted to see her as a half-open door to his new life in a country that wasn't his home. But he still hadn't recovered from being parachuted back into the changed and alien world of his own country.

Maddie got up and pulled her blanket tightly around herself, leaned forward and kissed him on the cheek. "I really care about you, Jackson. You know that, right?"

He grinned. "Yeah, I know."

After he left, she stood at the window and watched him walk down the street with his tall, rangy stride. He was fragile and a little broken, but she didn't want the responsibility of carrying him. It might have been selfishness. Thea would have called it fear. But Maddie had no wish to be the doorway to Jackson's dreams, to be the one to light his way. She was in search of her own dreams, a bird on the wing, and even though she wasn't sure of where she was going, Maddie knew she wanted to fly alone.

☙ C₰

"You can't leave." Thea stamped her foot on the floor.

In other circumstances, it might have been funny but Maddie knew that if she laughed, Thea's rage would spill over and drown them both. They had been given their eviction notice after the fire and Maddie was packing, filling boxes with books, separating Thea's from hers. Remnants of the pink and gold sunset fell in a band across the faded carpet and already evening shadows had begun to invade corners of the room. Bob Dylan's raspy voice filled the room with *One Too Many Mornings*.

Maddie knew Thea was afraid to leave, worried about where she'd go. "I guess we're outta here," she'd said to Maddie a few weeks before. "*Ex post facto.*"

"Meaning?"

"Meaning, *in light of subsequent events.* Subsequent to the fire, we've been forced to leave. Booted out. It's my word today. Or words."

Upstairs, footsteps padded across the floor. A body settled onto a squeaky bed. A woman's laughter. Once Thea stormed upstairs and banged on the door of the suite above theirs, shouting at the woman and her lover that their bed squeaked and their afternoon lovemaking was disturbing Maddie's sleep. Maddie had been in bed with the flu at the time. The woman slammed the door in Thea's face.

"You're running away," Thea said.

Maddie sat down on the edge of the couch, a pile of books in her lap. Through the grimy windowpane, she could see the distant mountains. For a moment, she felt as blank as an empty page. Her mind soared from the room, over the purple mountains, far from where her body sat. An old memory hijacked everything else that had been in her mind until that moment. Her mother: *You run away from every good thing in your life, Maddie. That's what you do.* She hated it when her mother said things like that. As though Maddie hadn't been present in her own life.

But was that what she was doing?

"Is that what you think?" she asked Thea.

Thea turned the record over on the stereo and ignored the question. "You know, we had something once, my mother and me," she said. "A life. We had a real life once. I've never told you about it, what our life was like before my father left and we moved across the street from you."

"No."

Thea had told Maddie very little about her father leaving. She was not someone you asked questions of lightly. If the timing was wrong, she could tear you to pieces just for asking. She held the keys to the vault of that particular piece of her history and was the only one who would decide when to open it.

"He's gone," was all she had said then, closing the door on the conversation as quickly as it had opened.

"We had *things*," she said now. "A house. A beautiful house. And a car. An Oldsmobile. It was one of those two-toned jobs, red and white with lots of chrome. God, I loved that car."

"And what happened? To all your stuff, I mean."

"My father took it away."

"Just like that?"

"Just like that."

Thea got up from the couch and punched one of the pillows off the arm. "He left us and took everything away. I was thirteen. Just becoming. You know."

Maddie did know.

"And when he left us, our entire life was over." Thea kicked the pillow and sent it tumbling across the floor. "My mother, who had never worked a day in her life, had to get a job. At first, we lived in an apartment. We'd never lived in an apartment before. I didn't even know anyone who lived in an apartment. Nothing was ever the same after that."

Thea would let little diamonds of truth like this escape when she chose, when she needed the attention or a bit of drama, although these things were often one and the same.

"I'm so sorry," Maddie said.

"You're so sorry," Thea mimicked. "You have no idea how it was. Who's ever left you?"

What she wasn't saying, Maddie knew, was the real story, the subtext to their conversation. She was angry because ever since the fire, Maddie had reneged on their plans to wait until summer to take their vacation time together and hitchhike to San Francisco. Thea wanted to follow the hippies to Haight Ashbury with her blanket, bells and drums, and with flowers in her hair. Instead, Maddie had decided to live alone and go back to school. She had chosen her own life over Thea.

They were living in a renaissance, a world turned upside down. Sometimes, Maddie felt removed from it. *Turn on, tune in, drop out.* The mantra of the day. The music was a testament to their dreams; the pot and the acid were the icing on the cake. But at night Maddie wanted her head on her own pillow in her own house. Dropping out would only have made Maddie dependent on others for the thing that meant the most to her – a place she could call her own.

She and Thea thought of themselves as hippies. But Maddie felt a hint of lingering shame, believing that she wasn't quite bona fide, just a hippie with a job. Maddie could never be a real hippie because she had money in her pocket and a place to live. She liked the security of the paycheck every two weeks.

More often though, Maddie was going to work high, yearning for freedom, a change, anything different. She didn't want to be a weekend hippie either, one of those girls with long ironed hair, love beads and flowered gypsy skirts who hung around The Retinal Circus or The Afterthought, or wandered Fourth Avenue on Saturday nights looking for long-haired boys and free dope.

Sometimes the drugs scared her, but she hadn't told anyone that. Not even Thea. The bad trips always convinced her that she was being made to pay for surreptitious crimes. Or sins she hadn't yet committed. So when she had a bad trip, she prayed. For forgiveness. For absolution. Most of her bartering with God involved a promise to give up getting high. Bad trips were God's punishment. *Please God, just get me through this one and I swear I'll never touch drugs again. Don't let me fall over the edge here.*

Maddie prayed for the possibility that whatever transgressions she had stumbled into could somehow be struck from the record. *Make me a better person.* But by then it always seemed far too late for that. Then she'd resort to *Get me out of here. I'll do anything,* but knew that was a lie too. She'd do anything then, in that moment, but the next day and all the days after that, she would be just trying to survive, to keep her head above water in ways that had become habits. And Maddie knew she'd probably keep getting high. There were no other wings to fly with, no escape route out of her life. She had her wits but also a frightened heart. Mere crumbs to live by. In the end, her prayers felt hollow, meaningless.

"You're running away," Thea said again.

"And what is it you think I'm running away from?" Maddie said. "Grace me with your wisdom, Thea."

"Go ahead, mock me," Thea said. "I may be a bitch, but I'm no fool."

"No. No one would ever mistake you for a fool."

"What you're afraid of," Thea said, "is what might happen if you stand still. What might happen if you have to think too much about the religious insanity of your childhood. About your grandfather. What might happen if you let yourself get closer to Jackson. Or me. Or anyone else, for that matter."

They had only talked about Maddie's grandfather once and neither of them had ever mentioned it again. But Thea hadn't forgotten. She took out a bottle of white wine from the fridge. "Want some?"

Maddie shook her head.

"You. Me. Jackson. We're all strangers in this universe. You know that. We're all scared. All running."

"You think I'm afraid? You think I'm running? And you hardly know Jackson."

"You're afraid of anything and anyone," Thea said, "who gets too close. And do you know how I know that?" Thea shoved her face mere inches from Maddie's. "Because, *you're just like me.*"

"How clever of you, Thea," Maddie said, "but you're dead wrong. I'm *nothing* like you."

"You don't want to be," Thea said, "of course." She took a thick green mug out of the cupboard and poured wine into it. "But you are. There's only one important difference between you and me." She took a long drink of wine. "I know who I am. I *know* that I don't want anything or anyone in this goddamn world getting too close to me."

"And me?"

"And neither do you. But it terrifies you. You still want *something.* You're still waiting."

"For what?"

"Who knows?" Thea drained the mug of wine and dropped it into the sink. Rubbed her mouth against her sleeve. "This is a shit way to drink wine. Maybe what you're waiting for is something as stupid as love."

You're in love with him. It was something Thea had said before about Maddie's relationship with Jackson, always with a tone of accusatory disbelief. Maddie knew she wasn't in love. She didn't know anything about love except for the fearsome and all-consuming love of God that had compressed her world into something small and claustrophobic. Or the oblique and disquieting love of her parents. As for what she thought of as "real" love, a boy-girl, man-woman kind of love, she had been able to sidestep that for this long. Even the idea of it terrified her. Thea was wrong about love.

Maddie stood up. "I'm going out for a while. And as far as leaving, Thea, we *have* to leave. It's not as though we have a choice."

"Yes," Thea said, sitting back down on the couch, "I know that. I'm fully aware of the situation." She stared up at Maddie. "Here's my word for today: *cognizant.* Of the situation. Which I am." She picked up the pillow from the floor and wrapped her arms around it, pressing it against her chest. "I know we have to leave, Maddie. But *you* don't have to leave *me.*"

∞CB

"So, is there anything else?"

Maddie's father had stopped on his way home from work to fix a lamp that kept shorting out. Maddie asked him to do it because their landlord was in the hospital recovering from back surgery and there was nobody else to call. Thea and Maddie weren't good at fixing things and neither was Maddie's brother. Her father used to try to teach Tom, dragging old clocks or kitchen gadgets up from the basement to show him the basics of household repairs, but it never took. Or perhaps Tom just refused to learn.

Maddie's brother had been angry with his dad most of his life. Angry for the things they couldn't have: TV, radio, record player. A normal life. He still raged against the rules they endured while growing up. One of the rules Maddie's brother never seemed to mind though, was having to occasionally look after her. When they got home from school, he'd take her on his paper route if their grandparents – who sometimes looked after Maddie while their parents worked – were away or busy. In the winter, it was almost dusk by the time they got out of school at four and collected Tom's papers from the paper box at the community center.

Tom's route wound through Wellington Crescent, a tree-lined avenue that curved along the Assiniboine River. Grand manors were stately testaments to far-flung wealth and power. The houses were graced with facades of Tyndall stone, gabled roofs and leaded glass windows. Coach houses with lamp-lit driveways. Stone lions stood guard outside wrought iron gates. In the garden, a few straggly winter roses leaned against a stone wall. A sweet-faced angel knelt under an oak tree, alone, with her blind eyes and folded wings. Vestiges of a golden past. Nobility. All gilded in the wash of old money.

There is one day Maddie has not forgotten. It has stayed with her like a dream, nuanced with a recognition that was imprinted on her skull a long time ago. The streets were already dark and driveways to the houses long and shadowy. Maddie waited outside the gates, kicking her boots against icy ridges of snow left after the sidewalks had been shoveled, while Tom trudged up to the house and dropped the paper on the veranda. The door opened and a V of yellow light streaked out into the dark. Tom was speaking to someone, leaning into the shadow of the doorway. From somewhere inside the house, Maddie heard a dog bark, the distant drift of music. The streets were dim and ghostly and the eerie light filled her with a gentle kind of lonesome. She had no words for this feeling. She was thinking of other things.

She was remembering the long walk home from school in the early winter gloom. Past the houses with their lit windows, small squares of yellow light, the warm glow from the kitchen filling the darkening street. The smells of evening dinners, families living their lives. Mothers bending over cooking pots, children sitting at the kitchen table reading or drawing. Some back and forth squabbling, but with an overlay of tenderness and laughter. All of them waiting for the door to open and the cold night air to rush in along with the father who had been at work all day. There might be music on the radio. She sometimes saw the flickering blue light of a television reflected in a window.

Maddie's dream family.

Tom came back down the driveway holding something pressed against his chest. "Let's go," he said.

"What have you got?"

"A record."

"What record?"

"Just a record. Elvis Presley." He turned it over and read the label. "*Heartbreak Hotel.*"

"Where'd you get it?"

"A girl," he said. "A girl in that house gave it to me." He pulled his mittens on and picked up his empty newspaper bag. "Anyway, I don't want it."

"Why not?"

"Why would I?" His voice cut her, sharp-edged and shivery, like the icicles hanging from the eaves. "What good is it to me? Do we have a record player?"

Maddie had no answer. She knew they didn't. The only music allowed in their house was hymns. Her grandmother at the piano, twisted, arthritic fingers stumbling over the keys. Somewhere in another room, her grandfather's rusty old voice sings: *Rock of ages, cleft for me.*

What is cleft?

Maddie's mother saved her singing for church. She was proud of her perfect pitch. As a child, Maddie had no idea what *perfect pitch* meant, but she suspected it had something to do with pleasing God. She knew how important this was to her parents.

Maddie had always had her own conversations with God. Night time prayers. A special prayer for the children: *Jesus, tender shepherd, hear me, bless thy little lamb tonight, through the darkness be thou near me, keep me safe 'til morning light. Knees pressed against cold, wood floors.*

But no music. No television or radio. No record player.

The devil's business.

Maddie knew her family was different. *Not friendly,* she heard one of the neighbors say. *Very religious. Crazy.* The neighbor woman was Ukrainian, wore a babushka and carried her shopping home from the A&P in a basket hung over her arm. Maddie's mother thought the Ukrainians were the odd ones. *DPs* she called them. When Maddie was a child, she explained to her that a DP was a displaced person. Someone who didn't belong. Maddie felt like a DP.

"Does she like you?" Maddie whispered to Tom. "The girl in that house?"

"Yeah."

"Do you like her?"

Tom didn't answer. He picked up the empty bag and slung it over his shoulder. He started walking.

"Follow me," he said.

Maddie knew that Tom was suggesting something out of the ordinary, because following him on his paper route was what she did almost every day after school. Thin bands of winter light fell through the tall oaks and maples, casting eerie shadows along the empty boulevard. The moon appeared from under a bank of clouds, washing the road in a cold, silver light.

Tom stopped at a caragana bush, a winter skeleton now, stripped of its leaves and any sign of life. He pushed his way through and started down a path that led to the river.

"C'mon, Mad."

Maddie hesitated in the black space between the safety of the street and the darkness of the river. She didn't want to go with him but she didn't want to stand alone on the street either.

They edged down the path, felt their way in the dark. Maddie saw the cars on the other side of the water, a slow parade of lights crossing the Maryland Bridge. Tom took off his mittens. He pulled the record out of his newspaper bag, slid it from its paper sleeve. His fingers, light as bird wings, glided over the grooves as though they were reading Braille. That small, black circle of wonder with its unspoken possibilities, its hidden magic. He stood on the bank, silent, looking out over the river as though it were another country.

Then in a slow dance, he spun the record out in a wide arc, sent it soaring into the slate blue night. It plummeted, sliced the water with a soft *kerplunk*, carrying with it all its promises, its secrets. All the stories left untold. And disappeared as though it never was.

Tom picked up his paper bag and hoisted it over his shoulder, then motioned for Maddie to follow him back up the path to the street. Neither of them mentioned that day again.

"No," Maddie said now to her dad. "I don't think there's anything else." She laughed. "We've got mice but you can't fix that."

"I can put down traps."

"Oh, no. No traps."

"You'd rather live with mice?"

"I'd rather live with live mice than dead ones."

He laughed too. Then dropped his tools on the kitchen table and sat down heavily in one of the chairs. He ran one hand through his thick mass of curly hair that was beginning to gray. "There are some things I wish had been different," he said.

Maddie was startled. This was not like her father. She wasn't sure what he was trying to say, and didn't think she wanted to know. All conversations with her father led to scolding Bible quotes, recriminations of one sort or another and – inevitably, on Maddie's part – guilt.

"Like the time you got burned," he went on. "That shouldn't have happened."

He was referring to the time Maddie was two or three, sick with pneumonia. Her mother was steaming her in her crib with friar's balsam. Henry, her parents' boarder, had stumbled over the extension cord in the hallway and knocked the boiling water onto her.

Out of the landscape of their past, from all the roads they had travelled together as a family, this was the one big thing he regretted?

"It was just an accident, Dad."

"Well, yes. But I should have been more careful."

"You didn't do anything. It was Henry."

"Henry?"

"Henry. The boarder. He was the one who tripped over the cord."

"Where on earth did you get that idea?" he said. "It was me. I tripped over the cord."

"But I thought . . ."

Why had her mother lied? She'd told her it was Henry's fault.

"Anyway," Maddie said, "no matter who did it, it was an accident." It was obvious her father wanted to talk more, but she didn't. She wanted him to leave. "So, Dad, thanks. For fixing that lamp."

"Nothing else, then?" He got up and pulled his jacket from the hook on the wall.

"No, nothing else."

He shrugged. "Okay, then." He put his hand on the doorknob. "You know I'm here." He hesitated, "If you need anything."

"Thanks," Maddie said. "If I do, I'll call. I promise."

The sound of his steps faded down the narrow wooden stairway, giving way to the hollow sound of the thin pane of glass rattling in the door to the garden as it closed behind him.

She sat down on the sofa feeling strangely unsettled. Out of all the craziness he had imposed on her with his mad beliefs, why had he chosen this one thing to feel guilty about? And why had her mother lied to her?

୫୦୪

Maddie paused on the landing of the stairs leading to the basement. Her mother had asked her to get potatoes from the burlap sack under the stairs. It was Sunday evening and her grandparents were having dinner at her parents' house as they did every Sunday. This week, Maddie's mother had called and invited her too. "It's been too long," she said. "Come and have Sunday dinner with us."

Maddie hated basements. They scared her. For most of her childhood, they had lived with her grandparents, and her grandfather's room was in the basement. Ever since she had been a child, he had lived in exile below her grandmother's rooms, which smelled faintly of violets and lemon polish and did not invite company. They shared their meal in the evenings and her grandfather sat upstairs by the fire while her grandmother played hymns on the piano. They spoke sometimes, not often, and occasionally Maddie's grandfather would make Gran laugh. The laughter would escape, then evaporate before her voice chilled again and all the old walls were made visible.

Home for Maddie was not a place of shelter or of love. Days were blurred in a veil of bitterness, cloaked in an incomprehensible aura of regret. Her grandparents had lived with them for so many years, and it was through the straitened world of her Victorian grandmother that she learned to navigate love's opposites: the withdrawals, the betrayals. The silence.

Her grandmother glares at her still, with her hardened heart, from a photograph on the wall. A cameo brooch at her throat pinned to a black velvet ribbon. All those years her grandparents lived with them, Maddie watched, vigilant for any signs of unraveling family secrets. She understood the measure and the weight of what her grandmother carried to her room each night, a room that was far away and separate from her grandfather's. Her Bible, her reading glasses, her silver combs. Sometimes a book: *John Halifax, Gentleman,* or *Pilgrim's Progress.* A long braid down her back, a white flannelette nightgown. Her bitter mouth.

But why did basements haunt Maddie still? Memories of what her eyes could see above the weight of him on her body, beyond his thin, bent arms holding her down. Birds' wings and dead leaves trapped against the window. Dead images of dead places. *So long ago. Nothing to be afraid of now.*

The basement smelled of sawdust and nails. A sharp, acrid smell caught in her throat, pulling her back to the basement smell of her Winnipeg childhood. She tossed some potatoes into a wicker basket and went back upstairs.

During dinner, Maddie told her parents she was quitting her job and going back to school.

"You're doing what?" her mother said. She paused, waiting for Maddie's answer, a forkful of roast beef suspended halfway between her plate and her mouth.

"Foolhardy. Quitting a good solid job like that." Her father mopped up the last of the gravy from his dinner plate.

"It's not foolhardy," Maddie said. "I want to go to school. I want to be a writer."

Maddie's grandmother unfolded her napkin carefully. "You're already too clever for your own good. Going back to school at your age. What do you think you have to write about, anyway?"

Maddie might have known she'd have something to say. She wished she had the courage to say what she wanted to say: *None of you ever wanted me to get an education. You are all so terrified of the big world out there and how it might corrupt me.*

"It's a little silly, don't you think?" said her mother.

"Mom, I want to do this. And no, it's not silly."

Maddie's grandmother shook her head, dismissing anything Maddie might say. Her grandfather reached for the bowl of potatoes, his left hand propped under his right elbow to take the weight off his arthritic joints. Maddie hadn't spoken to him for years. Hardly anyone else spoke to him either.

Maddie's grandparents rarely spoke to one another. They had been torn apart by old arguments and hurts and long-buried secrets that had grown between them like gnarled old roots, binding them together forever. Gran was the undisputed monarch of the house, Maddie's grandfather more like a reluctant visitor. He told stories in which he was the hero, the desperado who rode on wings of bravado and glory, and this always invited her grandmother's scorn.

"He's been everywhere and done everything, he has," she would say in her cold, derisive voice. She was not willing or able to allow him even those few moments of self-importance.

Maddie wanted to believe his stories. She wanted to believe that he had ridden shotgun on a stage traveling through Sonora in old Mexico, wearing buckskin and dust. And that he had pounded the hard dirt trails through the hills, bunked down by a *mesquite* campfire, its glow the only warmth in the desert night. Maddie loved the idea that he had bucked the wild currents of the Ottawa River, ridden across the Prairies in an open freight car and survived all of it through sheer will and grit.

She wanted to believe that somewhere in her grandparents' life together there had been some love, some shred of tenderness. She watched for it, imagined it as though she was waiting for a new spring shoot. But her parents and grandmother, she knew, thought he was nothing more than a crazy old man. And maybe he was that too.

Gran had discovered one day that his name was not Thomas, as she had always thought. She had married him as Thomas and called him Thomas all their married life, but when he applied for his pension, it turned out that his name was Samuel. They had even named Maddie's brother after him. Gran was enraged, Maddie's mother indignant. This news somehow made his name invalid, a mockery. They were convinced that it was the work of a deranged mind. They would give him nothing, allow him no camouflage.

"Well, I'm doing it," Maddie said. "I'm not changing my mind."

Her mother gathered a few dishes and went into the kitchen. Maddie could tell she was annoyed, even from the back. "No," she called back to her, "I don't suppose you will. You've always done exactly as you pleased. Always."

Maddie's mother had maintained the same position for as long as Maddie could remember: *Maddie is willful and obstinate. She refuses to listen to reason.*

"There are those who don't know what they've got," Gran said. "Always wanting more. Never enough." She picked up her empty plate and carried it into the kitchen. Maddie's mother returned to the dining room and Maddie saw her glance quickly at her father.

Maddie pushed her chair back from the table and got up. She picked up her plate, still streaked with slivers of roast beef and gravy, and followed her grandmother into the kitchen. In the living room, the mantel clock chimed six.

"Six bells," said her father quietly. It's what he always said, but no one listened anymore.

Maddie put her plate on the counter. Her grandmother was repinning one of her gray braids to her head. She had pushed her pale blue sweater sleeves up to her elbows and was running water into the sink for the dishes.

"That's not fair, Gran. Wanting more is a good thing," Maddie said. "It's about getting a better education."

Her grandmother stared at her evenly, looked straight into her eyes. "And just who do you think you're going to be with all this education?"

Maddie had not been the child of her parents' dreams. They both knew that. She was the black sheep that had strayed too far from the fold. And the older she got, the farther she strayed. Her parents resented her solitary inner life, the one that had grown over her like a new skin. The place to which they had no key. But the world that Maddie had claimed for herself, colored with her own intention, was fragile and her tenancy there was still uneasy.

As a child, all Maddie had ever wanted was what she thought of as a normal life, a life that felt the same inside and out. Her home life had never in any way resembled the world outside its doors, the world inhabited by her friends, Saturday afternoon movies, Girl Guides, proms, summer camp. She had longed for a world where God was not the constant, fearsome companion.

Maddie's father's proselytizing came from a fierce belief that those who had been given "the truth" – and he certainly saw himself as one of them – were bound by their faith to spread the word. Though he was driven by his unrelenting faith, the true master her father served, Maddie knew, was fear. Fear had ruled his life, had brought him to his knees, until he was bent under the pronouncements of an angry and unforgiving God.

The state of their souls was Maddie's father's greatest challenge and out of fear Maddie had been saved when she was thirteen. He knelt with her there on the floor beside her bed and prayed for her salvation. She wished she could have felt the joy he told her he had felt as a young boy, the day he had been saved in the middle of a horse field on a steaming summer afternoon, kneeling in the grass, praying to his God. Maddie had managed to feel only relief, as though she had been snatched from the pathway of an oncoming car. But she had sinned so much since her own saving, she could hardly believe its power still held.

Maddie had resisted her parents' fierce religiosity with the only defense she knew: silence and a gradual withdrawal from the life inside their home. Tom had chosen to live in exile from the family. His was a deliberate refusal to engage in family life. From the time he was ten years old, he had jobs: his first paper route, his job as a delivery boy at Humphrey's Grocery, then his elevated status as a stock boy at the A&P. He was hardly ever home. His withdrawal grew from a surfeit. Too much of everything. Too much family. And especially too much praying, too many reminders of their inherent wickedness. Maddie's estrangement from family was a choice too, but a choice born from a sense of impoverishment. Not enough. Not enough recognition of the world she inhabited. No honoring of the life that was hers.

Maddie walked into the living room and gazed out the window at the falling snow. Her mother came up behind her and put a hand on her arm, a hesitant, uncertain gesture. They didn't touch much and neither of them knew how to do it without feeling awkward.

"Maddie . . ."

"It's none of her business," Maddie said. "She has no right."

"It's not easy for your grandmother."

"Just how is it not easy for her?" Maddie's voice trembled with anger. "She runs the whole show. And yours too." Maddie knew this was dangerous territory. "Gran's the boss of all of us. Always has been. She thinks she can say anything she wants."

Her mother closed her eyes for a second as if in pain. "We need to talk." She beckoned Maddie into her bedroom and closed the door. Maddie sat down on the nubby white and pink chenille spread and her mother sat down beside her. It had been a long time since Maddie had been in that room. On her mother's vanity sat her tortoise shell brush and mirror set and a silver-framed picture of Maddie and her brother as children, taken in Assiniboine Park.

"I've been wanting to tell you this for a long time." Maddie's mother pushed back the dark curls that had escaped from her bun. "I guess this is as good a time as any." She nervously crossed her feet at the ankles then uncrossed them. "I know she's hard to deal with," she began. "And she can be cranky."

"Cranky? She's a bitter old woman," Maddie said. "She hates her life."

"Yes, that's true. There are parts of her life she hates," she said, "but for good reason."

"And that would be?"

"Your grandfather."

"Well, obviously. She despises him. All of you do. They should have divorced years ago."

"That just wasn't a possibility so there's no point in even bringing it up."

Oh, because you're all so religious? Maddie wanted to say. *Because God wouldn't approve?*

"Anyway, it's more than them just not getting along."

"No kidding. You've all made him a pariah."

Maddie had always refused to be part of that alliance of women who hated him. It was the women – her mother, her grandmother, Aunt Annie, Aunt Cilla – with their chilly smiles and silent contempt who had frozen him out, exiled him from the family.

Her mother paused. "He did things."

"Like?"

"When we were kids. To your aunts and me."

"You mean . . .?"

"Yes." It was obvious that she didn't want to say it any more than Maddie wanted to hear it. "He sexually abused us."

Silence.

"From the time we were babies," she said.

"And she did nothing?"

"She didn't know. Not for years."

"How did you finally tell her?"

"We didn't. She caught him."

"When?"

"Not until we were about nine or ten. She heard him in our room one night and walked in on the whole thing."

Maddie didn't want to imagine what *the whole thing* was.

"And you've all hated him ever since."

"I guess you could say that."

"It's been obvious all *my* life."

That explained it then. Nothing could ever have come from Maddie's watchfulness, from those years of vigilance, waiting for some sign of love between her grandparents, a chance kindness, an accidental, caring gesture. Despite what she knew he had done to her, Maddie had never been able to feel anything for her grandfather but pity. He had been as exiled in the family as she had felt. And that pain of exile had always felt greater than the pain of what he had done.

So Maddie had protected him. She had pitied him for having had to live with her grandmother's sullen contempt. All those years and all those miles between them. No gentleness. Gran's smiles measured and few. Certainly never an embrace. Maddie knew how it felt to be in exile. As though she'd been born into the wrong life.

Maddie tried to imagine her grandmother's head on her pillow at night, her dreams knotted in the longstanding roots of contempt for her husband, the man who stalked his daughters' rooms at night with unspeakable demands. The man who did the same to her, sometimes in the bright light of day on blistering summer afternoons in his own room, right in her parents' house. In that world of Bible readings, prayers, and intimations of hell.

She felt sick.

"All I'm trying to say, Maddie, is that this is what she's had to live with. All her life with this man."

"And she did nothing. She just put up with it. With him." Maddie stood up. *And he kept going to church. All of you did. Still. Now. And you all said nothing.* There was a voice inside her shouting, *Tell her. Tell her what he did to you too.* But she couldn't.

"Some things just have to be borne," said her mother. She got up and put her hand on the doorknob, paused, then opened the door and left the room.

Maddie felt numb. Her mother and father spoke in low tones in the dining room. Dishes rattled in the kitchen sink. The clock chimed six-thirty.

Maddie went to the front hall and put on her boots, jacket, scarf. She quietly opened the door and stepped out into the snowy evening.

How could her mother not have told her this before now? Maddie felt as though her life was a train flying through the landscape, a train that had forgotten to stop at the station where she was waiting to climb aboard in all her innocence, her naïveté. The world inside a dark silhouette against lighted windows as it sped through the night. Her life hurtling by. A huge piece of it missing.

She headed into the darkness toward the bus stop, then decided to walk home. Big, wet snowflakes fluttered against the light of streetlamps. The streets were deserted, shuttered against the darkening night and the soft, drifting flakes. Maddie was alone, but in a warm, bittersweet way, unseen in that silent, snowy world. Down in the harbor, deep two-toned foghorns moaned.

Most of the houses were lit, silhouetting dark shapes that moved to some other rhythm of a life within. Some houses still had Christmas lights shining on cheerful garlands of green, red, and blue. When Maddie was a child, both her parents worked and in the winter she came home from school to darkened windows and cold, empty rooms until her brother, who went to a different school, came home to look after her or until her grandparents arrived home from wherever they had been.

How she longed for that welcoming light in the window, for a voice inside, laughter perhaps, anything familiar. Eventually though, as Maddie grew older, she came to love that time alone and welcome it. Choose it, even.

Maddie thought of times that were good, when she sometimes felt safe in the family fold. Winnipeg in the summer, the drive from her house to Aunt Cilla and Uncle Victor's. The hot, sticky leather in the back seat of the Austin in the heat of the day. Then coming home, on the Pembina Highway, past the oil refinery, a black and silver skeleton of pipes flame-lit against the night sky, and past the rotting animal smell of the packing plant. Maddie would blink her eyes against the tiredness, determined not to miss a thing, not the swift flash of light as each car approached then swished by, or even her mother's soft humming of *Amazing Grace* from the darkness of the front seat. So long ago now.

She walked along the street, moving to her own rhythm, her footsteps quiet in the falling snow. On Broadway, the flakes seemed even bigger, a storm of white against the yellow streetlights. Cars hummed along snowy roads not yet ploughed. Past Lucy's store, closed because it was Sunday, White Spot, her old school, and all the way home.

She didn't want to, but she couldn't stop imagining those young girls. Her mother, Aunt Cilla, and Aunt Annie. So alike, yet different; fair and dark, three little girls in a photograph over the mantel, wearing pinafores and high button boots. Three little girls shamed and silent. Like Maddie. Children lying in their rose-papered rooms, waiting. Even now, it was easier to feel pain, to summon anger for what her grandfather had done to those small girls than it had ever been to feel it for herself.

All that silence. All those secrets. Why hadn't she been told? And how many more lies and secrets were waiting to be revealed?

ဆၢၵၓ

Evening, dark and still, wrapped itself around Maddie. None of the other tenants appeared to be at home. Thea was working the three to eleven shift and would probably walk in at any time. On the radio, a guitar riff and then a soft voice picked up the rhythm and the tune: *Tennessee Waltz*. Maddie turned it off and put a Billie Holiday LP on the record player. Her voice, as always, scraped raw by booze and drugs and bad love.

Maddie went outside and stood on the wooden balcony that jutted from the living room. Below her stretched the deep shadow of False Creek, spanned by the Granville Street Bridge with its streaming ribbon of lights. It was cold. A few snowflakes drifted against her cheek like slivers of ice. *Too cold to snow.* That's what people said, although Maddie was never really sure what that meant exactly. She lit a joint, breathed in the hot, acrid smoke and waited for the edges of her thoughts to soften, to cool. She thought of her old life, her parents in another part of the city, wondered what they might be doing on this winter night. It was just a few days past Christmas, a time when Maddie always felt lonesome and lost.

Maddie didn't have traditional Christmas memories. No bright lights strung through the boughs of a tree. No tree, in fact. No carols, no Santa, no stockings, no choirs of angels. No angels of any kind. Her family didn't celebrate

Christmas. Her parents' extreme fundamentalism ordained that celebrating Christmas was a perverse form of idolatry. For Maddie's brother and her, that made them different, freakish even. They weren't Jewish or Muslim. There was no acceptable reason for their celebration-less Christmas. And no explanation. It was a time of year that always left Maddie feeling hollow.

She wondered what her friends from high school were doing. Pursuing their dreams probably, those visions of their future, proclaimed in the pages of her yearbook. *Diane looks forward to marrying her high school sweetheart. Larry plans to travel through Europe before attending UBC to pursue his goal of becoming an engineer. Maddie's dream is to lace on her highway shoes and hotfoot it as fast as she can into her future. "No one can stop me now," she says. "Freedom is my brass ring."*

She wished she had said that but she'd played the game like everyone else. Well, almost. *Maddie plans to take a few trips before she enrols in a nursing program.* "Trips" in Maddie's lexicon meant getting high, so she thought her entry was clever. No one in her class would know what she was talking about. Most of the girls graduating just wanted to get married - the sooner the better.

Maddie took another toke on the joint and pinched it out. Flicked it into a brass ashtray shaped like a cupped palm. It was strange thinking about other people's lives, comparing them with her own.

Maddie had never had a serious goal beyond getting away from home. Getting married and having children didn't appeal. It meant you'd have to live part of somebody else's dream. Beyond getting her nursing course under her belt so she could work and be independent, further education hadn't even been a consideration. Her parents had never suggested such a thing or offered to pay for her to go to university. She could end up taking courses like philosophy and start questioning the very truths her parents held dear. It was the slippery slope of the nonbeliever.

She didn't want plans. Somebody else's plan was what she had lived by all her life. She wanted to drift free, live each day, one at a time, the way she counted out her penny candy as a child. Saving the sweetest for last.

She went back inside and lay on the bed with Leonard Cohen's new book, *Beautiful Losers*, reading by the light of the candle on her bedside table. The only other light in the room was a soft, red glow from the artificial grate in the fireplace. A disc circled beneath fake coals and shadows performed a restless dance across the floor. In a yellowing black and white photograph on the wall, Maddie's great-grandmother, her mother's grandmother, posed like Queen Victoria. Her hair was white, severe, and she was wearing a dress of stiff, dark satin with an uncompromising bodice and a white lace shawl. Around her throat she wore a black velvet ribbon. Maddie hadn't known her, of course, but liked the photograph. Billie Holiday sang *God Bless the Child*.

A few records leaned against the back of the wicker armchair by the window. Debussy's *La Mer*, *The Freewheelin' Bob Dylan*, Stravinsky's *Firebird Suite*, a Miles Davis album, *Kind of Blue*, and an old Louis Armstrong LP. The bed was heaped with Thea's clothes, which she had brought back with her after visiting her mother. Thea's mother had moved to the Fraser Valley to be nearer the psychiatric hospital where she worked as a ward clerk. Thea visited her every couple of weeks.

Maddie remembered how Thea came home one day high on speed, full of insolence and bravado. How she quickly grew restless, paced the rooms as though the place was too small to contain all her thoughts and ideas, the sheer glory of *Thea*.

She got amphetamines from a nurse who worked with Thea's mother, a naïve Australian woman who had no idea that Thea just wanted to get high. The nurse gave her a bottle of one hundred Dexedrine. Thea didn't know where she got them. Didn't care.

"What're you gonna do with these, anyway?" the nurse had asked Thea.

"Oh, just take them as appetite suppressants," said Thea. "I've really been porking up lately. Probably from the birth control pills." It was blatantly untrue, but the Aussie fell for it.

"That goddam son-of-a-bitch landlord," Thea said the next morning before she left for work. She was still high, hadn't slept at all. She slammed a quick right-hand jab into the back of the couch. "Tossing us out in the street like garbage." She threw herself into the La-Z-Boy and flipped up the leg rest.

"Thea, he's giving us an extra few months."

"So what. It's still not fair. And don't start packing, either. We can't give in to that nasty little man."

"To him we're a risk," Maddie said. "Burning things. I don't think there's much we can do about it. He's the landlord."

Thea got up and walked over to the window, looked away from Maddie. Maddie remembered waiting for Thea to turn on her for the remark about burning things, but instead she traced the outline of a greasy stain on the glass with one finger.

"It's not fair, is it, Pauley?" she said sadly.

Thea had called Maddie 'Pauley' several times recently and was always surprised when Maddie mentioned it, as though it was inconceivable she could have made such a mistake. Pauline had been a friend of Thea's before Maddie. She had died having an abortion. Thea had refused to tell Maddie any more than that. Brutal. The damage, like the knowledge, unthinkable. Unalterable.

Distracted from reading *Beautiful Losers*, Maddie sighed, tossed the book on the bed and got up. She dragged her dad's old steamer trunk from the closet. The trunk was filled with her treasures, all the things she wanted to keep. Records and books; high school yearbooks; a school newspaper where her first poem was published, something on the theme of spring; a pressed rose given to her by a sailor she'd met at fifteen. He was spending the summer with his grandparents, who lived next door to Maddie's family.

He wasn't a real sailor. He'd joined the navy a few weeks before they met and was taking the train to Halifax at the end of the summer to do his basic training. They sometimes met in the park after dinner to sit on the swings and twirl and talk while it was cool and growing dark. Or, *he* would talk. Maddie was shy with him and could never think of anything to say. She'd had no experience with boys and felt anxious with him, afraid that he would want something from her, something she didn't want to give. Or couldn't. He called her Princess.

Maddie was startled from her memory as the front door opened, then slammed shut. Thea came in, bringing the cold, damp night air with her. She yanked the captured hair from her collar and took off her steamed-up glasses.

"It's colder than a whore's heart out there," she said. "Shit, it's cold." She looked around the room. "Why've you got your trunk out?"

"I'm packing. I've got to get it done some time."

"Oh, Maddie, are you still on about that? You can't just leave. We'll get another place. Together. Somewhere with a lot of light and more room. And where there's no mice." Thea took off her coat and flung it onto the sofa. "We'll have a real bathroom where things work."

Maddie didn't answer, afraid to tell Thea she'd found a solution for herself that very morning. She'd been reading the paper with her coffee and saw it in the classifieds. *Room and board in exchange for babysitting a seven-year-old child.* She called and the woman sounded excited about meeting her. Told her to come by the next morning.

"Don't make me beg, Maddie," Thea said irritably. "Just think about it."

Thea went over to the mirror and practiced her smile. Maddie was glad to see she and the mirror were on friendly terms again. A few weeks before, Thea had discovered a new wrinkle and from that day on she and the mirror had been enemies. She consulted her mirror daily, as one might consult a horoscope in the newspaper, reading in the lines of her face the traces of where she had been and might be going, as though each mark betrayed a secret, interpreting her own signposts of failure. But she stalked failure, hunted it down. It was her identity, her reason to rage, her skewed way of winning.

Thea had disappeared into the bedroom. Maddie found her sitting on the bed, crying.

"I'll never forgive you if you leave me," she said. "What am I going to do on my own? You've always looked after things. You know. The bills and stuff."

Maddie put her arms around Thea and laid her head on her shoulder. "I have to do this, Thea. You'll be fine. We'll visit. We'll still do things together." But even as she spoke, Maddie knew something deeper and darker was haunting Thea. She was missing her Sundays in the woods. She was missing Charlie and Dogface.

What happened?

"You miss Charlie, don't you?" she said.

Thea stiffened in her arms. "I don't want to talk about it, Mad. You have no idea. You can't begin to know."

"So tell me. Tell me, Thea. What happened?"

"Maybe another time. Not now. Or maybe not ever." She pushed Maddie away and got up. "I've got things to do."

"But Thea –."

"Maddie. I can't."

The next day Maddie went to see the woman about the room. It was a cold, bright morning, a day that skirted the edge of winter, still gripped by that last persistent uncertainty of a changing season before spring took the world under her wing.

The room was in a tall two-story house with high wooden steps and a long porch framed by two immense cedars. The porch was furnished with a faded brown sofa and two green armchairs that had seen gentler days. Glass wind chimes hung from the rafters, but the small glass pieces were broken and too tangled to chime. A child's battered bicycle with a blown-out tire leaned against the porch railing below a few tulips that had been jammed into a precariously placed glass milk bottle. There was an oval of thick, leaded glass in the door, and when Maddie rang the bell, the sound reverberated eerily from somewhere within.

The woman who came to the door looked harried. She rubbed wet hands on her knees and pushed long strands of damp, dark hair behind her ears. She was wearing pink, floppy slippers, tight blue jeans, and a threadbare black sweatshirt that announced *Vancouver Rocks.*

"Yes?" she said impatiently.

"I'm here about the job," Maddie said. "I called yesterday."

"Oh," she said and her face lit up. "I'm so sorry I look such a mess. Come in, come in." She opened the door wider and motioned Maddie into the dark hallway. "I'm Dawn," she said. "You have no idea what a relief it is, finding you. I've just gotten this new job." She darted into the living room, called out for Maddie to follow, and cleared a space on the couch where she had been folding laundry. "I work evenings and need someone to stay with Daisy. If we could do a room and board exchange, it would be perfect."

"Are you offering me the job?"

"Well," she said, "you look like a nice person. Daisy's not here right now, but I'm sure she'll like you. When can you move in?"

Maddie moved into the upstairs bedroom a few days later, bringing the few belongings that had been stored in Tom's basement. She piled her books on the shelf made of bricks and boards, lay her Indian bedspread across the bed, and set up her bamboo table and screen. She would buy incense and candles later in Chinatown.

Dawn hung around and talked while Maddie unpacked. Maddie learned that she worked as a desk clerk in a low-rent hotel on the lean side of downtown on the three-to-eleven shift. She raged against being on her own with a child, spoke of her ex-husband with bitterness and contempt. There was no forgiveness, no concession, just the brittle stance of someone who must be right to survive. She reminded Maddie of her grandmother.

Maddie could still see Thea's face, full of contempt and rage as she'd stood in the doorway and watched Maddie pile all her books and records into boxes, fold the Indian bedspread and carry her bamboo table and screen, and the boxes out to Tom's pickup truck. Although the landlord had given them the extension, Maddie had decided to move out as soon as she could. Maddie and Tom walked in silence, back and forth along the stone walkway, arms loaded with books, cushions, and boxes of dishes.

When they were ready to go, Thea stood leaning against the doorway in the rain, arms folded across her chest, watching. Her hair was plastered to her head, glasses streaming, but still she stood there in bare feet, shivering in a long, yellow print summer dress even though summer was a long way away. She was wearing her big, loopy silver earrings. Maddie got out of the truck and went to her.

"Thea," Maddie said, "we'll still do things together. I'm not far away."

"No," Thea said. She looked at the rain sluicing down the stone steps and pooling at her feet. "When people leave, they don't come back."

She waited there but would not say goodbye, even when Maddie climbed into the truck, her potted fern balanced precariously on one knee, and waved. Thea went inside and shut the door.

Maddie went to classes three days a week when Daisy was in school and in the evenings sat in her room and wrote on her pad of yellow lined paper, leaning back on the bed, listening to the rush of traffic on the street below.

She thought of calling Thea, who was still in their old place, but most days she just wasn't in the mood, and was also struggling with her most recent assignment, a short story on exploring fear. She had plenty of material for that topic, but where to begin?

Maddie had always been a fearful child, besieged by creeping apprehensions. Being struck by a bolt of lightning as punishment for long-forgotten misdemeanors; stepping into traffic and being struck down in the prime of her as-yet-unlived life. Or traveling in a plane that unaccountably fell out of the sky, exploding in a burst of flames like a bottle rocket against the night.

There were other fears too, more secret fears. She could be sitting quietly in a chair, her head leaning against its back when she might be overtaken by the irrational conviction that whatever combination of skin, sinew or ligaments that connected her head to the rest of her body had simply collapsed and refused to hold her head up. She imagined her head was like a giant peony, too heavy for its delicate stem, wobbling, then simply crashing.

For some reason, the neck was an area of Maddie's focus. Its defenselessness horrified her. She had developed a phobia about the backs of men's necks, a strange obsession that began in high school with Norman Rabinski. Norman sat in front of Maddie in Mr. Simon's grade nine science class. It was a muggy afternoon in June and all the classroom windows were open. A fly droned against a dirty windowpane. The summer heat and the weight of a long school year had pulled them all down into a dreamy ennui. Maddie wasn't participating in the class discussion; she rarely did. She was just there. Heavy with boredom. Daydreaming.

"Are you with us, Madeline?" asked the teacher. "Disturbing your reverie, are we?"

"Sorry, sir." Maddie pulled her thoughts away from the world outside the classroom window and focused on what was right in front of her. Norman's head. Fine, pale hairs curled in the soft hollow between the frail cords of his neck. His reddish blond hair curved from the bottom of his earlobes and drifted into a silky V at the base of his skull. It was then that Maddie was struck by the delicacy of that small continent of skin, a place as open and imperfect as the soft spot on a baby's head. Vulnerable as an undefended island. Its tender nakedness frightened her.

Maddie's greatest terror was her fear of enclosed spaces. Elevators were off limits. If riding in one was unavoidable, she would wait until someone else got into the elevator with her. If she was going to smother to death trapped in a dark elevator, at least she wouldn't die alone. Even with company, she would spend the entire experience battling panic, balanced on the edge of terror. Escorting hospital patients up and down gave her no comfort. In their vulnerable and weakened state, they would be of no use at all if they crashed or were trapped in the dark, hollow coffin of an elevator shaft.

Maddie wasn't sure where or how her fear of confinement began but like a knitter unraveling a sweater, she could follow the thread as far back as childhood, back to her father tucking her into bed, tightening the sheets and blankets around her until she couldn't move, shoulders, arms, legs, even her feet imprisoned in the sarcophagus of bedding. His dark presence. The walls a screen of shadows and moonlight. *Unwrap me. Let me go.* But Maddie had been too afraid to say that to him because she could not disappoint him. His darling child. So she'd lain there frightened and trapped, until his footsteps fell away down the long hallway to her parents' room. And even when she shifted her arms and legs and inched free, she felt guilty.

As though she was a traitor to his love.

ꙮ

Maddie's time with Daisy was undemanding. She would watch anything that came on television. Her favorites after school were *Frisky Frolics* and *Gilligan's Island.* Maddie fed her from her mother's meagre stock of food: beans or canned soup, or toasted cheese sandwiches. Daisy didn't seem to mind. Curiously, she asked for very little. Maddie had just enough money saved to buy her own food and kept it simple: rice, fruit and vegetables, cheese, a rye loaf, and sometimes a package of cookies as a treat. She hid the cookies from Daisy and felt guilty about it.

Daisy didn't mind her mother going off to work, and didn't in fact appear to notice her leaving. She seldom spoke and Maddie found this strange and disconcerting in a child.

"Why are you here?" Daisy asked a few days after Maddie had moved in. "Where's your husband?"

"I don't have a husband," Maddie said.

"Are you gonna get one?"

"I don't know. Maybe. But not now. Lots of people don't have husbands."

"We don't have one either," she said, and paused to pull a dress over the head of her Barbie doll. "Are husbands bad?"

"No, Daisy, of course not," Maddie said. "Why would you ask that?"

"Because my mom said. She said they're all the same. They're bad."

"Well, it's just not true that they're all bad," Maddie said. "There's good and there's bad everything. You know that, don't you?"

"My mom made her husband go away. Sammy. That was his name." She switched on the TV.

"You mean your dad?"

"No, my dad's dead." She adjusted the tuning. "Sammy was her husband, he wasn't my dad. But he was bad."

"Why was he bad?"

"He drank too much whiskey. Then he'd get mad at us," she said. "He'd yell. And he didn't work."

"He got mad at you?"

"Sometimes. But mostly at my mom. But we . . ." She drifted off mid-sentence as the *Gilligan's Island* theme song came on. She sang along with it, loudly and off-key: *The weather started getting rough, the tiny ship was tossed.*

Maddie wanted to ask her more but knew it was delicate territory. Uncertain ground. A place she wouldn't go.

৪০෬

Maddie stood beside the flowerbeds, green now and sprouting new blooms of tulips and daffodils. She was in the yard of the house where Thea was still living. She looked up to the balcony off the bedroom. One of Thea's uniforms was draped over the railing, fluttering lightly in the breeze. There were no lights in the windows, but the door from the balcony to the bedroom was slightly ajar so she thought Thea must be home. So, she hadn't moved out yet. Maddie walked around to the front, climbed the stairs to the top floor and hesitated at the door. Would Thea even want to see her? It had been two months since Maddie had moved out. She tried the knob. It was open.

"Thea?" she called softly.

There wasn't a sound in the apartment except for the humming of the fridge. She put her backpack on the floor and quietly shut the door. "Thea?"

She peered into the bedroom through the half-open door. The bed frame was gone. Thea was asleep on the new mattress on the floor, her hair spread across the pillow and one knee pulled up to her chest, left arm flung across the bed, and fingers trailing over the edge. Her glasses were carefully placed on the ledge that ran around the room and beside them an overturned book of poetry – Palgrave's *Golden Treasury* – looking as if it had been placed there hastily, just moments before she fell asleep.

Maddie looked around the room at the boxes stacked against the wall, the last remnants of their life there together. Debussy's *La Mer* was on top of the pile of records. Thea must have been listening to it recently. In the kitchen, the tap dripped into an empty pot, just the way it always had. One of the plants on the window ledge had withered and died, its brown leaves scattered beside a broken coffee cup. A river of spilled coffee had etched a pattern on the ledge that ran down the wall to the floor. Thea sighed in her sleep.

Pale sunlight shone through one of the grimy, rain-streaked windows and fell across the faded imitation Chinese carpet. Maddie walked over to the window and looked down onto the familiar scene below: scrap yards and factories under the bridge, the grit and smoke of industry. Jackson once told her that when he drove over the Granville Street Bridge, he always looked up to the spot where he knew the house was and waved. She hadn't called Jackson in weeks and wondered what he was doing. She was lying low, studying, and in no hurry to see anyone.

Maddie looked around the room again. *Why have I come? What did I expect to find?* She knew she had to go. On her way out, she shut the door quietly to not wake Thea. These rooms were her past, not her future and she had no wish to disturb Thea's sleep, let alone her life.

ଞୠଔ

Maddie saw Thea only once that spring; it was early April. A cold mist hung over the city and foghorns bleated from the harbor. Maddie was looking for a bookstore on Broadway. She stepped off the bus and stopped, shivering in the wind and wondering which way to head when someone called her name. Maddie glanced up to see Thea running toward her from halfway down the street, long auburn hair blowing across her face.

"Maddie." Thea put her hand on Maddie's arm in her proprietary way. She was wearing soft black leather gloves. Her hair had grown and she had new glasses. She held her dark suede coat close to her body, as though it might blow away. "I've wanted to see you but I didn't know where you were."

"You look good, Thea," Maddie said. "You look happy."

"I've moved," she said, "and I'm with a new man. A musician. He's the one, I know it this time. You have to meet him." She was out of breath from running.

"I'd like to," Maddie said. *But not now.*

"Come to his place with me now," Thea said. "I'll cook your favorites, meat loaf and baked potatoes. I've told him all about you, Maddie."

"I can't, Thea, not now, not today. But that's a sweet offer." Maddie could have gone but she didn't want to. She wasn't ready for Thea yet, her questions, her recriminations.

Thea looked defeated. "Call me, then. My number's the same as our old one." The wind gusted and she wrapped her coat even tighter, shivering. "You know what he did for me? How I know he's the one?"

Maddie shook her head.

"He gave me a brass bed. Remember how much we always loved that song?"

Yes. Maddie remembered. *Lay Lady, Lay.*

"He gave me a big brass bed, Maddie. For when I move in. Don't you think that must mean he really loves me?"

"Yes," Maddie said, "he must."

"Well, I have to go now," Thea said abruptly, "if you're not coming with me."

She yanked her leather bag over her shoulder.

"I'll call you, Thea."

Thea didn't move. She just looked at Maddie.

"You were stupid," she said. "You know that. For leaving and ruining everything." Then she turned and walked away.

Maddie watched her disappear down the street and tried to think of something to say. In the end, she just called out "Bye, Thea," but didn't think Thea heard. Maddie meant to call her later that spring but never did.

Six
The Island

*M*addie is back from the airport, pulling her tote bag up
the rutted road of Gully's Grove, but she feels as
though she's left her heart somewhere back in the
burnt hills of *caliche* and cactus that surround Lita's *pueblo*.
She'd lain awake most of her last night in Mexico, listening
to the crickets sing from doorways and stone niches.
Morning came too soon, pink and dove-gray light. Then
the bus ride south to Mexico City. An overnight in the old
hotel *Isabel la Católica*, then winging home once again to the
cold north and back to Gully's Grove.

Smoke drifts from her chimney. It's still morning.
Claudine must have started her fire. Maddie had e-mailed
from Mexico a few days ago and told her she was coming
home but didn't hear anything back.

Maddie wants all Joey's things gone now. This is what
she knows even before taking her jacket off. She walks
through the cabin turning on lights. The antique one on the
bookcase with a frosted glass shade like a soft pink

scalloped shell, the tall Mexican lamp beside her bed, and the small lamp on the kitchen counter that has a parade of elephants around a golden shade. She decides she'll go over to Claudine's later to pick up her plants that Claudine was caring for while she was in Mexico. She'll unpack her bags later.

Before Maddie has time to think about it, she's thrown her jacket onto the couch and is pulling Joey's things from shelves: CDs, books, his *Texas Highways* magazines. She stops to put the kettle on for tea, then stokes the fire, stirring up embers until they raise geysers of new flames. She opens a drawer in the kitchen and pulls out a few green plastic garbage bags and drags them from room to room, filling them with everything of his, anything that reminds her of him. Anything she hasn't already burned.

She doesn't try to wipe away the tears that blur her vision. Maddie knows this has been coming for a long time, knows that it's right. The tears anger her more than anything. Although Joey's absences have been more frequent over the last few months, it is the lack of his presence now that feels strange – the recognition that the abyss that lies between them is permanent.

A knock at the door startles her. She opens it and a stranger is standing there in the cold on her rickety back stoop, balancing her potted fern on one arm and her jade plant and trailing philodendron on the other. He grins at her. "Maddie?"

"Yeah," she says. "Who are you?"

"I'm Claudine's brother." He leans toward her, frowns. "I saw the lights were on. Are you okay?"

Maddie remembers that her face is stained with tears and the mascara she put on for the plane ride home is probably smeared across her cheeks from where she's ground her fists into her eyes. "I'm okay," she says. "Where's Claudine?" She takes the fern from its precarious perch on his arm and carries it into the kitchen. "Thanks." He follows her and sets the philodendron and jade on the counter.

"Katy, Claudie's youngest, is having some trouble with her pregnancy." He shrugs. "Not sure what exactly. Claudie wanted to be with her. She flew to Denver yesterday."

Maddie had never heard anyone call Claudine *Claudie.* "So you started my fire?"

"Yep," he says. "She left me clear instructions."

He's tall and fair, about Maddie's age, with gray eyes. Eyes that smile. He doesn't look anything like Claudine. In fact, Maddie didn't even know that Claudine had a brother. Although they've been neighbors for years, they've never been close friends and Maddie doesn't really know a lot about her.

"Well, thanks." Maddie puts her hand on the doorknob to let him know that leaving now is an option. He seems like a nice man but she wants to be alone. "I'll come by later and get the rest of the plants."

"Okay," he says. "Anytime. I'll make tea."

He's walked down the path, crossed the dirt road, and climbed the porch steps of Claudine's cabin before Maddie realizes she didn't ask his name.

It's almost dusk before she finishes hauling boxes and garbage bags full of Joey's things out to the shed. Lights are on in Claudine's cabin and every so often, while crossing the yard to the shed, she sees the lean figure of Claudine's brother silhouetted against the square of yellow light. Maddie wants to go over and pick up the plants before he decides to bring them over himself. She doesn't want phones ringing or strangers showing up at her door. She'd much rather be the one to invite communication if she wants it at all.

Before she lifts her hand to knock on his door, it opens. Van Morrison is singing *Madame George.*

"Hey, I love this song." Maddie speaks before she realizes the words have come out of her mouth, friendlier than she wants them to be. She really doesn't want to have to talk to anyone.

He waves her in and closes the door. "I'm a Van fan myself," he says. "Tea? I've just boiled the water."

"Sure." She meant to say no but now the yes is out. "I haven't asked your name. Rude of me. Sorry."

"Max," he says. He puts the teapot and two china mugs on the table in front of the sofa.

"So how long are you here for? Is Claudine going to be away long?"

"Don't know," he says. "She was talking about maybe staying until the birth. She's a little concerned, I think." He pushes one of the mugs toward her and waves his spoon in the direction of the honey jar. "I've had some recent changes in my life so I told her I'd take care of her place for a while." He settles himself into the wicker chair across from Maddie.

He talks of his life easily. Retirement from his job as a publisher of a small community newspaper in a prairie town. A recent divorce. Like Maddie, no kids. He's affable and loose, easy with words, easy in his own body. Maddie tells him about Joey, that they're splitting, carefully avoiding the dark parts. He doesn't need to know the details. She hardly knows him.

After Maddie leaves, she stands out on the road for a minute watching the moon rise over the mountains, before heading up the path to her cabin. How many moons, Maddie wonders, has she seen rise over Mt. Strachan? Tonight, it's a January moon, a Full Wolf moon in native legend. Maddie was just a girl – eight or nine – when she read about the native tribes who gave names to the monthly moons. Her favorite is December, a Full Long Nights Moon. For years she has watched it lift over the mountains and shine on the sea, its light filling the deep darkness of those long winter nights. Edging the whitecaps in silver light, flooding the meadow and the pathway that winds through the Grove.

When she told her father the moon stories, he refused to listen. *I've never heard of such a thing,* he said. *Nothing in the Holy Word about that.* Maddie never spoke of the moons again, but kept the stories to herself, named them – Strawberry Moon, Full Corn Moon, Hunter's Moon – and held them like treasures in the secret shallows of her heart.

The wind is cold and the iced-over puddles crunch under her boots like broken glass. The cabins in the Grove are being torn down one by one, and there are only a few left now. During the winter, neighbors feel distant from one another and lamplit windows are often the only sign of life. Neighbors and visitors become dark, faceless figures hurrying along the gravel path, sliding over frozen puddles, throwing seed down for the hungry, scrabbling geese that have wandered up from the beach.

Maddie remembers the first time she saw Claudine on this road. It was a summer night, one of those nights when she couldn't sleep. She was walking toward the ballfield where she could breathe in the fragrance of the tangled mock orange, and the lilac and sweet honeysuckle that grew alongside the edge of the field.

Claudine appeared out of the night, a shadow on the dark road. She was tall and barefoot, and wore a long denim skirt. Huge silver hoop earrings and a jangle of silver bracelets glinted in the bright moonlight. Her hair was tied back in a scarf and she was tugging on a purple shawl that had slipped from one smooth, bare, tanned shoulder. In the shock of moonlight Maddie could see clearly what she carried, balanced carefully in one hand on a silver platter - an elegant and superbly beautiful lemon meringue pie.

Maddie watched her head down the path lined with wild roses, which led to the sea, then cross the wooden bridge over the creek and head across the moonlit field toward the hillside that led to Walker's place. There could be no other place she was going. The Queen of Hearts, carrying her gift on a silver platter to the king's parlor. Maddie was stunned and amused. This object of such beauty, such devotion, was being carried to Walker, the mad poet of the Grove, the man who glued his front teeth together with Krazy Glue.

Walker was a hermit of sorts. A mystery to all of them. There was talk of a blind cat that he took out only at night when he strolled across the field under the silence of a full moon and the sleeping village. His cabin was perched on a steep hillside, high above the other cottages. It was slowly crumbling to the earth like all the rest, but still glorious with its white-painted tower and flagpole. It held a place of honor, yet it was always apart, in the same way that all of them in the Grove kept themselves apart, separate from the larger island community that sheltered them.

Some nights, from the winter darkness of her cabin, Maddie would watch Claudine head across the meadow and into the woods, then emerge some time later with a bedsheet full of firewood. Blown-down branches, rotted stumps, anything that would burn. Sometimes when the house was quiet, she would hear the soft dragging of the sheet along the frost-heaved road and over the frozen puddles. Claudine would pause then, to catch her breath, stand tall, unapologetic and unbowed.

Claudine's cottage smelled of wood smoke and kerosene, and on the table, were dried blue hydrangea, silver-framed photographs, and bowls of bean seeds. Queen of Hearts, collector of dreams. Like all of them in the Grove, she weathered the inner storms of just living, while the wind outside rattled the windowpanes.

Maddie fills the fire and closes the damper down for the night, hoping it lasts so she can get a few hours of uninterrupted sleep. She brushes her teeth, finds her warmest long underwear, then climbs in under the down quilt, getting up only once during the night to fill the fire in a sleepy haze. This ritual is second nature now. From the bathroom window, she sees a light in Claudine's bedroom glimmering through the trees.

Maddie stumbles awake in the morning from a dream that has already vanished like smoke, but it has filled her with a sense of deep and grievous loss. She has known for so long that her life with Joey was wrong, not just wrong for her but wrong for both of them. The addictive behavior that typifies him is a part of who she is too, and has been since long before he was in her life. The pain is from knowing that one of those addictive things for her has been him.

Maddie makes a cup of Earl Gray tea and sorts through the mail she gathered from her post office box on the way home from the ferry. The lawyer's letter is there, as she's known it would be. Her mother's estate has been settled.

She's been thinking about this time; the day when she could buy her own house on her beloved island. Build her own life. Stand on her own two feet, lean on no one.

After her tea, she washes the cup and turns it upside down on the counter, then dials the real estate agent's number. They'd spoken before Maddie left for Mexico and the agent told her that she'd keep her eye open for Maddie's home-to-be.

"I don't need much," Maddie had said. A little house, her very own, tucked away in the woods. A bit of land for a garden and flower boxes, maybe a flowering cherry tree. A roof that doesn't leak. Windows that don't freeze over in the winter. A big wicker chair where she can sit in the sun. A place just for her. Her own home.

A place where she can take back her life.

෨෬

It began with muffins. Bran muffins, full of sweet dates. After the muffins, Max brought soup. Chicken soup, thick with root vegetables, or spinach lentil soup. He tells Maddie he loves to cook and hasn't had much of a chance to do it. Playing around with food, he calls it. The first time he brought food over, she wasn't home so he left it on the porch railing and hoped she'd find it before the crows or Steller's jays did. It's a comfortable place, this being taken care of, a place Maddie recognizes as too easy for her to slide into. She figures the gods have sent him to test her, to see if she really is ready to stand on her own two feet without a safety net. So she tells him. No more food.

Maddie has never told Max anything more about Joey, the shameful things she can never tell anyone. How walking to the post office or the General Store felt like navigating land mines. How afraid she was of running into someone who would look at her and immediately perceive her disgrace, as though she were wearing her shame like a tattoo on her forehead. The wretched, useless tears that left her humiliated, feeling forever tainted. She has told him about Joey's ultimate deception – his affair with a woman in Mexico, and her own stupidity for not knowing.

Maddie offers him scraps of her life. Stories of her grandfather's roaming hands, her fear of riding in elevators, of being trapped, smothered, obliterated. The isolated life of her childhood, her parents' fierce religious beliefs and her mother's recent death. It's freeing, this talk. It seems so long since she's opened up this much with anyone other than Lita.

When Maddie talks with Max, there is always a hesitancy as though both of them are standing in front of a door, hands on the doorknob, not entirely sure whether either of them wants to open it. Maddie senses her own hesitation in the pauses between the words, feels the pulling back, the shutting down. Sometimes the room is dense with the knowledge that there is a road not taken.

Max asks a lot of questions. He wants to know how Maddie escaped the prison of her family's religious life, how she avoided getting bent under the burden of the church's teachings.

"Oh, I'm bent," Maddie tells him. "We're all bent. You couldn't live in that world for so long and not be."

"So how did you escape? You don't seem bent to me."

Maddie admits to Max that she hadn't known how to let go of her parents' faith at first. How she wasn't certain there weren't perhaps a few flecks of gold amongst all that bitter ash.

"And? Were there?"

"I'm not sure. It was fear that kept me hanging on. The old fire and brimstone. That kept me in line for a long time."

Max talks about his ex-wife Becky and her passion for cats. She's a woman Maddie thinks she would like. His "ex-life" he likes to call her. "You know," he says, "I don't see it so much as a failed relationship. We just needed to move on. She loves cities and was tired of our life in such a small place. She has things to do and so do I. And they're different things."

"I wish I felt like that about Joey," Maddie says. "As though it wasn't just a big, stupid mistake. Because it was. And I knew better. I'm smarter than him."

Max has offered to drive Maddie to the recycling depot and they're in the car with all the windows open. "I hate the way I feel," Maddie says. "All the years I've lived with Joey, and now I don't even want him on my radar. That feels pretty bitter. And shallow."

He pulls the car into the depot parking lot. "It's not shallow." He hauls a bunch of folded cardboard boxes out of the trunk. "It's just honest."

Max tells Maddie about his childhood terror of dentists, a fear he still hasn't mastered and about his latest plans for the novel he's writing. "I need a routine, a discipline," he says, "and a place for my writing to happen."

Maddie asks if he might stay on the island and he says not likely. She's glad. Max would like more from her, she suspects, but that's territory she has no wish to explore or be charmed into. For so much of her life she's ridden on the coattails of someone else's dream, waited for the trail ahead to be blazed by someone – anyone – braver than her.

Maddie flew tandem in those early days of her youth, soared on Thea's wings and imagined that through some inexplicable piece of magic those wings would someday morph into something that grew out of her own shoulders.

It was the first promise of sheltering wings that had lured her into Thea's world. Although her caring was unpredictable and out-of-the-blue, Maddie had found comfort in her friendship as she'd found comfort in the community of women in the nursing world. Women who sometimes called her Little One, and who mothered her with the gentle concern she had never experienced from her own mother. Maddie yearned for that kind of affection and is disconcerted, even now, by the memory of how it warmed her when the other nurses called her Honey Child or Sweet Pea. It was as though they all sensed that missing piece in her, that empty space that was hungry for the love and protection of a mother. But if she has learned anything in all those years with Joey, it is that it's time to ride alone instead of looking for love in the eyes of anyone who drifts through her life.

On the way back up the path to her cabin, Maddie grabs an armful of dry fir from the woodpile, then stands for a few minutes and watches the sunlight against the mountains across the bay fill the cut on the ski hill with a golden light. *When I leave the Grove, this view will be lost to me. And I'll miss it.* She stokes the fire and puts a pot of soup on the stove before she notices the red light on the phone blinking. It's a message from Joey, the message she's been waiting for, and dreading. He's coming tomorrow to pick up his things. "Coming home," he said, and she wishes he hadn't. She reaches over to the stove and turns off the burner under the soup. She's not hungry anymore.

Just scared.

Maddie is drinking her morning coffee and reading her Thoreau quote of the day on her computer – *Simplify, simplify* – when she hears his van pull into the driveway, tires spitting out gravel. Every part of her body is rigid, closed tightly against the knowledge of him being this close. The door of his van slams and his boots crunch up the path to the house. She waits for his knock. Or will he open the door and just walk into what he may think of as still his home? Then she remembers that she locked the door last night before she went to bed. She didn't want any middle-of-the-night surprises.

She opens it before he can either knock or try the door. He leans toward her and she quickly steps back. He looks sheepish. *Pretend sad*, she thinks.

"Maddie." He's wearing a wool toque. He pulls it off his head and jams it into the pocket of his jacket. "Are you okay?" He reaches out and puts his hand on her arm. She moves it away.

She sees the hurt look on his face but doesn't care.

"Of course, I'm okay. All your stuff is in the shed." She knows she can't really stop him from coming in.

He steps back. "Well, can I come in and talk to you before I leave?"

She wishes he wouldn't. "I guess," she says. "If you have to."

She doesn't owe him anything beyond what is piled in the shed. They've lived a simple lifestyle all these years and accumulated very little together. Most of what Maddie has now she had when he came. All those years together

173

have amounted to almost nothing in the material sense. There will be no division of property, no arguments over *things*. He was happy to take on her life, to wear it as though it was his own. But she's reclaiming her home and her life now and doesn't even want him on the periphery.

Maddie is stunned by how dispassionate she feels toward this man who has been her life for so many years, how easily she can cut out her past with such icy finality. There are a few images that linger still. Long walks in the woods on cold December nights under a Full Long Nights Moon. Deer tracks in the snow. An owl hunched on a power line.

Slow dancing on the grassy slope outside the cabin under northern lights. No music that day. Just the light tinkle of glass wind chimes in a breeze blowing in from the sea.

In a matter of months, she will hardly remember him. She plans on that. To forget the curve of his face, the way he walks, the sound of his voice. To forget how it felt to ever love him. She already has. These are the tricks she learned a long time ago. They served her well in her childhood. They saved her, in fact.

"Forget it then," he says, and leaves. She shuts the door behind him.

She lays out books and historical photographs on the table and tries to launch herself into a new research project, one she's looked forward to. She's been hired to write the history of not just her island community but the smaller community of Gully's Grove, her home for the past fifteen years. The cottages here were once part of a larger historical landscape, an integral part of the cruise boat era of the twenties, thirties, and forties. This cluster of cottages, long before they were sold to George Gully, were owned by a steamship company as part of a resort that encompassed hundreds of acres. Cruise ships steamed out of the Vancouver harbor carrying thousands of revelers from the city to the shores of this island, where they danced the nights away to the sounds of some of the best big bands of the era.

Maddie has spent long afternoons walking the lagoon trail below the hotel – torn down long ago – known then as Bridal Trail. She's discovered remnants of a time long gone. A beautiful bottle of thick, green glass, a dented silver engraved cigarette case, a gold wedding band. It's not hard for her to lose herself in this history. The lamp-lit bridge over the lagoon, echoes of voices drifting across the water as boats steam out of the harbor, ladies strolling through the rose arbor in their long skirts and bustles, a man who perhaps dropped a silver engraved cigarette case. It is this journey into the past that stirs memory, haunts her dreams and ties her irrevocably to this small piece of ground under her feet.

But Maddie can't work. She paces through the house, back and forth, waiting for Joey to finish. To be gone. She steals looks out the window at his van, willing it to disappear in the same way she waited at the same window and willed his van to bring him back to her all those months ago when he began coming home late, then not coming home at all.

She hears him piling his things into the van. She smells the smoke when he lights up a joint. He's playing an old Stones song from *Sticky Fingers* on his CD player. Maddie tries to remember when it was that she realized why he would never consider buying a truck even though it made more sense for his work as a welder. It was his getaway vehicle. He needed to know that he'd always have a place to live. A place to live the way he lived in those days before she knew him. A vagabond living on the banks of the river. A drifter on the run. He was a man who, one way or another, had always been running from something. Or someone. Joey needed to carry his home with him like a turtle in its shell, always prepared to escape.

Eventually the crashing and banging stops and Maddie waits for his footsteps on the stairs. He knocks on the door, then opens it and comes in with an armful of wood.

"Thought I'd bring some wood in for you." He carries it over to the stove, drops it into the wood box, then reaches out to open the stove door, but Maddie stops him.

"I don't need you to do anything for me, Joey." *I don't need you.*

"Can I sit?"

She says nothing.

He sits in the wicker chair by the fire, tentatively, on the edge of the seat. "Maddie, I'm sorry for all this."

"I can't see why you'd be sorry," she says. "You're doing what you want."

"But I'm not. I don't think I am."

"Too late, Joey."

He gets up from the chair and just stands there, staring at the floor with his usual hangdog look.

For God's sake stand up straight like a man, she wants to scream at him. She moves toward the door as if she's about to open it and usher him out. In the second it takes to do this, he is beside her, his arms wrapped around her.

"Please, Hon," he says. "This is hard for me too. Please don't hate me."

It takes a second for it to register that he has actually called her *Hon* before she steps out of his embrace.

"Get out."

176

"But I still love you." There are tears in his eyes. Real tears.

Maddie laughs out loud. She can't help herself. His body goes rigid and a wave of rage washes over his face. She realizes she's been stupid, incautious. Laughing in the face of a violent man. Fear slides in. Memories of crouching in corners, crying like a child. She feels humiliated again as she remembers.

"Get out," she says again, and opens the door. He steps outside onto the porch and pulls his toque out of his jacket pocket. It has begun to rain, a fine mist that brushes her face like an early morning spider's web.

"If you need anything . . ."

"I don't."

He leaves without a word. Trudges down the stairs and across the path to his van without looking back. Maddie's glad he's leaving her with this last image, this dark, terrifying memory of cowering in the corner of the bedroom as he towered over her, fists balled, enraged. She doesn't want these images. She doesn't want the rage that tears through her body.

But in this moment rage is all she has.

&⊙ᘓ

As soon as Maddie sees it, she knows she's found her home.

"I've got it, I've got your house," Sandra, her real estate agent said when she called that morning, just days after Joey left. Maddie was in the middle of trying to organize the notes she'd fanned out like tarot cards on the kitchen table. This is where she does most of her first handwritten drafts on yellow lined notepads before moving into her office and onto the computer.

Sandra sounded excited. "I'll meet you out there at noon."

The house wasn't even on the market yet. The woman who owned it had died recently, leaving no living relatives and Sandra finagled the listing from the woman's bank. Maddie sees Max on his porch and yells across to him that she might have found her house. He yells back that he wants to come with her to look, but Maddie says no. It's something she wants to do alone. That first look. That first rush of possibility.

It's a twenty-minute drive across the island from Gully's Grove. Sandra drives. Maddie doesn't have a car. She dislikes driving and has had no need of one. If she moves, she'll have to get an island car, a beater just to get her to the shops in the Cove and back. It's been a while since she's crossed the island. She's forgotten its hills and valleys, the stillness as the road winds farther and farther away from the Cove and the ferry dock. The road narrows and climbs through forested highlands, past fields of grazing sheep. Occasionally they catch a glimpse of blue-gray sea, distant islands, and a curve of dark coastline. Sunshine is draped like a soft shawl of pale light against the far-off mountains.

Despite the difficulties of living in Gully's Grove, Maddie will miss it. She knows she'll grieve for the loss of those days that have defined her life for so many years. Campari and soda on the porch of Claudine's cabin, watching the northern lights dance across the summer sky. Her laundry strung out over the sloping green like prayer flags - empty, untenanted bodies billowing in the wind. Opera falling from a house far above the highest cliffs over the ocean, cascading out of windows, tumbling over cliffs, dropping into the cluster of cottages in the Grove.

Summer nights, days when all of them sat on a log by the ocean drinking margaritas during a lightning storm, cheering each glorious explosion of light across a rose-colored sky. Later, in the dense night heat, lying damp and sleepless on tangled summer sheets, dreaming half-awake dreams, sweating salt and tequila. And from her haze of half-sleep, listening to the sound of voices carrying across the water, the rattle of ice cubes against glass from inside the nearby pub, short bursts of laughter, music drifting through the night air. Plum blossoms falling on an empty lawn. Candles that she lit and put in the window to honor the day Angela died. And sometimes, the sound of weeping in the night. Bewitchings and betrayals. Loves gained and lost. Lives scarred by the fires of need, by the chill of love. A place where she started out as one and became two.

And now is one again.

They pull into the driveway. The house is barely visible through the trees. A stone chimney stands against the backdrop of the green mountainside. Above it, blue sky and cirrus clouds. *My house is on the side of a mountain.*

The house is hidden away in the trees just like Maddie has always imagined her home would be. They climb the stone pathway and follow it around the side, past a laburnum with its long chains of golden blossoms, rhodos in full bloom: purple, yellow, and a deep blood red. Alongside the path to the back of the house, a creek tumbles through a ferned gully, over smooth rocks, rattling pebbles under a wooden bridge that spans the creek and joins the property to the one next door. *A creek. My own creek.*

Sandra points out the trees: dogwoods, a tall maple, rhododendron bushes, dozens of cedars and firs, the laburnum, and a mountain ash. The house is small but solid. Two bedrooms, a deck that will need some fixing, mossy stone stairs to the front door and all on a half-acre of forest. Its two jewels are a massive stone fireplace in the middle of the house and floor-to-ceiling windows in the living room that make Maddie feel as though she'll be living in a tree house. She's in love with it already. This is a place where her heart can open and grow, put down roots. Heart roots. Something she's run from all her life.

She wanders outside to the backyard and sits on the rock wall encircling a small garden, rampant with ivy and lemon thyme, tall purple and white foxgloves, creamy-blossomed dogwood. She savors the sun's warmth on her shoulders, watches a couple of juncos fly back and forth to what must be a nest in an Arbutus tree, listens to the soft sounds of the creek. Maddie tries to imagine what it would feel like if this world were hers. For so many years, she's resisted the idea of settling, of community, fought against the notion of being so connected to a place that its loss would cause pain. But despite her best efforts to stay free, the shy tendrils of her life in Gully's Grove took root and grew, against her will, against any planning she might have done.

Sandra comes around from the side of the house. "So?"

"Yes," says Maddie. "Yes, yes, yes."

My new life. My own life. There is freedom in those words. At last. She used to love being alone and knows she'll love it again. Over the last few days, she's found herself looking out toward the sea while leaning against the window in Gully's Grove where she used to stand waiting for Joey to appear. Glad he's finally gone.

Every day now she finds herself standing on that bridge between two worlds. Breathing. Practicing just being in the moment. *I'm here*, she thinks to herself over and over. *I'm here*. Somewhere between an ending and a beginning.

But not lost.

෨෬෬

Maddie has been filling boxes for weeks now, and piling them in the storage shed. Because the new house is empty, she's been taking boxes over there every day. She's borrowed her brother's truck to make the move. He and Max have offered to help, but she's got a lot of time to do this one on her own. It's what she wants.

Maddie stands in the Grove, in the middle of her yard, and looks at her cabin, framed by a hawthorn tree and the wild cherry that hasn't produced fruit for years, the place that has contained her life for so long. She picks up the box of books just packed. *I'm ready.*

She piles the last of the boxes in the truck and opens the window all the way so she can fill her head with the warm blossom-scented wind during the drive across the island. The journey is becoming familiar now. She's already found her guideposts. The black-faced sheep grazing in a pasture of rolling green and yellow hills, the break in the woods where she can glimpse the river, dark, running swiftly, the curve that heads up a gravel road to a place called Shepherd's Hill.

That night Maddie calls Lita and tells her about the house. And how every morning before the move she'd looked out her bedroom window in the Grove, down onto

181

the mud flats and tall reeds at the water's edge, filled with gratitude for her new waiting life, her new home.

"And Lita, I'm so afraid I don't deserve this."

"Maddie," Lita says, "I understand. I do. But if anyone deserves a good life, it's you. I know Joey's my brother, but he was never good for you." She sighs. "I'm not sure he's good for anyone."

Maddie asks her about Sebastian.

"Wow," Lita says. "Yeah, the relationship thing."

"Tough?"

"Yeah, tough. And scary."

"Well, yes, Lita. *Hello.*"

Lita laughs. "I know," she says. "I guess it's kind of ridiculous to have thought it could be otherwise."

"What's the scary part?"

"Well, I've met his family."

"And?"

"And they love me."

Maddie hears Lita open the door and walk out into her courtyard. The crickets in the stone wall sound as if they've transported themselves from Mexico into Maddie's living room.

"They have an old hacienda, a working ranch, really. And olive groves. It's in one of the villages near Lake Pátzcuaro. It's so beautiful. They're so beautiful. And the country is spectacular," Lita says. "Pine forests and waterfalls and blue-green mountains. And his *Mami* is the mother of all mothers. She adores me. I feel a little bewildered. Maybe even a little bewitched."

"Bewildered by them or the landscape?"

"Both. But them, really. We went to his niece's *quinceañera* yesterday. All those girls. Just fifteen. But so beautiful. They're such a warm family. So loving. And I haven't felt that for so long, Maddie. That family closeness. Not since Ange died."

Maddie likes the way Lita is never afraid to say the word out loud. *Died.* She has never said "She passed away" or "We lost her," as though Angela has somehow simply been misplaced. Lita is always direct and clear. She looks life in the face.

Maddie drops a teabag into her cup and pours boiling water over it. "I'm so glad you've come to this," she says. "And that you're okay with it. That you're happy."

"I guess I'd just stopped believing in happiness," Lita says. "In its possibility. I thought I'd used up all the love I had on Richard and Ange. Sometimes I still wonder..."

"Lita, stop," Maddie says. "That's a country you don't need to visit."

Lita laughs. "So what, you're my travel guru now?"

"If I have to be." Maddie laughs too.

"And Joey? That's going to be okay?"

"I'm getting my old self back, Lita. My own power," Maddie says. "I gave everything away to Joey. That was my fault. I gave it willingly. Gave myself away, piece by piece. It was a long, slow process, but that's what I did."

"Yeah, you did, Maddie."

"And that's what I'm getting back."

"I'm glad," Lita says, "that you're thinking that way. Because I watched you and didn't think I could stop you. I saw you let the reins slip out of your hands. You don't know how many times I asked myself if being a true friend meant telling you or waiting for you to see it for yourself."

"You did the right thing. I wouldn't have listened. I was stupid. Obsessed with the idea of being loved. If anyone was bewitched, Lita, it was me."

Maddie lies in bed long after her call to Lita and thinks about their conversation. And how she's feeling now. *Bewitched. Beguiled. Enchanted.* Fairy tale words.

Maddie has been reading *The Red Shoes*, the folktale about a little girl who was so hungry for love – a love manifested in a pair of beautiful red shoes – she was carried away by a fierce mad dance she could neither control nor stop. And that, Maddie thinks, is what these last few years with Joey have felt like. Until now. She's finally desperate to connect to those lost, wild parts of herself instead of what she's been doing all these years. Dancing out of control to someone else's song.

ॐ

Maddie looks at her bed covered with the new rust-colored Indian spread and orange and blue hand-printed pillows, her bedside table piled with the books she's reading, a few magazines, her copy of the *I Ching*. She hangs an ornate brass cross on the wall above the bed, just like the cross that hangs over her bed in Lita's house in Mexico, and recreates her altar on a small wooden table in a corner by the window. On it she puts a blue candle in the shape of a woman, a statue of the Virgin of Guadalupe in her star-spangled green cloak, a tiny *retablo* from a long-ago trip to Oaxaca, a brass Kwan Yin – goddess of compassion – a silver bowl of shells, and a red box in the shape of a heart. She switches on the lamp with its pink shell shade and it casts a pool of rose light on the wood ceiling.

In the soft light, Maddie sees the edge of something poking out from the pages of a book that's lying on the table. An old copy of Joseph Campbell's *The Masks of God* that she hasn't read in years. She found it in one of the boxes during her move and is eager to read it again.

She tugs on the corner and a card slides out, a card with a picture of a rabbit in a field of grass and flowers. Imprinted over the field of grass is written: *I hold you in my thoughts and in my prayers.* Curious, she turns it over. On the back, it's signed: *Love, Mom.* Just that. Maddie has no recollection of ever having seen it before, but it has most likely been in that book for ten years or more.

She holds the card against her heart, tears running down her face. Ever since her mother died, Maddie has waited and hoped for a sign, something that would tell her that her mother has made the journey to the other side safely and that she is at peace. And perhaps that she has forgiven Maddie for her anger, her hurt, her selfish wish for a different sort of mother. And it has come. *Thanks, Mom.* She hopes that her mother, wherever she is, can hear her.

On an impulse, she digs through one of her boxes and pulls out a small framed picture of *The Gleaners*. She'd found it in a second hand shop years before. The frame is old with flaking silver paint. On the back Maddie has given it her own title: *Ruth amid the Alien Corn* from Keats's *Ode to a Nightingale*. Her mother's name was Ruth.

She finds her book of poems and reads the poem again, thinks of her mother, the girl Maddie imagines she was. Standing tall on her high school stage when she won a prize for poetry: *The Golden Treasury of Verse* in soft burgundy leather. The one Maddie holds now in her hand. Perhaps her mother was hopeful then that her life would come with gifts, with the promise of some small, sweet glory farther down the road. In her wedding picture that stands on Maddie's bureau, her smile is uncertain. Her mouth soft and sensuous, her eyes wistful. Thinking perhaps of other things. *Through the sad heart of Ruth, when sick for home, she stood in tears amid the alien corn.*

Her mother had stories too.

It was 1942, wartime. Maddie's father and her uncle were conscientious objectors and spent six months in a prison camp near Clear Lake, Manitoba, building what was later to become a resort area. Maddie's mother always referred to it as "the time the boys were in camp." She had photographs of them dressed in thick woolen pants and shirts, leaning in the doorway of a wooden hut. No smiles. They were just boys. Serving their time as traitors and fugitives, the dispossessed.

There were other pictures Maddie's mother had taken at the lake after the war, of Maddie's father and uncle leaning against wooden lamp posts or strolling down the long pier, gray fedoras tipped at a jaunty angle. How could they have returned, even as visitors, to such a place? But they did return, like veterans who went back to Europe after the war to the sites of battles, perhaps to remember or to learn to forget the thing which had carved out such a part of their lives.

Maddie's mother was just twenty-one when her father was transferred from camp to the Vaughan Street jail in Winnipeg. She was pregnant with Maddie's brother Tom, and alone. She bore the scorn of neighbors for having a husband who refused to fight, rode the street car across the city every day through that long winter to visit him. Even then, she was powerful in her willful determination. Her body a sharp, angled certainty, leaning into the wind.

She and Maddie's father traded stories through jail bars. Held hands and prayed. He called her Ruthie. They came together on stolen time, created their own place of safety, even behind prison walls. A place Maddie could never know. But this she does know: The weight of fear has not been hers alone to carry. Her father's fear was for the safety of his own soul, even though he dropped to his knees in that farmer's field all those years ago, offered his life, seeking a savior who would redeem him and bring him peace from his own childhood terrors. Her mother learned to tame her fears by hiding behind walls of forgetting, creating a façade of safety within the silence of empty rooms.

And Maddie stands now in the truth of what has become her legacy. A last gift. The final chapter of her parents' story. Her home.

She walks outside into the back garden, picks tall stalks of purple foxglove and arranges them in a silver vase that was her mother's, then leans the rabbit card against it. She digs through her CDs until she finds her favorite Emmylou Harris, and listens to her voice fill the house. Emmylou stumbling into grace. Just like her.

And then, all by herself, in the last sun of the day, Maddie does something she has rarely ever done. She dances.

ಬಿಂದ

"I had a dream last night."

Maddie is having an acupuncture treatment for her restless legs and the fibromyalgia that leaves her muscles taut with remembering. Muscles armored against the invasions of her body from so long ago. This is what Ruta, her acupuncturist, has shown her – that the message her body carries is the one that tells her she is safe only when her body is moving, dodging that invisible enemy. A body confined in a prison of sheets. Legs that could find no rest, that long to run wild down the dark hills of night. There is truth and healing in her skin, Ruta tells her, and in her muscles, deep in her bones. Deep in the place where the stories live.

Ruta had left her alone with the needles in place and is now back to give them one last spin. The window is open and Maddie hears a red-headed sapsucker's persistent tapping against a mountain ash. A faint breeze stirs the glass wind chime that Ruta has hung in the window.

"Ah, tell me," Ruta says, "about that dream."

So Maddie tells her. It's just another version of a dream she's been having for years. This one though, was the most vivid, the most frightening. "I'm in a prison," Maddie says. "I'm a reporter, there to learn about and tell the prisoners' stories. I have a notepad and pen, and am ready to write things down." Maddie winces. The needles in her legs have always caused pain. An ache in a place that feels so deep it has no bottom.

"Prisoners are crowded around me and they all want to tell their stories. But the prison guards are trying to stop this. They're attacking me with everything they've got. One of them lunges forward with a syringe full of something that will paralyze or put me to sleep. They will go to any lengths to silence me, to stop me from telling the prisoners' stories. With all my strength, I reach for a locked door to unlock it, to escape, just as the needle is about to be plunged into my thigh. That's when I wake up."

The sapsucker has stopped tapping and the breeze is still.

"Wow," says Ruta.

"Yeah."

"So who is trying to silence you?" asks Ruta.

"The prison guards."

"Who are those guards?" she says, "And who is the prisoner?"

Maddie lies for a few minutes in silence. She's been studying dreams for years, has even worked with dream therapists. She knows that her dream cast of characters are all parts of herself. This one's been staring her right in the face.

"I've been the prisoner," she says, "and I guess I've been the guards. But why?"

"Well, what have you been guarding all this time, Maddie? Who have you been protecting and why?"

Ruta pulls out the needles and with every one she dislodges, Maddie feels a slight ache, a deep hurt, but fainter now.

Maddie remembers the dream and sees the anguish on the faces of those prisoners, their desperation to have their stories told. The prison guards, faces contorted with rage. And fear. There is fear in their faces too, in their narrowed eyes, in their desperation to stop her. Then there is Maddie, caught between them, almost childlike in her ignorance, her innocence of the battle in which she is trapped. She's ready with pen and notebook and all she wants to do is tell her story.

"It's my father," Maddie says. *How do I know this?*

All those nights of her childhood trapped in his love. Bound in bedtime rituals, Bible stories, visions of hell, the place where she would go if she didn't believe. All those nights of her childhood that left her with a lifetime of nightmares. A legacy of pain.

"You've opened an interesting door here," says Ruta. "Something to think about."

Maddie decides to walk the few miles home. She's not ready for conversation with anyone. The day is fine and clear, bright with new spring growth. She takes a path through the woods that runs alongside the river. This life flow she has always loved, a pulsing vein through the body of Mother Earth. A place that can carry her anywhere if she has the courage to step into its depths. She thinks of her brother and all the rivers they swam together as children. The cold river water that smelled like rust and dank earth. The rough hands of the preacher, the offering of holiness that never quite took, but left its scar.

I'm free to tell my story. She says this in her head again and again. *It's time to listen to the river.* There has never been anyone stopping her but her. She thinks she's always known that the story is not about her grandfather at all. That's just the story she's remembered. The real story is about her father. That's the story that wants to be told.

The night sky is framed in the window. Maddie is not alone. Someone is in her bedroom. There is a soft collapse, like a sigh, as someone sits on the side of the bed. A hand against her cheek, not cool, but hot. She peers deeply into the past. His face hovers above her, his mouth, his eyes. Looking for what? Her father.

Her father sitting on the side of her childhood bed, stroking her hair, telling her Bible stories. And ever since, her body has shut out those memories, resisted truth, armored her against the fear of those nights. Armored her too against every intimacy. The unwelcome touch of a stranger's hand. Because all she could associate with her father's hand stroking her hair, tucking her into bed, too tight – always too tight – were those terrible stories that left her frightened and alone in the night after he left her room.

Maddie had heard the stories a thousand times. But no matter how many times she'd heard them, she still felt guilty and stained with sin. Why was it that she was convinced, always, that she was the one who was doomed to end up on the side that was wanting?

There would be the five wise virgins, her father told her, who put oil in their lamps before the wedding feast. Beautifully arrayed and with their lamps trimmed and ready, they waited for the call of the bridegroom. But, her father said – there was always a *but* – there were also five foolish virgins who didn't bring enough oil to keep their lamps lit while they waited. All ten fell asleep and when it was announced that the bridegroom was near, the foolish virgins realized that their lamps had gone out. Because the wise virgins did not have enough to share, the foolish virgins rushed out to buy more oil, but while they were out, the bridegroom came. Too late, the foolish virgins arrived at the wedding feast only to find the door closed. In response to their pleas to be let in, Jesus told them, *I do not know you.*

"And you see," Maddie's father told her, "if you are not prepared for the coming of the Lord, you will not be able to enter the Kingdom of Heaven. No matter how much you call out and plead and weep, it will be too late."

As a child, Maddie had no idea what a virgin was, but she imagined her to be angel-like, dressed in white silk and lace, possibly with a halo, always beautiful, pure of heart. She couldn't imagine being turned away from her own wedding feast, even if she had forgotten to fill her lamp. But all the stories her father told her were about someone being left behind, and that someone, it always seemed, was certain to be Maddie.

During the years before Joey, Maddie hid from her fears in undemanding relationships. Christopher, David, Lorenzo. Easy love. A life buffered, always, against what might lurk inside that pared-down, razor's edge hollow place. That place inside her. And how well she learned to abandon her body, disclaim her father's touch, his hands that imprisoned her in those nighttime sheets. Disowned all memory. And now she lives in the physical pain that armor has created. Her body has paid a high price for not knowing, for all those years of denial. Maddie thinks of something Carmelita said not long ago during one of their long evening chats.

"I have a theory," Lita said. "About you. You and your obstacle course." She'd teased Maddie for years about how Maddie turned her cabin in the Grove into what she called "an obstacle course." A bright shiver of asparagus ferns hanging just low enough to run into; doorways partly blocked by shelving full of books; a wrought iron plant stand; framed pictures hanging in the narrow hallway that would come crashing to the floor if anyone were to accidentally brush against them.

"This is how you've protected yourself," she said.

"But why?"

"Think about it. If you keep enough stuff around you for people to trip over, there's no way anyone could get to you in the night when you're sleeping without you being warned. Of course, it's unconscious. It's not as if you planned to do this."

Maddie was stunned. It was possible. Maybe even probable. Her father's nighttime visits. It was always her nights that were invaded, in the dark, where she most needed to feel safe. She's told her story to Lita, little by little over the years. Lita has pulled the stories out of her, memory by memory, and with each telling, the door to Maddie's heart opened a little wider. And with each telling, Maddie has known a little more.

"Tell me about you as a baby," she would say, "sitting up on your father's shoulders. How he showed you all the trees in bloom, and named them for you. *Cherry tree. Wild plum.* Tell me about the time you were sick and had to be steamed with friar's balsam, when someone tripped over the cord of the kettle and burned you with scalding water."

Maddie doesn't remember being scalded by hot water. She only remembers the story she's been told. But she does remember her mother telling her how much her father adored her. How he had always wanted a daughter. Maddie has never forgotten how her mother scolded her for not loving her father enough. Maddie turned from him, her mother said, refused his love. Denied the man who came into her childhood room in the night, tucked her in too tight, as though he were wrapping her into her winding-sheet. Whispered Bible stories with thinly-veiled allusions to the perilous state of her soul. Maddie's blood ran wild in her veins, her sleep hijacked by the terror of the Lord coming in the night.

An unloving child, her mother called her again and again.

The deepest cut of all.

Maddie remembers some of those things. Her father carrying her in his arms, holding her up to smell the blossoms on the tree in their backyard. A child's bicycle with fat tires leaning against a white picket fence. A vegetable garden filled with beets, carrots, and lettuce, encircled by smooth, round rocks. Or maybe that's not a memory at all but a picture in her mother's photograph album.

Over the years Maddie has told Lita stories until her life was spread out before them like a patchwork quilt, cobbled together out of Maddie's dreams and memories. Maddie has told Lita too, about the dream of the guards who try to prevent her from telling her story.

And Lita just said *yes*, as if she knew already.

Maddie hears the rushing of the river, closer now. The path underfoot is damp, rich with the smell of earth and rain. Memories pour in. Didn't her mother know? Couldn't she see how frightened Maddie was of her father? Why did she let him go to her night after night?

It hits Maddie like a slap on the head. *Satori*. What Kerouac called "a kick in the eye." Her father was the captain of the ship. He made the rules. And that's why Maddie's mother didn't tell her that it was her father who tripped over the cord and spilled the boiling water on her. She didn't want to think about him skulking near Maddie's room. She wouldn't ever have thought of it as anything untoward. Through his stories, he was simply attempting to save her from the everlasting darkness of hell. It was the only way he knew to subdue his own terror: the belief that after his death she would be lost to him.

The finality of this truth leaves Maddie feeling empty. She finds her way down to the riverbank where she sits, comforted by the river's familiar rhythm and its swift, sure presence. Remembering another river from another time. The baptism. The fragrance of sweet gale on the riverbank. Cold river water closing over her head. The preacher's rough grasp. The place where she tried to live her parents' truth.

Maddie feels as though she's waiting for something, although she can't say what. She sits by the river until all the light has drained from the sky and then makes her way back to the safety of home through a slender path of shadowed moonlight.

Seven

Vancouver

It was late summer when Dawn told Maddie that she and Daisy were going back to Toronto to live with Dawn's parents.

"Before Daisy gets too settled in school," Dawn explained. "It'll be better for her."

Although she loved her writing courses, Maddie had been thinking for a while that she'd have to get a real job, and knew that meant going back to the hospital, at least part time. She called Jackson to check out the work situation.

"Wow. She finally surfaces," Jackson said. "Where've you been? I've got to say I've felt a little hurt that you haven't called me for so long."

"I know," Maddie said, "and I'm sorry. It's been in a self-imposed exile. I just needed to lie low, write, and not be tempted by anything."

"Like friends?"

"More specifically getting high with friends. That's gotta go. I can't be high and do my writing work."

In the quiet of those days living with Dawn and Daisy, Maddie had begun to write. There had been the stillness of the moment, accompanied by the gifts only solitude and necessity could bring. It had begun long ago with poems and musings on the pages of an old notebook. She'd always written. Journals, poems, the odd short story. She'd taken writing workshops, but it was through the long nights looking after Daisy that new words had begun to hum through her veins. As Maddie began her classes, writing against deadlines, she learned to coax those words from some deeper place, then sculpt and polish them until she could imagine them sending out shards of silver light. She'd finally decided that she needed to claim her life in black and white by putting words on a page.

"I'll keep taking writing courses," she told Jackson. "I want to study short story writing. Fiction. Nonfiction. Nursing has never touched me in any way that matters. It's never filled me the way words do. But it has been a means to an end. Money. Freedom. I have no regrets."

"Will your parents help you financially?"

"No. Never. Higher education scares them. For them, the idea of seeking knowledge is dangerous territory. Anyway, I want to do this myself. I'll work for the next year and save. Live cheap. Eat lots of brown rice. Stop smoking weed. Stay out of trouble. I can do it."

"So, you're coming back to work?"

"I think so, yeah. But I'll work only as much as I need to. Like I said. Means to an end."

৪০৪৪

Maddie found a place to live, a three-room suite in a big old house on the other side of the Burrard Bridge, but still close to downtown and the hospital. It was small but comfortable. It even had a postage stamp-sized backyard with a patchy garden and a square of yellowing grass. She was living alone for the first time in her life, and for the first time felt the sweet pull of the whole idea of home, her own home. A place of sanctuary.

She bought herself a black-and-white TV and night after night watched the familiar litany of war, boys younger than she was coming home in gray, steel coffins and handed over to mothers, fathers, wives. Sometimes Jackson came over and they both watched. The blood of Vietnam permeated their consciousness, stained even the simplicity of a summer sky, left little on which to hang their thin hopes. With every nightly newscast, the innocence of their generation felt as though it was being torn away, piece by piece.

Jackson told Maddie that he knew of a few openings at the hospital, so she made an appointment with Miss Wainwright, the nursing supervisor. She offered Maddie the position of on-call evening shift float. That meant Maddie signed in and then went to whichever ward needed her most. She often worked in two or three different wards in one evening. She liked the freedom it gave her, the casualness, and loved that she could choose her shifts and the number of shifts to work. It was Miss Wainwright who told her about Thea.

"We've had to suspend her, Miss Kaslo. Temporarily. She was taking drugs from the drug cupboard. They weren't narcotics, but just the same."

The only drugs that were easily available and not counted were 292s, Valium, and Placidyl, a mild sleeping pill.

"Has anyone called to see how she's doing?" Maddie asked.

"Not that I'm aware of," said Miss Wainwright. "But she's due back next week. It's her responsibility to deal with her problems."

Miss Wainwright knew that she and Thea had been roommates, and Maddie managed to convince her to share Thea's address and phone number. When Maddie called the number, a woman answered.

"She isn't here," said the voice. "This is a communal phone. I don't know a lot about her but let me ask someone."

Maddie heard her calling off into the distance. In the background, a door slammed over muffled laughter. Maddie wondered what had happened to Thea's trumpet player with the big brass bed.

"Hello," said the voice again, "Annette thinks Thea's in the hospital, the psych ward at University Hospital. She told Annette she was going to admit herself and no one's seen her for a few days."

Thea in a psych ward? It was hard to believe she would have put herself there willingly. She was too clever. Always liked to be just one step ahead of everyone else. She would outwit them all, make fools of them. Clearly, Maddie thought, she had not told Miss Wainwright.

The madhouse. That's what Thea would call it, just for the high drama in the retelling.

Maddie traveled by bus to the university the next afternoon after calling to confirm that Thea was there. The grounds of the hospital were perfectly manicured, bordered by rust-colored asters and sweet alyssum. A group was playing volleyball in a patch of yellow grass next to the main building. A few played with enthusiasm, leapt for the ball, shouted wildly when it was missed. Two or three were stretched out on the grass, not playing, or refusing to play. Three others stood near the net as if they were part of things, but their eyes were dull, distanced from the game, bodies rigid as if camouflaging invisible wounds. They all looked normal, like anyone Maddie might have passed on the street and that surprised her. What had she expected? Faces hollowed out with madness like vacant, grinning pumpkins? Lunacy?

Inside was cool and quiet, pale green walls, parquet floors, hanging asparagus ferns and philodendron. Behind the main desk a young woman with long, straight hair and owlish eyeglasses poked tentatively at a typewriter and ignored Maddie. When Maddie asked for Thea's room number, she looked startled but told her. "I don't think she's there, though."

Down the long, cool, white hallway, past numbered doors. An undercurrent of conversation, then a shower of bright laughter from behind one of the closed doors marked STAFF. Thea's door was partially open. At first the room appeared unoccupied and Maddie thought for a moment that the owl-eyed receptionist was right and that Thea wasn't there. Then she saw her, in bed with the covers pulled up over her head.

"Thea?"

There was a beat of silence.

"What are you doing here?" said her voice, muffled by the covers.

"I could ask you the same thing."

Two arms slid out from under the sheets and Thea slowly pulled them back from her face, briefly glancing at Maddie. She picked a bottle of purple nail polish from the drawer of her bedside table, opened it and began lacquering her nails, stretching each finger out in front of her on the bed. "So, ask."

"Why are you hiding in bed?"

"I'm refusing to cooperate," Thea said. "I won't bare my soul for their salacious perusal."

"Didn't you come here for help? One of the women at your place told me you signed yourself in."

"Yes, but they can't make me do anything I don't want to do."

"Of course not, Thea. No one can. No one wants to."

Thea blew on her wet nails, admiring the gloss. "A lot you know."

Maddie ignored the remark and sat down on the edge of her bed. "I've missed you."

Thea gave her a long, angry look. "Then you shouldn't have left. Have you seen Jackson?"

"I've talked to him," Maddie said. "Briefly. Why? I didn't know you even knew Jackson."

"Of course, I know Jackson. He's been working at the hospital for over a year now." Thea held up her hands and inspected her newly painted nails for flaws. "I just know him a little better now."

The remark felt like a trap and Maddie wasn't taking the bait.

Thea opened the drawer and tossed the bottle of polish into it. "He wanted to get your phone number." She slammed the drawer shut. "But *I* didn't know where you were." She said this accusingly, as though Maddie had been hiding from her.

"Have you seen him?"

"He's come over a few times in the last couple of months," said Thea. "Just to talk. Sometimes we've gone out for coffee."

"I didn't know that."

"Well, God knows where *you've* been. *He* didn't know." She began smoothing out the long, silky strands of her hair, checking for split ends. "I read him *Oft, in the Stilly Night.*"

Thea's favorite poem.

Maddie wondered why Jackson hadn't said anything to her about seeing Thea.

Thea swung her legs over the side of the bed. "You know I've moved," she said. "You'd love my new place. I have a room in one of those big old houses in Shaughnessy. There's lots of dark wood and stained glass windows. Big gloomy hallways and massive staircases. A *Jane Eyre* kind of house."

"What happened to your man?" Maddie asks. "Your trumpet player. The one with the big brass bed?"

"Oh, him," was all she said.

"What do you mean, *oh him*?"

"He treats me like a child. I hate that." Thea pulled her feet up onto the bed and inspected her toenails. "Anyway, I think he's on the road right now. With his band."

"Was he good to you?"

"He's a lush," she said. "You should see him. He carries a silver flask with him everywhere he goes. Gin, of all things." She rooted around in the drawer of her bedside table again. "What guy drinks gin?"

"Are you still with him then?"

"No. Though he may think so."

"So why don't you want to be with him?"

"He's too good to me."

"And this is a complaint?"

"For Christ's sake, Maddie, he gave me a big brass bed. Just because I wanted it. And he hates Bob Dylan. How can I be with someone who hates Dylan?" She kicked the sheets off the bed, yanked open the drawer of her bedside table, slammed it shut again. "He's just *too* good. I mean *boringly good.*"

Thea paused and picked at the bedspread. "I went to Los Angeles for a week with another man," she said. "When Mr. Music and I were living together. And he let me come back."

She looked disgusted. She told Maddie that she'd met the other man when he was a patient in orthopedics. He'd had knee surgery. He asked her if she would go with him and she told him yes.

"Simple as that," Thea said. "On the back of his Harley, all the way to Los Angeles. That coastline made me crazy with its beauty." She closed her eyes. "Big Sur. The lonely, lost roads that climbed the Santa Cruz Mountains. All the literary ghosts living in those hills. The farmers in the Salinas Valley. Doc in *Cannery Row*. Kerouac drying out under the Bixby Creek Bridge. The Joads. And the ocean, Maddie. The ocean. I cried because I wanted it to be my history too. Not just stories. I wanted those stories to be mine. Wanted that life to be mine."

This was the Thea Maddie knew. The one with the heart full of dreams, the one who had a divining rod for beauty.

Thea sat up straight. "I had a dream, Mad. I think it was telling me something. Something important."

"A dream about . . .?"

"Nine birds singing."

"Exactly nine birds? Not ten or eight?"

"Nine," Thea said. "I read that the Hebrews believed the number nine is a symbol for truth." She rummaged around in the drawer and pulled out a copy of *Vanity Fair*, her glasses, and a hairbrush. "I was standing on a street corner right downtown. It was raining, cars flying by, kicking up waterfalls of rain. I heard birds singing and looked up. And there they were, strung out along the power line. Nine of them. And you know what killed me?"

"What, Thea?"

"No one else heard them or saw them. It was dusk, not dark yet. The time my mother used to call *owl light*. All of us standing there waiting for the light to change and not one of them knew what was happening right above their heads. They all had on their going-home-mad-at-the-rain faces."

"Birds singing in the rain," said Maddie. "What kind of birds were they?"

Thea turned her head upside down and began brushing her hair. "I don't know a damn thing about birds, Maddie. You know that." She tugged on a knot. "I wanted them to be nightingales. Such a beautiful word. *Nightingale*. But of course, they couldn't have been. They were just regular old birds. Dream birds."

"So tell me, Thea. What happened to this man you were telling me about? The one with the Harley."

"He drove me to the top of Griffith Park in Los Angeles and told me he loved me," she said. "I just laughed."

"Why?"

"Because he *didn't* love me. He only said it to try and keep me there."

"Where is he now?"

"Who knows? I took the Greyhound home. Alone." She threw herself against the bed. "And who was waiting for me, big wide arms and heart all bruised and open?"

"Your trumpet player."

"Of course. And I didn't want him anymore."

"But Thea, that seems so . . ."

"So what?"

"So . . . unforgiving."

"I can't imagine what I've ever done," she said, "that would make you think I'm a forgiving person." She grinned and Maddie did too.

"What do you do here?"

"We make ashtrays out of tiles," Thea said. "Red, green, and blue. That's it. I thought it was a good idea at first. *Oh, ashtrays. Sweet. Something I can use.* But they're the stupidest bloody things I've ever seen. We all make the same thing. Ashtrays. Red, green, and blue. That's it."

She showed Maddie the blonde streaks she had put in her hair. "I thought it would make me feel better. Before I came in here."

"Did it?"

"Don't be stupid."

Maddie laughed.

"I'd move out of my place in a heartbeat," Thea said, "if you changed your mind about us getting a place together."

"I can't, Thea. I need to get my feet on the ground, get my life together." Maddie told her about school, her writing.

"And I'll be stuck at St. Simeon's, going nowhere."

"You're not stuck anywhere, Thea. You can do whatever you want. Why do you always forget that?"

"I am stuck," she said, "in ways you can't imagine." She slapped the mattress as though it had reared up and challenged her. "Maybe I wouldn't be if you hadn't interfered."

"Interfered?"

"A nice quiet sleep and it would've been over."

"Are you talking about the fire?"

"What else?"

"You wanted to die?"

"It wasn't a plan, Maddie. It's not like I woke up that morning and decided, *today, I'm going to die.*"

"It wouldn't have been the first time."

"A clever deduction considering you haven't been around for the last few months. Anyway, I didn't need you playing Pollyanna."

Maddie shook her head. "Why, Thea?"

"Why what?"

"Why did you sign yourself into this place if you aren't prepared to try and get well?"

"To get well? You think it's that easy? Do you think it's even possible?"

"Yes, Thea, I do."

"I hate you, Maddie."

"That's it? That's all you can come up with? You hate *me*?"

Maddie's anger felt huge, too big for the room. She felt as though she were running out of air, as though the space wasn't big enough to contain both of them.

"You think I'm not trying?"

"I can't carry you, Thea. I'm so tired of this shit."

"So now you're carrying me?"

"What I'm carrying," Maddie said, "are my fears for you. And I don't want to do it anymore. I can't."

"I never once asked for you to be my emotional Sherpa," Thea said. "I don't need a Sherpa. I don't need anyone. And now I want you to leave." She lay down on the bed and pulled the covers back over her head.

Maddie started to leave the room, then turned back. "Do you have any new words?"

Thea slid the blankets down until they uncovered her mouth. "As a matter of fact, I do."

"And?"

"*Untenable. Not defensible against attack or objection.* My life here has become untenable." She yanked the covers over her head.

Maddie left her there, hiding under the sheets in exactly the way she'd been when Maddie first came into the room. She wondered what Thea meant – whether her life in the hospital had become something she could no longer defend, or whether her whole life had, for her, become untenable. Maddie thought of her lying under Heathcliff's car, breathing in the exhaust fumes. And of Heathcliff telling her he'd had enough.

I've had enough too.

Maddie asked the secretary if she could speak to Thea's doctor before she left.

"You may be in luck," she said. "I think he just came in." She disappeared into a room behind the front desk and came back a minute later. "He'll be here in a second."

The Muzak played something popular, vaguely familiar. The volleyball players drifted in from the outside, fatigued, clumsy, stupid with the heat, or the drugs. Maddie thought of Thea's disappointment with the ashtrays in her occupational therapy group. As though she had truly thought that making an ashtray or putting blonde streaks in her hair could ever make her happy.

The psychiatrist arrived, tieless, short sleeves, cool. He hadn't been playing volleyball.

"Well." He shook Maddie's hand with the strong grip of a professional hand shaker. "A friend of Thea's. What would you like to know?"

"What's going to happen to her now?"

He shrugged. "It's up to her. If she carries on the way she has – refusing to accept responsibility for herself – then we'll have to insist that she leave. There's no free ride here."

"But can you help her?"

"Not unless she's willing to help herself."

"And if she is?"

"Then of course we can help her. If she's willing to get involved in the programs. If she participates in group. Takes the meds we suggest. But frankly, Miss . . .what did you say your name was?"

"Maddie."

"Frankly, Maddie, at this juncture I don't see any of that happening."

Maddie sighed. Neither did she.

"And if you want my honest opinion . . ."

"Yes?"

"I don't mean to be crude, but there's nothing wrong with Thea that a good kick in the ass won't fix."

༄༅

Maddie had been shopping at the Chinese market down the street and heard her phone ringing as she was unlocking the door. She dropped her bags and dashed across the room, grabbing the phone mid-ring. It was Thea. She was crying.

"Thea, what's the matter?"

Maddie pulled her bag off her shoulder and sat down on the edge of her bed, which was also her sofa. The last light of the day streaked across the cushions flung across the quilt.

"I have something I need to tell you, Maddie. Something big. I've done something unforgivable. I wanted to tell you when you were here, but . . ."

"Nothing is unforgivable, Thea."

"You're wrong, Maddie. Stop. Listen to me. It's about Charlie and Dogface. I know you've been wondering what happened. Well, I'm going to tell you."

"Thea . . ."

"Dogface is dead."

"You've heard from Charlie? Where is he? What happened?"

"No. I haven't heard from Charlie. Maddie, this isn't about Charlie. It's about Dogface. And me. I killed him, Maddie. I killed Dogface."

"Thea, you're being dramatic."

"Don't, Maddie. Don't try and turn this into something that's okay. That it's something that can't really be my fault." She'd stopped crying. "It *isn't* okay. It's never going to be okay."

"Tell me what happened."

"We were up in the woods, in one of the places we used to go to shoot and hike. Way up in the middle of nowhere. We stayed later than usual that day. It was getting dark. There's an old abandoned shack there. No doors or windows, just a falling-down wood frame. Probably abandoned a long time ago. I'd left my backpack in there and went in to get some water. We always brought water with us."

She paused. Maddie heard the scrape of a match as Thea lit a cigarette. Inhaled. Exhaled. She must have been in the hospital's sunroom where they were allowed to smoke. "I could hear Charlie and Dogface talking. Just low murmurs. I couldn't hear what they were saying. They were just sitting on the ground out front, leaning against the shack. Shooting the breeze."

Maddie waited as Thea took a deep breath before going on.

"At least that's what I thought. Shit, Maddie." She stopped. Started crying again.

"Then what? Please don't cry, Thea. Just tell me." Maddie felt the story's darkness encompassing her, rushing through her veins. She really didn't want to hear any more.

"I picked up my rifle, settled it on my shoulder. Didn't plan to shoot it. I'm not even sure why I picked it up. I ran my fingers along the barrel thinking how smooth it felt. Then I looked through the empty window frame toward the horizon. The sun was fading into night. There was still a faint rim of light on the horizon. I remember that. I was looking out at nothing, really. Thinking nothing. The night was warm. The light was low, almost gone." She stopped.

"I didn't see him. He crossed in front of the window about twenty feet away from me. He'd picked up a couple of pieces of firewood. I guess he was going to bring them into the shack to keep them from getting wet. We did that sometimes. There was a fire pit outside and sometimes we would cook food or sit by the fire to get warm before we headed back to the city." There was silence. Maddie waited.

"That's when it happened. I just shot through the empty window frame into the dark. Out into nothing, I thought. And he fell. He . . .he didn't make a sound. He just fell."

"Thea, it wasn't your fault," Maddie said. "You didn't mean to kill anyone."

"Those are just words, Maddie. I killed Dogface. Nothing can ever change that. Certainly words won't."

"What did you do? What did Charlie do?"

"Charlie didn't say a word. Not one word. Not then, anyway." Thea's voice was harsh and cold. Like the truth of what had happened. "Once he realized Dogface was dead, he hiked into the bush, dug a grave and buried him."

"Just like that? He had a shovel?"

"You know Charlie and all the shit he carries around with him in that truck. Tools for every job imaginable. Even a shovel for digging a grave."

"And the gun? What happened to the gun?"

"Charlie threw it into the lake on our way home. It had never been registered. Thank God."

Maddie couldn't find the words to ask about all the things she wanted to know. "Do you think he'll ever be found?"

"Never. No one will ever know."

"Where's Charlie now?"

"Charlie's gone. I don't know where. He said it's better if I don't know. He said we can't ever see each other again. He made me promise to never ever tell anyone. But Maddie, I couldn't carry it alone anymore."

"You've got to tell someone, Thea. Someone other than me. Your psychiatrist. A priest. Somebody."

"I can't do that Maddie. Charlie and I made a pact. We've closed the door and thrown away the key."

"What about Dogface? Doesn't he have family somewhere? Isn't somebody going to be looking for him?"

"No one knows anything about Dogface. Not a thing. That's the only reason Charlie could even consider doing what he did. We were all he had. Just Charlie and me. He was a man without a history. American, Charlie knew that much. He thought he'd been to Vietnam, hence the name. Dogface. No one, not one single person knew his real name. He never drove. No driver's license. No papers of any kind. That's the saddest part of all. He was a nobody. He lived and died a nobody."

"I'm so sorry, Thea, that you've had to live with this. Carry it alone."

"Sorry's no use to anyone now," said Thea. "It's a forever truth. Nothing will make it better or make it go away. I'm guilty. There is punishment due."

"It's no use thinking in terms of punishment, Thea. You can't live your life waiting for some kind of retribution to rain down on you. You can't live like that."

Thea laughed, a harsh, broken laugh. "Those are just words again, Maddie," she said. "Nice words. But here's the real truth: it's obscene that someone's life should end like that and that no one should be made to pay."

Maddie knew there was nothing in the world she could do or say that would change what Thea had told her. But the mystery of the past few months was falling into place.

"Oh, Thea."

"I am not looking for or expecting *propitiation*."

Maddie could sense the rueful smile on Thea's face.

"*Atonement*. My word for today. There is no atonement for me."

"Thea, we need to talk about this, but not on the phone. I'll come and see you tomorrow. We can talk then."

"Sweet Maddie. Always trying to fix everything. Even the unfixable." Thea's voice was light now, drained of emotion. "You'll have to forgive me my persiflage, Mad." She waited for Maddie to ask but Maddie said nothing. "*Persiflage*," Thea said. "*Banter; light raillery*. It's in the Oxford Dictionary. You can look it up."

⁖⁗

The ringing phone woke Maddie, pushed her to the surface of sleep. It must have been ringing for a long time. The woman in the suite above her ran across the creaky floor and slammed the bathroom door. The clock on the bedside table said it was just past nine o'clock. Too early for anyone Maddie knew to be calling on a Sunday morning. She reached behind her and pulled the curtain back to let in some of the gray morning light, then picked up the receiver.

"Maddie?" The voice was barely audible. "It's Verna." Thea's mother.

"Hi, Verna." Maddie shivered in her thin summer nightgown.

"She's. Dead." Verna dropped the words like rocks into a cold sea.

What is she talking about?

"What?"

"Thea's dead."

Maddie couldn't understand what she was hearing. Was Verna speaking a foreign language?

"Maddie?"

"But I just saw her. In the hospital."

"She's dead," Verna said again. "She checked herself out of the hospital and went back to her room. They couldn't keep her, you know. She'd signed herself in."

Maddie sat down on the side of the still-warm bed. "How?"

"She took pills. Must have saved them up from work. Painkillers, sleeping pills. Even aspirin. She took a lot, they said. With half a bottle of scotch."

"Who told you?"

"One of the nursing supervisors. Miss Wainwright. She told me Thea phoned in last night to say she wasn't coming to work this morning, but she wasn't even on the schedule. This Wainwright person said she knew something was wrong. Thea was slurring her words, so she sent over an ambulance."

Maddie sat in stunned disbelief.

"Maddie?"

"I'm here, Verna."

"You'll have to go there. Please. I can't."

"Go where?" Maddie yanked the curtain back across the window.

"They want me to identify her body at the morgue," she said. "I can't do it."

"You want *me* to go to the morgue?"

"You have to."

Maddie hung up the phone and leaned against the wall. She thought about Thea's psychiatrist and what he said to her that last day. *A kick in the ass? You bastard.*

The room was hostile. The day had all at once become treacherous.

৪০০৪

Maddie took the bus to the police station at Hastings and Main. The bus was empty and stank of empty lives, hopelessness. It was a gray, cold day and the streets were nearly deserted. They had told her to come early because the autopsy had been scheduled for noon. She was waiting for the detective who was to meet her at the front desk and take her to the morgue.

Maddie was scared. She didn't even know what she was scared of. She'd cried when she called her parents to tell them.

"Do you want Dad to drive you?" her mother offered.

"No," Maddie said. "I'll be okay."

Her mother had said very little beyond, "That's a shocker."

Maddie wished she hadn't called them. Her mother's voice had been distant, unemotional, and it left Maddie feeling emptier than she'd felt before making the call. But she hadn't wanted to carry the knowledge of Thea's death alone and didn't know who else to call.

Maddie was angry, then felt guilty for being angry. How could Thea have done such a thing without warning her or leaving some message? After she'd told her she would come, and that they would talk. Verna didn't mention a message or a suicide note.

The detective who met her at the front desk wore a shiny gray suit and yellow tie. Expensive. He introduced himself as Detective Bryant, then shook Maddie's hand briskly, told her the morgue was in another building, and motioned for her to follow him. Outside, he stopped and lit a cigarette, flipped the dead match onto the damp pavement

"This is very unusual," he said. "We normally only allow family members to identify a body."

As though he was granting her a privilege.

"Unless, of course," he went on, "there is no family. But we did talk to her mother."

They were in a narrow alley littered with cigarette butts, stray boxes, scraps of the debris of other lives. Street lives. Above them hung a maze of power lines and beyond that a ragged gray patch of sky. Maddie looked for birds on the power lines, but there were none. There was only silence.

They continued across a cement walkway between rectangles of dead grass to the back door of a building that was adjacent to the police station. He pushed the door open and ground out his cigarette on the pavement with the toe of one polished shoe.

He led her up a narrow iron stairway that circled the black pit of an elevator shaft. Maddie decided it was used to transport bodies up and down when she saw the empty trolley and the wooden platform where the bodies may have been placed. With each hollow, tinny echo of their steps, the structure swayed and wobbled. There was silence, except for the ring of their steps on the stairs. Death loomed like a cold, impenetrable fog.

When they reached the second floor, the detective led Maddie down a long narrow hallway. She felt like a prisoner, scared and vulnerable. He motioned her into a small room. To her surprise, Verna was sitting there in a dark green wool suit, leather-gloved hands folded in her lap, hair smooth and blonde. Her fake fur coat hung over the back of a chair. Everything about her was so unlike Thea.

Maddie gave her a quick hug. She expected Verna to say that she had changed her mind, that she was there to identify Thea's body after all, but she was there only to sign the papers for the release of the body and to pick up Thea's wallet and whatever other things had been brought with her to the morgue.

"Do you think she really meant to do this?" Maddie asked the detective.

Could she have changed her mind partway through, too late? Or had she hoped that someone, anyone, would find her and stop her?

"Miss, from what we can tell, she took enough pills to kill an elephant. So, yeah, I think this is the result she wanted."

"The death certificate . . ." Thea's mother leaned forward in her chair toward the detective. "I would like it to say that she died of a cerebral hemorrhage. Can you do that?"

He slid the papers across the desk for her to sign. "No, ma'am, I can't. That would not be the truth. This is a legal document."

Verna was crying now, quietly, without passion. Tears ran silently down her face and she made no attempt to stop them or wipe them away. "You'd better get her name right on those papers," she said.

"Ma'am?"

"That birth certificate you found in her wallet," said Verna. "It's not her real birth certificate." She took a white, lace-trimmed handkerchief out of her bag and dabbed at her eyes. "I don't know where she got it, but she said that not having a Canadian birth certificate was a hassle. We're Swedish."

The word *hassle* sounded so unnatural coming out of Verna's mouth with her precise Swedish accent, so like Thea's. But it was what Thea would have said. Verna

217

folded the handkerchief carefully and put it back in her bag.

"Her name isn't Thea," said Verna. "She just picked that. She liked it because it's short for Theodora. *Gift of God*. That's what it means."

"She changed her name?" Maddie couldn't believe she hadn't known that.

Verna nodded and began crying again. "I named her Ingalill," she said. "She hated it." She smiled suddenly. "But isn't that just like her," she said to Maddie, "to change her name to suit herself?"

Oh, yes.

Verna stood up and held her hand out to Maddie. "Well, goodbye, then. I'll call you tonight. We'll have to make some arrangements for a service." She left the room.

We?

There was no place in that room where Maddie's mind could go for comfort. Even the bleak, pale sunlight that lit the walls was not bright or warm. The sunlight had become like everything else that day, an instrument of trickery and deceit. Maddie watched Verna walk away, a petite, pale figure, too bewildered to have begun to comprehend the enormity of what had happened. The detective motioned Maddie into another room, smaller than the one they were just in. Suicide was illegal, apparently. There were questions to be asked.

"I didn't want to say this in front of her mother," he said, "but do you know why she did it? Was she pregnant?"

"I wouldn't know," Maddie said.

She would never have killed herself for that reason, anyway. Maddie knew that. When they lived together, Thea sometimes talked about having a baby, but never with any reference to a man. "I'll call her Ramona," she'd said. Ramona, after her favorite Bob Dylan song *To Ramona*.

Thea never doubted that any child she had would be a girl, an ally.

"She was a good-looking girl," said the detective. He tipped his chair back and laced his fingers behind his head. His eyes and his attention shifted from Maddie's face to her body. There was a new kind of tension in the room now. Maddie was wearing her orange beaded cotton Indian shirt and jeans that were probably too tight, bare feet in leather sandals. She hated shoes. Maybe she should have dressed more conservatively for this situation.

"Were you good friends?" he asked.

"Yes." There was no container of words that could frame their friendship, nothing Maddie could pin down or name as this or that. There was nothing more to say. She felt the weight of Dogface and his death, and the terrible weight of what she knew. She averted her eyes from the detective's gaze. Afraid that the truth could somehow declare itself through the look in her eyes or the nervous way she swung one leg over the other.

He got up and opened the door, then motioned for Maddie to follow him. He showed her into the room next door and pointed to a wooden chair. She sat.

"I'll see if they're ready." He went out and closed the door.

Who are they? Ready for what?

There were no windows. Just a bare light bulb hanging from the ceiling. In the corner was a filing cabinet and a desk and on the wall, a blackboard. On the blackboard a list of names. Beside each name, a crude description of the victim's cause of death. All were women. Maria Johnny:

gunshot wound, left temple; Jane Doe: hanging; Theodora Knudsen: barbiturate OD.

Maddie didn't want to have to look at those names on the wall, the evidence. What kind of people ended up in a city morgue? Suicides, homicides, people with no known identities? People with no families? Or is this where everyone ends up?

She thought of her grandmother, who once said that she was afraid of being buried before she was dead, imprisoned in the dark earth without a voice to call out, unable to struggle or escape from the narrow, cold box. As a child, Maddie had dreams like that: her bed was a prison, a coffin, unyielding sheets solidified around her like cement, too heavy to lift. Nightmare dreams during measles and mumps and pneumonia. Strange and unfamiliar sounds filtered through sickroom smells: lemon tea, Vicks VapoRub, steaming kettles laced with friar's balsam. Dreams of her father kneeling in dry prairie grass, praying for forgiveness. The sun hot on his back as he crouched and made his peace with God.

Maddie was afraid of dying alone.

Stop.

The door opened. "We're ready for you now, Miss."

She wished he'd stop calling her *Miss.* They walked toward a large room. There were rows and rows of steel doors, and one that was open. The smell of anesthetic hung in the air. Hospital smells. Maddie felt the bile rise. This must be where they do it, or near here. The autopsy.

The detective pulled a gurney through the open door. Even from where Maddie stood in the middle of the big, empty room, she could see it was Thea. Her long auburn hair had fallen back from her face, highlighted with the blonde streaks she had put in just days ago.

"It's her," she said to the policeman.

"I'm sorry, Miss, you'll have to get closer."

But Maddie's feet wouldn't move. She felt like an animal that smells its own death and will not be led any farther.

I can't.

"Here, I'll hold your hand," he said. "I know this isn't pleasant."

Maddie let him hold her hand because she was afraid. Afraid of what, she couldn't say exactly. Maybe that Thea would moan or suddenly sit bolt upright. Or that she would open her eyes and curse her for not caring enough, for allowing this to happen.

Maddie looked down at Thea. She didn't look dead. The expression on her face was contemptuous, mocking, as it so often was in life. There were bruises on her face where the blood had clotted. She had been in the cold morgue, alone, for so many hours. Maddie loosened her hand from the detective's. Thea wasn't asleep or simply waiting. She was dead and she would not come back, not ever.

Maddie thought of what Thea had told her just days before: *There is punishment due.* Was this what she'd done: meted out her own punishment?

Maddie wished she could have done something, anything, that could have stopped this from happening, but Thea would have cursed her for believing such a thing was even possible. A crash landing was a certainty. Thea's only regret would have been that she hadn't gone out in a blaze of astonishment, like an exploding rocket that lit the sky in all its terrible glory.

If she could have, Maddie would have set Thea free from the ghosts that haunted her. But Maddie had no key to Thea's secrets and dreams, no map to the dark places where she hid. In the end, Maddie was just like everyone else, a witness standing on the sidelines, caught in the fragile web of Thea's life, helpless against the fury of her last and final story.

Maddie was reluctant to leave her there, alone with her keepers. She wanted to mourn for her, to make her own peace with her. To say goodbye. But she couldn't. It was too late now.

Too late for Thea.

⁎⁎⁎

"Jackson?"

"I know. I heard."

"I'm at the Blue. Can you come?" The Blue Canyon Hotel was across the street from St. Simeon's and it was where most of the hospital staff came for drinks after work.

"Give me five minutes." He lived just around the corner.

"I didn't want to be alone," Maddie said when he arrived, "and I didn't want to sit with all those people from work who didn't really know her."

"How many people really did know her, do you think?"

"Not many," she said. "Did you? She told me the two of you spent time together in the last few months."

"Not really," he said. "We talked at work sometimes. We talked about things that mattered, but our conversations always stopped short of the place where I could actually say I knew what she was feeling."

"I knew parts of her," Maddie said. "But then she'd shut me out. I never knew when it was going to happen. It was like a door slamming in my face. And most of the time I never knew why."

They sat for a long time saying nothing. Maddie could never ever tell Jackson or anybody else about Dogface. She'd have to live alone with that knowledge for the rest of her life. And what about Thea's trumpet player? The one who bought her the big brass bed. Who knew where he was now? And Charlie – wouldn't he want to know?

Jackson leaned back in his chair and downed the last of his beer, wiped the foam from his top lip. Behind them a glass crashed to the floor. A door slammed. The tide of voices rose higher above the music.

"That poem," he said after a while. "I wonder why she read it to me. *Oft, In the Stilly Night.* It seemed so important to her."

"She loved that poem," Maddie said. "She used to read it to me too."

"Do you remember it? How it goes?"

"When I remember all the friends so linked together, I've seen around me fall like leaves in wintry weather, I feel like one who treads alone some banquet hall deserted, whose lights are fled, whose garlands dead, and all but he departed."

"Do you think she always felt that alone?"

"Yes, I do," Maddie said. "Jackson?"

"Yes?"

"Will you come home with me? Just for a while? I don't want to be alone. Not tonight."

"Yeah. The ghosts are after me too."

ഩർ

Maddie and Jackson lay on Maddie's bed together, wrapped in an old, tattered quilt that Maddie had had since she was a teenager. She draped a gauzy, purple scarf over the lamp and lit a candle the way she and Thea used to when they were about to drop acid and embark on one of their inner journeys. An FM station from Seattle was playing the *Blonde on Blonde* album in its entirety. Maddie's Grateful Dead poster was hanging on the wall behind them.

Maddie was thinking of the last time she had seen Thea on the street. She was wearing a badge on her coat that said *Save the Whales*. It had taken her by surprise, but she hadn't mentioned it to Thea. Funny she should think of that now. Thea had never spoken about whales to Maddie, or about saving them. It was as though a tiny, previously hidden piece of Thea had surfaced – a part of her that had been so deeply buried that Maddie had not even guessed at it. How much more there must have been. *I feel like one who treads alone.*

"Do you know anything about her wanting to save the whales?" Maddie asked Jackson.

He was silent for a while before answering. "I remember she wore a pin on her uniform," he said, "but I don't know anything about where that might have come from. She never said anything about whales to me."

"It's strange," Maddie said, "that she worried about saving the whales when she so badly needed to save herself."

"Hmm," was all Jackson said, then, "I don't think it was our job to save her, though. I hope you don't think it was."

"No," Maddie said. "But I wish there was something I could've done. I wish she hadn't been so alone. I wish she hadn't died alone."

"Should we make love?" asked Jackson.

Visions of Johanna was just beginning to play and Maddie didn't want to make love with him because she knew it wouldn't have anything to do with the two of them. It would be about searching for some fragment of Thea, some essence of her. As though that was even possible. Or searching to appease some lonely part of themselves. Maddie didn't want to do that either.

"It's all right," Jackson said. He tucked the quilt under Maddie's one bare shoulder. The wind was gusting outside, rustling leaves, rattling the shells she had strung together and hung outside her window. Neither of them said anything for a long time.

"I think Thea was full of hidden rooms," Jackson finally said. "Private places she couldn't talk about. Or wouldn't."

Maddie nodded. Jackson couldn't know her secrets or what had lain hidden in her angry silences. And she could never tell. Those secrets were Maddie's now.

The memorial service was held in a small chapel high on a hill on the mountain side of the city. Not many came – a few from work, her trumpet player, Thea's mother, Jackson. A minister from a Unitarian church read from *The Prophet: Farewell to you and the youth I have spent with you. It was but yesterday we met in a dream.* Maddie read *"Oft, in the Stilly Night."*

Thea would have loved it.

Jackson stood beside Maddie in a cold wind under an icy blue sky while they listened to the minister's eulogy. He linked his arm with hers and held her close.

"I hate this," Maddie whispered.

"Me too."

"It'll be over soon."

After the service, Thea's trumpet player introduced himself to Maddie. His name was Lewis. He looked young, not anything like she had imagined. He was tall and lanky with straight blond hair that hung almost to his shoulders.

"I heard about the bed." Maddie said, "The big brass bed."

"Yeah," he said, "it was my grandmother's. My dad was born in that bed. I was never that crazy about it but Thea loved it."

"Yes. She did."

"Why?" he said. "Why did she do it?"

"I don't know, Lewis. I don't think anyone does."

"She knew I would always be there if she needed me. I would have done anything for her. I told her that. Over and over."

"I know. I want answers too, but there just aren't any."

"She went away, you know. With another man."

Maddie nodded. "She told me."

She had gone back and forth, he told Maddie. Living with Lewis, not living with him. Needing his help, rejecting it. Always angry.

"I would have done anything for her," he said again. "I offered her the world. My world, anyway. For what that's worth."

But Lewis would never know how or understand why his love had become a thing from which Thea ran. He didn't understand that it was not his beneficence she wanted. She needed to come up against things. She needed hard edges. Softness only crumbled under her touch. Anything that was not as steely as her will, or as intractable, had to be brought to its knees. A shameful thing.

Like a mendicant waiting for alms, she took his offerings only when she had to, but ultimately, she hated the almsgiver, cursing his benevolence, so ugly against her own naked need.

Maddie remembered something Thea had said that day Maddie had gone to see her in the hospital. "My sins are not venial," she had told her in her flat-footed self-deprecating way. "*Venial*. My word."

"Meaning?"

"Forgivable. My sins are not forgivable. Lewis forgave me and he was wrong. And not only was he wrong," she said, "he was stupid."

Verna looked lost. She wanted Maddie to have some of Thea's things. Records or maybe some of her books. Anything. She asked Maddie if she would go to Thea's room and take whatever was hers or anything of Thea's she wanted. Verna wanted someone to be there before she had to finally take away all her things. She needed a witness. Maddie understood that.

Maddie promised to go and have a look, told Verna to call anytime but knew there was nothing she could do for her. She left the chapel and stood for a few minutes alone under the hard, blue sky, gazing at the city across the water. Jackson offered Maddie a ride home. He dropped her off in a park near where she lived so she could walk for a while. She needed to be alone. All she could think of was the big hole in the day where Charlie and Dogface should be. Where they would want to be.

If.

She walked slowly at first, then faster, until she was running, light and free, weightless, as though a gust of wind could carry her away, high over the mountains and out to the sea. The inside of her skull felt cool and empty.

She ran until she couldn't run anymore, then sat down on the boulevard grass a few blocks from home and cried.

𝔰𝔬𝔠𝔰

Maddie had promised Verna she would go to Thea's suite and she wanted to get it over with. She wasn't even sure why she'd agreed. Verna had offered to meet her there, but Maddie refused, not wanting to be there among Thea's things with anyone else. She didn't want to be there at all.

The house was an old brick mansion on the edge of Shaughnessy. Narrow flower beds, empty now, lined a brick walkway. The stairs appeared untrustworthy and were badly in need of a coat of paint. The front door was unlocked. The house smelled faintly of stale cooking and bath oil. The carpets were shabby and worn from years of tenants' feet. The old wooden floor creaked underfoot as Maddie crept down the long, dark hallway. She felt as though she had stumbled into someone else's life, into a place she didn't belong. A massive oak stairway curved into the upper reaches of the house.

Maddie stopped and looked into the bathroom that was obviously shared by all the tenants on that floor. It was a beautiful room, the kind of bathroom Thea must have loved. Immense, shadowy and still, like the rest of the house. A deep tub sat on chicken legs beside an old-fashioned pedestal sink with porcelain faucets. An oval wood-framed mirror hung over the sink, reflecting pale sunlight from the stained glass window on the opposite wall. On the windowsill was a bottle of Vitabath, and a pair of pantyhose was draped over the shower rod.

A head peeked through a half-opened door down the hallway, then disappeared as the door was closed. Maddie felt in her pocket for the key that Verna had given her. Number eight. The heavy wood door slid open without a sound. She closed it quietly behind her. A purple Indian bedspread had been draped over the window, suffusing the room in violet light, creating at first a sense of unreality, of peace, even.

Then Maddie saw boxes. Boxes. Everywhere.

Boxes leaned against the wall, defeated. One was filled with Thea's books. Her favorites were on top. *Pride and Prejudice. Vanity Fair.* A book on astrology: *Linda Goodman's Love Signs.* Thea must have moved there months ago, but she hadn't unpacked a thing.

None of her clothes had been hung up; they spilled out of boxes. Jeans, a black turtleneck sweater, one of her uniforms, her purple silk dress. Clothes were heaped on a wooden rocking chair, more piled on the floor, tangled together. A green wool sweater, a white flannelette and lace nightgown, black leather gloves. Another box was filled with cushions that Thea and Maddie had in their apartment, most of them dark blues and purples, Thea's favorite colors. Once she had stolen an entire bolt of purple fabric from a nearby store and covered a whole wall with it. She wasn't afraid of getting caught. She'd simply hoisted the bolt over one shoulder, boldly walked out of the store and down the street for four blocks to the house where they lived. Thea stole things and gave them to Maddie as gifts: stylish sunglasses, an antique sterling silver evening bag, French perfume.

There was a box on the windowsill. Its blue velvet cover shimmered in the diffused sunlight. Maddie opened it. Lying on pale blue crumpled satin was a string of creamy-white pearls, like drops of moonlight. She picked them up and let them slide through her fingers. They were exquisite, a strange beauty in the chaos of the room. Maddie imagined them on Thea, the simplicity of those creamy globes, opalescent against her olive skin. They spoke of tenderness, softness. A Thea Maddie had only occasionally seen.

Who would have given her pearls?

Farther along the windowsill stood a wilted ivy in a clay pot and in the corner, a tiny jeweler's box. Maddie opened the box and inside, in a nest of white satin, was what looked like an engagement ring. Thea had told Maddie that Lewis with the brass bed had given her an engagement ring, but Maddie was never sure when Thea was telling the truth.

"It's a sapphire," Thea had told her. "He said he couldn't afford a diamond right away." She had looked at Maddie with a frown. "Do you think that means he doesn't really love me?" That was Thea. Always wary. Always on the edge of some uncertainty.

But Thea and Lewis did have a life together. At least for a while. Thea's memory didn't belong only to Maddie. It wasn't as though standing by her body in the morgue as the final witness had given Maddie squatter's rights to her heart. Thea had had her trumpet player and perhaps she had even loved him. He gave her a brass bed because of the song she loved so much: *Lay, Lady, Lay.* They shared a life about which Maddie knew nothing.

There was nothing of Charlie there. No photographs. Nothing to suggest that he had ever existed in her life. In the end, Thea had died alone in this room infused with violet light.

Maddie had been avoiding looking at Thea's bed. It was just a narrow cot pushed against the wall. It must have come with the room. Maddie wondered what had happened to her big brass bed. This bed was where she must have spent the last few hours of her life. Thinking what? Or could she have been thinking at all? Maddie wanted answers, clues. A note. Anything that could tell her what she needed to know: why?

One of Thea's words had been *insuperable*. "Some things are simply insuperable," she had said when Maddie ran into her in the cafeteria at work and asked how she was doing. "Impossible to surmount." And that was all she would say.

The bed had been stripped down to the mattress, covers and pillows flung to the floor. A pale blue nightgown was in a tangled heap at the foot of the bed. This was where they had put her on the gurney then taken her, too late, to the hospital. Why had they taken off her nightgown? She would have hated being exposed like that, to have suffered that last indignity, being taken naked to the hospital. They must have stripped her to try and resuscitate her.

Maddie could see it, even though she didn't want to. She shut her eyes to hide from the image. Ambulance attendants, cool and efficient. Indifferent even. They'd have glanced around the room for clues, pocketed the empty pill bottles. *Just another suicide.* If her heart had stopped beating by then, they would have tried to pump her back to life. If she'd been able, she would have screamed at them, cursed them.

Perhaps she did scream, far away inside her mind, all her rage imprisoned behind her empty skull as she plummeted, too late. Her body, cool and white, would have been placed on the gurney and covered with a sheet. The ambulance siren would have screamed through the early morning while in another part of the city Maddie slept, lost in the labyrinth of her dreams. Did they hold her hand? Did they pump her chest all the way to the hospital? Or had they decided even then that it was too late for Thea?

Somewhere in the tunnels of her mind, did Thea watch her life run out? Was she calling out from far, far away where no one could hear? Did she know she would die with only strangers looking on?

Maddie would never know.

Beside the bed was a low table that Thea had fashioned out of two glass bricks and a board. On the table, an empty bottle of scotch, half a glass of water. Her glasses. And under the bottle of Scotch, a folded piece of paper. Maddie lifted the bottle and picked up the piece of paper. On it Thea had written: *Elysian Fields: abode of the blessed after death.*

The last of her words.

Maddie gathered up the tangle of sheets and lay them across the bed. Hidden on the floor under the sheets was a piece of notebook paper. A poem. Words scrawled in Thea's clear, childish hand:

Sister Death, I ask one thing, and I ask this
only once: Release me, fill my soul
with light, so I can fly away. Fill
my heart with grace
and the truth
of nine birds singing.

Maddie knew that nothing in this room, not the soft slide of Thea's purple dress between her fingers, the crumbling box of books, the wilted ivy sprinkled with dust motes or sunlight against the windowsill could define Thea's life any more than Maddie could.

She took the brass fruit bowl, the candles, and the poem, and looked around. An empty room, visited, but never inhabited. She stood at the door and looked back into the violet light. Hesitated. She wasn't ready to close the door.

The stillness of the room was freighted with the unfinished sentence that was Thea's life. A life burdened with possibility, even now. It was as if Thea's dreams still clung like scent to these last few remnants of who she was.

And who she would never be.

൭൫

Jackson sat in Maddie's grandmother's chair and Maddie sat cross-legged on the bed across from him, a blanket around her shoulders. It was cold. Maddie told Jackson about Thea's room. The empty bed, the unopened boxes. Her last words: *Elysian Fields.*

"You've had to deal with all of this alone," Jackson said. "Going into her room. That must have been awful." His sweater was slung over the back of the chair and he looked very young and very tired. "I wish I could have been there with you."

"It wouldn't have made any difference," Maddie said. "I had to do it alone. I wanted to."

He got up from the chair and sat beside her on the bed, wrapped his arms around her. His smell was warm and familiar. Maddie didn't mind his nearness. They were quiet for a long time.

"Did she ever tell you I gave her pearls?"

In her mind's eye Maddie saw them in the box on Thea's windowsill. Milky pearls in a blue velvet box, nestled in pale blue satin. Did he hold them up to her throat, admire them, creamy white against her skin? Why did he give her pearls?

"No."

Thea would never have told Maddie that.

"I visited her a few times when you were holed up doing your writing and not seeing anyone. She invited me. She was so lonely. I just wanted to do something nice for her. She loved pearls." Jackson stopped. He looked as if he was about to cry. "They were my mother's. I had no use for them."

The cold cry of foghorns, like bruises on my skin.

He had slept with her. In that moment Maddie knew.

Coupling under the cool sheets. Wine glasses and a bottle of Harvey's Bristol Cream on the windowsill. The city below them, the rainbow arc of the bridge, the seductive velvet darkness. Maybe they smoked a joint and listened to *Firebird Suite*, like Thea and Maddie used to, chased through the forest of their smoke dreams after the elusive golden bird. Or did they listen to *La Mer* and pretend that the bed was their ark, their shelter from the relentless, crashing sea?

He gave her pearls.

Thea expected that from all her men, pearls in one form or another. Attention, desire, admiration, unquestioning loyalty. A big brass bed.

She had no shame.

In return, she gave her body, slender, dark and willing. Her clever insights, her dark and bitter humor, all her secret knowledge. No. Not quite all.

Life for Thea was an exchange, a trade-off. This for that.

She would never have told Maddie about Jackson, not even when it didn't matter anymore. That was the weight she carried: her aloneness. Thea was alone in the end because she couldn't be honest with anyone. Not even herself.

"Does it matter to you?" asked Jackson.

"No." *Yes.*

"It shouldn't. We were just two bodies trying to find some place to connect."

"I know that, Jackson."

Maddie had never offered Thea refuge or escape, or a map to the places she was looking for: illumination, instant wisdom, love without a price. Thea knew as well as Maddie that none of these things existed.

What words would tell Maddie who Thea really was? Impostor. Liar. A sorceress who could create truth out of fiction, fantasy out of truth. Friend. Thea and Jackson had leaned together in their loneliness. That was all.

"Maddie." Jackson reached out and captured her hand in his. "It had nothing to do with you and me."

"There was no you and me, Jackson."

"But there was," he said. "It was just different and it had nothing to do with her."

"It really doesn't matter now."

"I need to ask you something."

"What is it?" Maddie pulled the blanket off her shoulders.

"Is there any point in asking you to come to Montreal with me?"

"No."

Montreal. Thea and Maddie's dream place. For years, they'd talked of traveling there. Imagined meeting Leonard Cohen on the street. In Maddie's dream, he was barefoot and wore a white suit and a white panama hat. There was an old-world quality to the dream, a setting of ancient cobblestone streets, wrought iron benches, terracotta pots spilling red geraniums. He would be mesmerized by their mysterious inner wisdom, stunned by the grace and beauty of their thoughts.

"Montreal? Since when are you going to Montreal?"

"My sister's there. She's a nurse at the Jewish General. Says there's lots of work. There'd be work for you too."

"What brought this on?"

"I need a new beginning," he said. "It'll be a different kind of world there. Further away from my past. From my Nam nightmares. I thought you might want to start over too. We could get a place together." He grinned. "Just roommates."

"I am starting over, Jackson. But I'm starting over here."

"You're going to follow that one through?"

"Yeah, I am. I've already begun."

He stood up. Maddie slid off the bed and put her arms around him. "I'll miss you, but I'm so glad you're doing this. I think it's the right thing."

"I know it is."

"Jackson . . . there's something I want you to do with me. Before you go. I've been thinking about some kind of memorial for Thea. Someplace where I can go to remember her. A real place, not just a place in my head." Maddie picked up the blanket and pulled it back around her shoulders. She was feeling chilled again. "I want to plant a bush or a tree. Something that will last."

"Where?"

"That's the thing. I want a place where I can always go, and that got me thinking. People move. My parents are talking about getting a smaller place. And Tom and Julie will want to move once they have kids."

"So?"

"So, yesterday I walked down to one of those beaches off Point Grey Road. No one goes there with the main beach so close. I found a rocky path to the beach and at the bottom, a knoll, a grassy place. It's a perfect spot to plant a tree or a bush, something that won't grow too big. It's public land. No one would know and no one would mess with it. Will you come with me to plant it?"

"When?"

"As soon as I find the perfect thing. I'm sure it's not exactly legal to plant trees or bushes on city property. We'll go at dusk when no one's around."

"Call me," he said, "when you're ready."

He closed the door softly behind him and Maddie listened to his steps run down the stairs, light and full of energy and purpose, the way she had never heard them before.

From the window, she watched his back disappear down the sun-filled street. His steps were sure and determined, as though he was following old, remembered rhythms. Jackson looked stronger than Maddie had ever seen him look.

A few days later, Jackson stopped by Maddie's apartment and they walked down to the beach. The purple rhododendron and a spade were hidden in a black plastic garbage bag. Maddie chose purple because it had been Thea's favorite color. The last remnants of sunshine streaked the corners of the sky, shrouded in damp evening mist. A breeze carried the scent of freshly cut grass. They strolled along the narrow path above the ocean, then scrambled down the rocky trail to the beach and made a place in the sand to sit, leaning against a log that had drifted in with the tide.

Jackson opened his backpack and pulled out a bottle of wine, wheat crackers, and a chunk of jack cheese, and placed them on the log. "Might as well make it a celebration," he said.

"Yes," Maddie said, "but let's plant this first."

Jackson dug a hole in the grassy outcropping that arched out over the beach. Maddie put the young plant into the hole, patting the soil around it carefully, gently, as if she were putting a child to bed. She poured a jar of water around the roots.

"Come and sit down." Jackson took a sip of wine and raised the bottle into the air. "Here's to you, Thea." He passed the bottle to Maddie.

"To Thea," she said.

The mountains darkened against the fading sky. Lights from freighters moored in the strait rippled across the black sea like phosphorescence. Jackson put cheese on a cracker and handed it to Maddie. "So," he said, "tell me about something you and Thea did together. Something you've never told anyone else."

"We danced seminude once."

"You did? Where?"

"At my brother's. He and Julie weren't married yet but they lived together." Maddie picked up a thin piece of driftwood and traced a pattern in the sand. "We'd all had way too much to drink."

"Who was there?"

"Thea and me. Tom and Julie, of course, and one of Julie's girlfriends and her boyfriend."

"Just an impromptu thing? Somebody's crazy idea?" He laughed. "Whose idea was it?"

"Not impromptu, actually," Maddie said. "We'd kind of planned it. That afternoon Thea and Julie and I smoked a joint together and came up with the plan. We thought it was a great idea. Julie's a really good sewer so she whipped us up some pasties. Barely covered our nipples."

"Not much sewing involved there."

"God, no. She glued all this sparkly stuff on them. It was wild. We just wore bikini bottoms and pasties. That was it. We did this sinuous dance to Duke Ellington. *Take the A Train*, I think it was. Thea kept saying that we were such sluts. She insisted on lighting candles. No lights. Maddie laughed. "She could be such a prude. Never comfortable in her body." *Just like me*, Maddie thought. She hadn't recognized that truth before.

"What were you drinking?"

"Plonk. Some cheap crap wine. And smoking weed, of course. It's a good memory, that one. It warms me, thinking of it."

The tide was creeping in. A tug drifted by on the dark water, silhouetted against the skyline. "We'd better go."

They climbed up from the beach into the evening streets and the traffic on Point Grey Road. Maddie gave him a hug goodbye. They arranged to meet for dinner before he left for the East. It felt strange to Maddie, all these goodbyes. Thea. And now Jackson.

Maddie felt as though she was turning a corner onto a street she had never seen before – one of those alien streets you find yourself drifting along in your dreams. It all felt so close still, Thea in her purple silk dress. Laughing. Or sauntering, shouting out her elaborate indifference. Her face mocking, even in death.

The night was warm and Maddie wasn't ready to go home. She ambled toward a wooden bench on the grass near the trail to the beach, overlooking the ocean and the mountains. Someone was sitting there, a woman about

Maddie's age. She looked absorbed, lost in her own world and though Maddie really wanted to be alone, she sat beside her anyway.

Maddie's sudden appearance startled the woman.

"Oh," she said. "Hello. What a gorgeous evening."

She had a trace of an accent. Italian, maybe Spanish. She was arrestingly beautiful. Her blue-black hair hung to her waist. Her arms were crossed and her long blue-jeaned legs were stretched out in front of her on the damp grass. Green suede Frye boots. A hint of silver earrings hidden behind the sheen of her hair. Under the streetlamp, silver bracelets glinted against her brown skin.

"Hello," Maddie said.

"Beautiful place."

"Do you live around here?"

"Yeah. I just moved," she said. "From Texas." She leaned toward Maddie and shook her hand. "My name is Carmelita. I'm actually Mexican."

Before Maddie knew it, they were talking, words spilling, all in a rush like a river overflowing its banks. Her mother had died recently and Carmelita had come to Vancouver to be closer to her brother, her only living relative. He had come to B.C. a couple of years before through the underground network to avoid the draft. He was working on a ranch in the Kootenays. She was working as an assistant to the curator of a small gallery in the city.

She told Maddie about the village where she was born. A pueblo in the highlands of Mexico, a few hours north of Mexico City, a village known for its brick factories, painted tiles, and hammered tin. They had lived there until just a few years ago, before moving to Texas with their mother. Their father had left them years before.

Then she told Maddie about her daughter, Angela's, death just a few months ago. "My friends tell me I should try to forget," she said. "But I don't want to forget. I come here to remember."

Then Maddie was telling her about Thea, about her death, about the rhododendron bush she had just planted so that she'd always have a place to go to remember.

"Our stories should never be forgotten," Maddie said. "Not even the bad parts. The stupid parts. I'm so afraid that with Thea dead, without some witness, her life will just vanish and none of it will have meant anything."

Carmelita nodded thoughtfully, smoothed back the hair from her face. The streetlight glinted off the silver crosses in her ears. "Could we have coffee sometime?" she asked. "Maybe you could visit me." She pulled a pen out of her jacket pocket and wrote her number on the back of a matchbook.

"I'd like that," Maddie said.

Carmelita grinned and got up from the bench, wiping the dampness from the back of her jeans. "You know," she said, "your stories belong to you. And mine to me. They're ours forever." She shoved her hands into the pockets of her brown suede jacket. "And if you tell me your stories and I tell you mine, they'll never die." She started off down the street, tall and lean, certain and alive in her body. "Let's tell each other our stories someday," she called back to Maddie. "I'll be your witness. You can be mine."

She was right. Maddie's stories belonged to her. But Maddie knew she would have to learn to inhabit them, to live in their shadows and in the bright unfurling light of their truth.

Only then would she be ready to tell them. And in the telling, let them go.

ಐಲ್ಸ್

Maddie called her mother and asked to meet downtown for coffee. She chose one of her mother's prearranged shopping days and asked her to go where they'd often met before: Woolworth's soda fountain.

It was late in the day. Streetlights were already on, pooling into yellow puddles beside the curb. A cold drizzle belied what the calendar said – that it was spring – and turned the rain-glazed streets into a neon haze. Light from shops on Hastings Street – Sweet Sixteen, Modiste, The Only Cafe with its green neon seahorse, the White Lunch – spilled onto the gritty pavement, washing it in a luminescent sheen.

Hastings Street was beginning to look tattered around the edges, a little down at the heels, like an old, falling apart sweater. A lone woman hurried through Victory Square, past its crumbling tribute to fallen soldiers, carefully avoiding the dirty, outstretched hand of the grizzled vagrant curled up on the cold, wet grass. One hand clutched her coat to her throat, holding the mouton tightly against herself. The other hand grasped an umbrella that threatened to rebel and turn itself inside out at any moment.

Maddie's mother was sitting at the counter and had ordered her favorite: a baked apple wrapped in pastry and swimming in a sweet caramel sauce.

"I'm not going to need dinner tonight," she said, laughing. "This is such a treat."

Maddie ordered coffee, extra cream. A bran muffin. They talked about her parents' nursery business and how well it was going.

"It was a good idea" her mother said, "moving to Vancouver. It was the best decision for all of us."

"Meaning Gran and Grandpa too, I guess."

"Well, yes, of course. I wouldn't have wanted to leave her alone back in Winnipeg. With him."

"Mom, I have to ask you something. Please don't get mad."

"What? What is it?"

"There's something I need to know . . . after what you told me about Grandpa. The abuse, I mean."

Her mother put her fork down carefully beside her plate, as though what she was eating had suddenly lost its appeal. "It's so long ago now, Maddie."

"No. It's not about you. That's not what I mean. It's about me."

Her mother looked bewildered. She clearly had no idea where Maddie was going. The waitress wiped down the counter in front of them, all businesslike in her perky, pink nylon uniform.

"Top-up?" She pointed to Maddie's cup. Maddie shook her head.

Her mother pushed her plate away.

"Mom, Grandpa did those things to me too."

"What do you mean? How could he have?"

"Mom." It was all Maddie could do not to shout at her: *Why are you acting as though you don't know what I'm talking about? He abused me. Just like you.*

"When?"

"When I was a kid. In Winnipeg."

"But . . . when?"

243

"When you and Dad were at work. When you left me with them. After school."

She had grown pale. Her face looked shattered. "I didn't know."

"Of course, you didn't know. I didn't tell you. I was ashamed."

Her mother nodded.

"But I need to know . . ."

The waitress peered over at them, curious. Maddie shot her a dirty look and she went back to filling salt and pepper shakers. "I need to know why you left me with them. Why you left me in a place where he could get to me. I just don't understand that. After you, yourself . . ."

"No, I shouldn't have." She looked baffled. Diminished. For a moment, she wasn't Maddie's mother anymore. She was almost whispering. "I didn't think . . .I didn't know..."

There was no point in continuing. And no point in trying to talk about her father. Maddie could see that her mother's denial was that deep, that complete. Maddie knew she was never going to get what she wanted: her mother's outrage. Not even a story that could explain it, no matter how untrue the story might be.

After they'd finished their coffee, Maddie walked her mother to the bus stop, watched her climb the steps of the bus in the gray rain. She trudged for blocks through the stream of pedestrians, all of them with faces closed and dark, heads down, pushing into the wind like blind fish swimming against the current. Trolley buses groaned by, splashing rain from gutters.

So that was that, then. There would be no story, no explanation, no apology. But Maddie knew that her mother was innocent too. Naïvely innocent, but innocent nevertheless.

The story belonged to Maddie now.

Eight
The Island

It's early fall when Joey calls Maddie and asks if she'll meet him in the Cove. He's leaving the island, he says, and wants to talk. He's been living with his Mexican woman in Vancouver. Things have been thinning out workwise, and there are more opportunities for a welder in the city. They've finally decided to make the move back to Mexico.

Maddie agrees to meet him outside their old cottage in the Grove. She doesn't want to meet him but says she will, unsure why. *Maybe,* she thinks, *this will put that final stamp on our story.* Like those old-fashioned rubber stamps and stamp pad her dad kept in his office: *Paid in full.*

She stands in the lane and looks across to the cottage, the weathered split-rail fence, the black cherry tree, gnarled and fruitless now, the hawthorn tree, and then across the ocean to the mountains on the other side of the strait. She has no desire to invoke memories of those early days, the tenderness during that first bloom of love. And she refuses to remember the rest. The control he once held over her. Those words have crumbled and hold no power now. She no longer gives it living space in her heart. For her, Joey has become a hollow man, a straw man who lost his way in his search for Oz.

Maddie crosses the lane to the pathway and walks around the side of the house, past the pear tree and the empty piece of land, all overgrown now, where Frenchy's cabin used to be. The front steps of the cottage are in the sun so she sits there and waits. She doesn't look in any of the windows. It's a long-gone world Maddie chooses to leave unexplored.

She thinks now of the time before Joey came, when most of them in Gully's Grove were women who lived alone. Strong women: potters, poets, artists, weavers of words. Prodigal daughters, all of them. Those Grove Girls, they were called, when they showed up at a party on the other side of the island, uninvited and a little tipsy.

They spent one New Year's Eve calling old lovers and friends they hadn't seen in years. Voices from as far away as Australia, Hong Kong, the golden coast of South Carolina. Drinking scotch on the rocks and dancing to the Pointer Sisters. The fire stoked with chunks of dry cedar, snapping and crackling, melting frost on windowpanes. They took turns opening the creaky door of the wood stove and feeding it another log while the Squamish winds tore through the eaves.

It feels odd to Maddie, sitting on the steps of her old cottage that's empty and wild with vines. There is a faint breeze, just enough to stir the glossy leaves of the rhododendrons and rattle the wooden wind chimes she left behind. Out on the ocean the water is choppy, whitecapped. A boat cuts across the bay and slides into one of the coves along the coastline. The air is dense with memory.

She sees Joey in the distance and watches him walk along the boardwalk by the water. He climbs the trail from the beach and trudges toward her, a bent silhouette against the empty blue of the sky. There is something of endings in his posture, another reminder of what is past and gone. His appearance seems diminished, although he is not a small man. Something about him looks faded, insubstantial. His hair is grayer, thinner. He skirts the hawthorn tree where the day lilies grow and where two of her cats are buried. Looks down, then away. Does he remember? The day she carried Sammy in a cardboard box to the vet, then brought him back and buried him. If he does remember, he shows no sign.

"*Hola.*" He grins but his smile looks tentative, chastened.

Maddie doesn't answer or get up.

"Cabin needs a paint." He sits down on the step below her.

"Yeah."

"Everything's decaying. Falling down."

"Well, we've all moved on." Maddie stretches her legs out into the sun. "So, what did you want to talk to me about, Joey?"

He shuffles his feet against the clay brick path sprouting weeds and dandelions. Takes his time, filling the space between them with his restless uncertainty.

"I guess I just want to say . . .I didn't mean . . .didn't ever intend to do what I did. The way I did it." He slides a pack of cigarettes from his jacket pocket to give himself more time. Flips it open. Pulls the silver paper out and rolls it into a ball between his thumb and forefinger. "I shouldn't have left that way." He lights the cigarette and throws the match down onto the path. "I just wish I'd done it differently that's all. I wish I'd done a lot of things differently."

"Me too."

"So you're okay?"

"Of course, I'm okay," she says. "I've come a long way. I'm happy now."

He kicks a stone across the brick path. "It worked once, didn't it?"

Maddie doesn't answer.

They sit without saying anything. Out in the bay a ferry's whistle blows five long blasts, warning pleasure boats to get out of the way. The hollow sound of the whistle, its reminder of being left behind, its journeys back and forth across that stretch of sea, touches a nerve. Maddie stands up quickly as though she's been stung by one of the bees humming in the hawthorn blossoms. She's balancing on the very edge of a place she recognizes. A landscape traveled through so many times before. Someone else's story. She's only here because he asked her to come.

Am I still the girl with the red shoes? *No.*

"You know, Joey," she says. "I don't want to be here. I shouldn't have come. I have nothing that I want to say to you. And there's nothing I want to hear from you."

He's surprised. Shocked, even. And so is she. He stands up and looks at her, his eyes full of questions he will never ask. Then, "A last hug?"

She turns her back on him and walks away. She glances behind her just once.

Joey crosses the grassy slope to the trail and heads back down the path to the ocean. He doesn't look back.

After he's gone, Maddie walks back and sits for a long time on the porch, watching the sun sink behind the mountains the way she did so many times when she lived in Gully's Grove. It's strange being here, the solitary witness to this piece of her past. Her life here was quiet back in the beginning days, contained, safe. Then the dredgers came, tore up the mud flats to build a marina, ripped out the eel grass and sedge that grew where the creek ran into the ocean. She used to find arrowheads there, flung up by the machinery, the last legacy of the First Nations people who had stumbled on this piece of rock a long time ago.

Then came the sailboats harbored in the Cove, masts creaking and groaning, listing through her dreams. And the tourists who hiked through the Grove and hunted for a piece of their own past in the last of the tumbledown cottages. Like the cabins, all of their lives in the Grove began crumbling away, piece by piece, memory by memory.

The empty cabins have borne witness to all their dreams and memories. They speak even now as they inevitably slide into the earth, of Maddie, lying in her bed on a summer night, watching the Big Dipper cradled in the bowl of sky outside her window, listening to the rattle of limpet shells on her porch swaying in the wind, inhaling the scent of rain and roses.

The hesitation of oars splashing on water, creaking of sailboats listing on the tide, laughter of neighborhood children on the backyard rope swing. That was her life. The cottages tell the story of all of their lives. All those green beginnings and promises, and lofty dreams. All the days and nights, the beginnings and the endings.

The life Maddie created in Gully's Grove defined her nights and her days then, and their essence still coursed through her veins like a river. She could not have known back in those first years that every beginning held the seeds of the end, that every end was a beginning. She will probably be forever haunted by the moon over the water, the scent of honeysuckle on a summer wind. All these words, memories and thoughts, are just another kind of river. A world to explore. A gulf to traverse.

What's left for Maddie to do now is simply to say goodbye. Her own goodbye. There is no old rage to be soothed, no fragments of lives to be put back together. They all grew out of who they were in Gully's Grove, like new limbs from a pruned tree, lived their own stories culled from the collective dream.

They had lived it. And that was enough.

∞∞

When Lita arrives from Mexico for a visit she looks tall and strong and happy. "Oh, Mad," she says when she sees her house, "this is every dream you've ever had. And it's yours."

They spend their days sitting by the creek in the afternoons drinking homemade lemonade and Tanqueray gin. They cook together. On the hottest days, they walk to the beach and spend afternoons swimming in the salty bay, or leaning against beached driftwood, reading or doing crosswords, or simply continuing whatever conversation they'd been having from the time they got up that morning.

Maddie had said her goodbyes to Max before Lita arrived. She'd invited him for dinner at her new house, dragged an old left-behind picnic table down by the creek and they shared a bottle of wine with curried lamb and brown rice.

"You can cook." Max sounded surprised.

Maddie passed him the bowl of mango and pineapple chutney. "I never said I couldn't. Is Claudine coming back?"

"She'll come back for a while," he said. "Maybe in a couple of weeks. But I don't think she'll stay. She likes her role as grandmother. The Grand Mother. And Katie needs her."

"And you?"

"I've got my land in Alberta," he said. "It was left to me a long time ago and I've always dreamed of building my own house there. It's time to make some of my own dreams happen."

They hugged, promised to keep in touch, but Maddie knew they probably wouldn't.

On the day before Lita leaves to go back home to Mexico, she and Maddie make their annual foray into the city and spend their last afternoon together at the beach where Thea's rhododendron – almost ten feet tall now – is planted. Remembering Beach, they call it, and they have visited it together every year since they first met there all those years ago. For Lita, it has become a place where she goes to remember Angela, and every year she brings yellow roses that she tosses into the ocean and sends off with a prayer on the outgoing tide.

True to her word, Lita has become the vessel that has held all Maddie's stories and Maddie has been hers. To honor that, they made a pact years ago, that with every visit to Remembering Beach, they will tell each other a story.

Lita tells Maddie about her life with Sebastian in Mexico City. She has someone looking after her shop while she's away, but will never consider giving it up or giving up her *casita*.

"It's my home," she says, "and it will always be my home."

"And Sebastian? How does he feel about it?"

"Like me. That we have two homes now. We have so much, Maddie. Each other. And his family. It feels good to have a family again. To be surrounded by such love."

Maddie tells her about Joey and their meeting in the Grove. "I left," she says. "I was done."

Thinking about endings and beginnings reminds Maddie of a dream she's been having lately – a dream she's had several times with only slight variations. She dreams about a field, she tells Lita. She has come in on a train from the East, anticipating the muted green of the coastal mountains, her first glimpse of the familiar blue of the ocean. But the train takes her all the way to her island and stops at a greening field near her cabin.

The field is Gully's Grove, Maddie's past, her history. It is also her future because the field is only a stopping-off place on this particular dream journey. A field of possibilities. In the dream, Maddie looks beyond the field, past the mock orange bushes and honeysuckle and sees her cabin, the place that was her home for all those years. The old maple tree where the rope swing hung. The honeysuckle-lined path down to the sea, always alive with the sweet, peppery scent of wild rose. And across the yard by the wild quince is the split-rail fence where she would lean at night and watch the moon rise over the mountain.

From where Maddie stands, in her dream, she can see the glint of water like a diamond in a prism of light. She knows without really knowing, as happens in dreams, that it is a river, a river that waits for her. And it is in this river that she will unearth her beginnings, find that deep place of home through the hidden pathway to the tangled blackberry bushes and morning glory vines. This is the place that calls to her.

In the dream, the breeze rustles the high aspens and blows her hair across her eyes. The river's sound is soft, like the breathing of a sleeping child. Somewhere a bird sings, and then another and another. She remembers Thea's dream: Nine birds singing. Thea's perception of the truth. Singing birds. Not just in the city, strung across a power line at day's end, but here too. Everywhere. Their songs familiar, filling the cool river valley with sweet melodies. River spirits.

At Remembering Beach, the tide is out and Maddie and Lita lean against a log on the sand. They share a bag of plums they gathered from a tree beside one of the abandoned cottages in the Grove before getting on the ferry to spend the day in the city.

"There's one thing I've always felt strange about," says Lita, and Maddie knows that Lita has begun her real story. The story under the story. She tells Maddie about the days and weeks after Angela died, how she would sit for hours in her rocking chair in her house in Vancouver, looking out into her leaf-strewn autumn garden and back again to the cloisonné urn that stood beside Angela's silver-framed school picture on the mantel.

"No matter how much pain I felt," Lita says, "no matter how much rage and helplessness engulfed me, there was a voice inside me that said *this is good*. Can you imagine? *This is good*. About my own dead child. I was living in another world in those days and it was a scary world far away from reality. I just couldn't live with my own reality."

"What part of her death did you think might be good?" Maddie asks her.

"None of it was good," Lita says. "But in my utter desperation, I believed that her death meant the end of all the pain that could ever happen in my life. That the very worst that could ever happen had happened. Nothing could ever hurt me again."

"And it's not true, is it?"

"No. It's not. Pain is pain," Lita says. "I found that out when my dog died. It tore up my heart. It didn't hurt any less because she was an animal. It just plain hurt."

Lita lets a handful of sand pour between her fingers. "And you?"

"Me. Well, I've had a lot of time to think in the last few months. Packing boxes. Unpacking them. All those hours I had with myself while getting ready to move. I spent a lot of time inside my head."

"And?"

"And, I am endlessly amazed at how I was able to fool myself for so many years, tell myself stories about why I chose to be with Joey. And why I stayed."

"Tell me."

Maddie tosses a stone into the water, listens for the thin plunk. "What I told myself was that this was the man life had brought me. And there was that elephant in the room – the craziness I endured – that I refused to see and refused to talk about. I let him invade my life. I let him shame me."

"And how did you think letting him into your life could change anything?"

"I told myself it was time," Maddie says. "Time to deal with those memories of my past. Joey's coming to me, I thought, was an opportunity for both of us to heal. That was when he was telling me he was in therapy. And I believed him."

Lita laughs, a short, angry laugh. "Joey in therapy? Only with a gun to his head."

"Even my horoscope convinced me that he was the one for me, back when he was still living in the Kootenays: *Your true love is waiting for the chance to come close. Say yes, even if it's to a long-distance romance.*"

"I remember that," Lita says. "The horoscope part. I remember you reading it to me over the phone. You were so sure."

"But wait," Maddie says. "There's more. "The whole year before I met him and the whole first year we were together, *I* was in therapy."

"And you didn't tell anyone? Not even me?"

"Not even you. And during all that time, I didn't tell my therapist about his history."

"That must have been hard," she says. "Keeping all that to yourself."

Maddie nods. "Shame was what I felt," she says. "But I wanted him. And I knew that if I opened the door to what was really happening, if I opened it even a crack, I'd have to open it all the way and walk on through. So I told myself it was right, it was meant to be. That was my justification for loving him. For wanting him."

Lita nods and says nothing.

"I was an imposter. A liar. I didn't belong in therapy with all my shame and the stories I was afraid to tell, yet I carried them with me like a scar to every appointment. All Joey's secrets were safe with me."

After Maddie has seen Lita off at the airport, she drives a short distance, then parks in a gravelly roadside pullout nearby where the Strait of Georgia arcs into the land in a wide horseshoe, flat and glittering in the late afternoon sun. From here she can watch planes take off and land, something she's always loved to do.

She watches them lift off into the blue sky, filled with such a sweet sense of freedom, as though she's watching balloons or dreams being sent aloft, riding a vagrant wind without any real destination or plan beyond the simple act of being in flight.

There will be more flights for her, she knows, but they'll be real ones. South to Mexico over the Sierra Madres, where the sky over your head is as blue as a dinner plate, and the sun leaves a ribbon of lace smoldering like hot lava dancing on the skyline.

She's been in flight one way or another for most of her life. Dodging and evading all the stories that involved her and her father, and her and her grandfather. Keeping herself absent. Safe. Safe from truths that colored her life in countless ways. It's why she could never say no to the men in her life: her father, her grandfather, Joey. She became brilliant at the art of forgetting.

Now it's the remembering that really matters. It's in the remembering that she can make the choice to let it go. And in that remembering she needs to acknowledge some demons of her own. She is not without false pride. In her arrogance, she took secret pleasure in Joey's rages, gloated as she watched him crumble into something she could hate. *Look how ugly and cruel you are,* was the storyline that ran through her head. *And look how good I am. The victim of your abuse. I am so not like you.* She played her role too, spurned roads she could have taken. Chose instead to stay in his shadow and watch him grow viler, rather than find her way out into the light.

But her history has come with gifts too. It took half her life to understand that she didn't need anyone riding shotgun for her, that she could blaze her own trail through the rest of her life. Perhaps it was simply the fear that had carved itself into her body and mind that had prevented her from choosing her own life. The fear of an evil world that filtered through the even greater fear in her father's eyes.

Joey's gift was in finally teaching her how to say no. Lita's greatest gift was simply herself. The story of her — her light, her love. Thea's gift had been a double-edged sword. It was Thea who banged on Maddie's windows and rattled the doors, demanding a way into Maddie's heart. It was she who stood for her against her father and grandfather, forced her to open doors Maddie had not wanted to believe existed. Thea also passed on an unwanted gift: the burden of silence.

Thea would undoubtedly respond if she could, with scorn and derision. *Hyperbole,* she'd reply to Maddie's stories. *A deliberate exaggeration used for effect.*

Maddie has loved writing history, but this past year her journey through words has begun to take her to the heart of her personal history, has opened her to a world that soars beyond the place of fact or legend. The stories have been magical, as magical as finding the battered silver cigarette case on the abandoned Bridal Trail near the ruins of the old hotel. As joyful as imagining the dreaming couple that strolled along that trail during the flowering of their youthful passion.

Maddie has gradually begun to coax other stories out. The unfinished stories. The words that have lain unspoken for so long, like a field left fallow. Sentence by sentence, they are making their presence known. In her heart and on the page.

ഇഗ

Maddie can't sleep, called by the stillness of this late summer night. She opens the door and steps outside, bare feet on the still-warm deck, the sticky brush of a spider web against her cheek. Darkness pulses with scent and sensation, a soft green jungle of day lilies and mock orange. She feels her way to the old green wicker chair and sits down. Night, the old shapeshifter, alters what has become familiar in this new world of hers. The sky glitters with stars. Right above her, she can see the Big Dipper and Cassiopeia. The moon has not risen and the sky is dark as black ink.

Crickets are chirping in the dry creek bed, in the tall grasses and under rocks in the back garden. She planted a small garden this summer: sweet peas, pole beans, lettuce, spinach, a row of spindly carrots, a few pansies and impatiens – her first garden – but she knows this song of the crickets heralds the end of summer. Maddie has always waited for the changing of the seasons. Although she loves summer nights like this, she's always been a little in love with the dying season. Each turn of season has brought the bittersweet, the losses. And the gifts. Spring, with its eternal optimism, always unleashes an unbridled coltish delight in her, a soaring of blood in the veins. The soft green of new beginnings, the first delicate blooms, the purple flash of a hummingbird's wings. The creek, as it tumbles through grasses and ferns, spills over rocks and stumps, making its way to the sea.

As the landscape shifts into summer, the creek becomes a splash, a trickle, and then is silent. By the time the sound of moving water has drifted from her consciousness, the silence is replaced with the rasp of crickets that sing all night in the hot, dry grasses and the still creek bed. A doe brings her fawns through the garden, nuzzles the last of the low-hanging impatiens, nibbles on ferns.

The winter birds have already arrived, pecking at the bright orange mountain ash berries. Evenings cool as August creeps into September. The rains will soon arrive, along with the earthy smell of wood smoke. Endings are palpable.

This is that slow, sweet time before the end, a time not quite at the end, but when all her senses are contemplating endings. This is the time of letting go. A season of grace.

Maddie gazes at the lights across the water – the lights of Eagle Island and the Sunshine Coast. Then she hears a sound, a puzzling sound. *Is it the sound of singing?* A frail voice rises and falls, climbs then drops. She listens, sitting alone in the dark. Sometimes the voice is sad and quavering, other times it is strong and clear.

Then Maddie realizes that it isn't singing at all. It's praying. The words are mystical, alien. Hebrew, maybe. It's Misha, who lives next door. His wife died last year, and Misha is inconsolable. He sits in his chair late at night, under the starry sky in the woods by the creek, and sings his prayers. He is waiting, he says, for the darkness that sometimes threatens to bury him, to lift. For the lightness in his bones that will give him wings to fly.

Misha longs for peace, for an unfolding of the mystery that his life has become. For the arms of night to enfold him, to keep him safe. Maddie thinks of her mother in her last days, waiting for the final unveiling, for the keys to the kingdom and the streets of gold. Perhaps her father had already found that kingdom and was there, waiting for her in that final place for which they had spent their whole lives rehearsing.

Maddie listens to Misha shuffle across the wooden deck and go back into his house. A little while later his lights go out and the night is still again. Maddie waits too, but she no longer yearns for love or promises or anything outside herself. The idea of waiting no longer frightens her or demands answers. Waiting is simply a place of stillness.

Another kind of grace.

Acknowledgments

Thanks to:

UBC Creative Writing Professor Bob Harlow whose 'Harlowisms' and many encouraging words have stayed with me all these years.

My editors Davina Haisell, Lorna Lyons and Stephanie Williams for their invaluable help, and the cover designer John Dowler.

My publisher Carol Cram, of New Arcadia Publishing for her encouragement and support, her meticulous eye and her professionalism in her dedication to this project.

My CAA writing group: Rod Baker, Kay Schmitt, Suzanne de Montigny and Mellie Ceil de Young.

About the Author

Photo: © 2017 Debra Stringfellow

Edythe Anstey Hanen has published prize-winning short stories and poetry in literary magazines including *Room Magazine* and anthologies across Canada, in addition to articles in the *Globe & Mail*, *National Post* and the *Hamilton Bay Observer* and is a regular contributor to *Mexconnect*, an online travel magazine. She lives on Bowen Island in British Columbia, Canada, where for many years she was the editor of the *Bowen Island Undercurrent* newspaper.

www.ingramcontent.com/pod-product-compliance
Lightning Source LLC
Chambersburg PA
CBHW030102260626
47156CB00008B/2487